The List

the Snow book Three)

Christopher Coleman

Find a Rifle

1.

The alley was only a block away now and Danielle kept her pace steady, worried that a change of speed in either direction might trigger an alert. She couldn't afford that here, not this close to home.

Home.

It was an alley bar about the size of a boxing ring. Raise the Flagon. The kind of place even the college kids avoided, the theme of the place residing somewhere between biker bar and punk rock club. The stench from the bathroom on that first day was something Danielle would never forget, and the hours she spent cleaning it felt like prison-camp work.

But she called the place hers now, home, and though it wasn't exactly the Palace of Versailles, it had everything she needed to get through each passing night.

And most importantly, it was secluded.

The basement setting of the dive bar gave it something of a bunker feel, which, at first, made Danielle feel trapped, buried. Now, however, the underground location instilled security, advantage. As long as the white monsters never saw her enter the alley, she felt safe in this underground dwelling, like a gopher in its burrow.

Danielle stopped midway between Huntington and Poplar and turned on her heels, scanning the upper windows of the two-story brick buildings that surrounded her, shifting her eyes steadily along the openings, pausing for a second or two on each.

Empty as usual.

The desolation of the streets, even after all the time that had passed, still unsettled Danielle, making her feel as if she'd been kidnapped and dropped off in the middle of an abandoned movie set. Or that she had wandered onto an old nuclear test site, one that had left the ground poisoned with radiation while leaving the structures on top of it undamaged.

But the eeriness of her isolation lasted only a moment. She needed to stay focused on survival. It was the only thing that drove her these days.

Survival and her goals.

Danielle did a three-sixty and then another half-turn until she was facing forward again; and then, without another glance, she turned quickly to the right and strode briskly into the alley. She walked less than a quarter of the way down the side street until she reached an area between two dumpsters where a large, thin sheet of particleboard leaned against the brick wall of the alley. Danielle hesitated in front of the board and took one last peek behind her, and, seeing nothing, she swung the board outward, exposing a crusty iron railing and a narrow stairway that led down below the surface of the street.

She descended the first four steps toward the underground bar and then grabbed the thin board and replaced it against the railing, cloaking the entrance once again.

Danielle turned the wobbly knob and pushed open the unlocked door and then stepped into the tiny foyer. There, she instantly grabbed the candle positioned on a shelf to her left, lighting it quickly with the Bic that lay beside it. She replaced the lighter, closed the door behind her, and then walked past the stage to the u-shaped end of the bar. There, she set the candle on the bar top and then exhaled a gaping sigh.

The candle was largely unnecessary at this time of day, as sunlight was still shining in through the small recess window over the stage; but Danielle knew it would be dark soon, and at night, Raise the Flagon was a dungeon.

Candles, however, were a resource of which she had plenty. Candy's Candles sat directly across the street from Raise the Flagon, so Danielle had stockpiled dozens of the wax torches, and, if she ran low, a virtual limitless supply was only steps away from her front door.

So, she kept a candle lit almost constantly when she was home, and not just for the light it provided. Danielle's head ached almost constantly now—it was the tension, she assumed—and the fragrance of the wax and bounce of the flame offered at least a sliver of relief.

And, right now, she needed that relief as much as ever. Day two in the achievement of her next goal had resulted in failure.

No rifle found.

She wasn't discouraged though. Not yet. This current objective was ambitious, and she had given herself a week to cross it off. Finding a rifle—or a gun of any type—wouldn't be easy. Not in this town. Not this long after they had come with the snow.

It had been four months since the world exploded in a detonation of white death. That was Danielle's estimate anyway. Four months. It was a laughably short period, really. It felt much closer to four years. Tom's Diner seemed like a lifetime ago. The days when rescue seemed like just a matter of time, when she still clung to hope that her life of routine and monotony would resume as normal.

Danielle estimated it had been about six weeks since she'd been on her own, maybe miscalculating by a week in either direction. But not more. A month and a half seemed about right.

The weather was still relatively mild, and the leaves were holding steady. She figured it was mid-September, the cooler mornings suggesting fall was on the doorstep. The crippling snows of May had long since melted and it appeared the world had recovered to its normal seasonal patterns. But another month or so and warmth would again be an issue. A month after that and Danielle would be in real trouble.

Gotta hit your numbers.

Danielle snickered as the corporate idiom flashed in her mind, but it turned her attention to the list of goals hanging over the bar behind her. She never got much sales experience as a waitress—and before that as a receptionist at a veterinary clinic—aside from asking who wanted dessert as she cleared away empty dinner plates. So 'hitting her numbers' wasn't something Danielle could relate to from any real personal experience.

Still, though, she liked the urgency of the maxim, the implied consequences for failure, and she tried to apply it daily now to her current scenario.

She turned toward the bar and studied the list again, the light from the window shining on it as if it were a holy relic on an altar. She focused on the current goal—Goal 2: Find a Rifle—and as she continued further down the list, her heart rate increased with every number she read. When she reached the last one—Goal 8—her jaws were clenched so tightly it felt as if her teeth would shatter.

They were all there—she felt sure of it—the goals that would free her from this nightmare and avenge the misery that was her life for the past four months.

All she had to do now was capture them.

Hit the numbers.

She had begun this preliminary process of setting goals immediately after staking her claim to Raise the Flagon, almost two weeks after the helicopter had flown off without her, leaving her stranded inside the cordon alone.

At first, the goals she set were pedestrian things, easy stuff. *Eat. Secure water. Stay alive.* Things of that nature. But it wasn't long until Danielle quickly recognized these objectives as inadequate, even counterproductive. They were too vague, too existential. She needed specifics. Things that were measurable.

So 'Eat' became 'Find food.' Then 'Find vegetables' or 'Catch a fish' (the last of which turned out to be a joke of an effort, and fish was quickly eliminated as a diet possibility).

Still, though, even with the specifics, Danielle's daily aims were almost all food-related, and though eating was an obvious necessity, the goals weren't stretching her. Finding food, though angst-ridden, was not as difficult as she had expected; other than the menace of the crabs, it seemed she was alone inside the cordon, which meant competition for food was virtually non-existent. The non-perishable items that sat on shelves in supermarkets and convenient stores—not to mention in the homes of the now-dead or changed citizens—were hers for the taking. Cans of ravioli and tuna and olives and beans were plentiful.

So, too, were some of the more luxurious items like meat and bread and fruit, but those lasted only a few weeks, when the world—and the freezers—were still cold. And it was this failure of refrigeration that began Danielle's shift towards greater goals, understanding on a conscious level that the food wouldn't last forever. Besides, even if it did, the search for sustenance only kept her spinning in place, surviving the landscape like an animal in the jungle. If she ever wanted to reclaim her humanity, if she one day wanted to live a life outside again, she would need to expand her efforts beyond the basics, to strive toward things that would keep her not just alive, but moving forward, toward escape from the forsaken world in which she now existed.

So, her daily goals of food soon became broader objectives, most of which required either a broadening of her skill set or an expansion of her comfort zone. The first of these goals, which Danielle had accomplished and crossed off her list only days ago, was a mapping of the cordon.

Goal 1: Map the Cordon.

It wasn't an especially difficult task, as most of the boundaries Danielle knew already. The Maripo River Bridge and the natural southern boundaries in Warren County were obvious, but the areas that were still in question Danielle now had on paper, having made daily visits to the borders for two weeks, casing them with binoculars from afar until the map was complete. It was no Rand McNally in terms of specifics, but it was good enough. She now knew the lines of demarcation, the vulnerabilities that offered escape.

Escape.

The word popped into Danielle's mind several times a day now.

She had made four attempts to this point, two of which were earnest, but none of them had really come close to putting her outside the border. And that wouldn't get easier. She had been spotted at the edge of the cordon a few mornings earlier by a pair of soldiers, so now the military that was keeping the area on lockdown from crabs knew she was alive. The soldiers were a threat once again, and she assumed that soon other men, who had lately kept out of the interior, would be coming for her soon.

In any case, escape would have to wait. She wasn't ready for that goal yet. She had a few more things to accomplish first. Stones to step across. Preparations to make. Her past attempts had been failures, but they hadn't discouraged her. On the contrary. They had taught her about restraint and reflection, that her list should be arranged logically so that each goal could build upon the next.

Goal 2: Find a Rifle.

There would be no escape without a weapon.

She had had to leave her shotgun behind during the escape from Stella and her soldiers, but she had found a replacement almost immediately, another shotgun, resting by the steering wheel of a Buick, the previous owner beside it, tilted like a mannequin in the direction of the passenger seat, his head blown off from the mouth up.

That fortuitous find had not been a sign of things to come, however. It was the only gun Danielle had found since her getaway, and she was now down to her last few shells. She continued to keep her eyes peeled for more ammo, but bullets were only part of the problem. The truth was, she needed something with a little more range, something that could take the head off a crab or a soldier from a place high and hidden. She was no marksman for sure (though her shotgun acumen had been proven apt on the river cruiser), but she figured with a quality rifle and a decent sight she could do some damage.

But Maripo County was famous for its lack of gun retailers, so that left Danielle two options to reach her goal: attempt to cross the bridge back to Warren (no thank you!) or find a rifle in one of Maripo's private residences. The second option—investigating basements and scouring garages—was a process that offered the possibilities of cream-colored monsters around some corners and mercenaries around others. But it was her only real choice, maddening though it was.

And, indeed, the search on that day had been slow and fruitless. Pathetic really. Not a day's work about which Danielle felt proud. She had felt a bit more spooked than usual, her intuition a bit more heightened, particularly now that she was on the radar of the soldiers.

She had to strengthen her nerves, to keep them from fraying into uselessness. She had come a long way over the past few weeks; now was not the time to come apart at the seams.

In those first two or three days following her escape from the colonel and Stella, Danielle had wandered the landscape like a vagabond, distraught, barely feeling the need to shelter from the cold, almost welcoming the crabs to come and devour her. How much of a chance did she really have on her own, with hordes of crabs and an army of soldiers against her? She had watched helplessly as the helicopter flew off above the old D&W building, heading north out of Maripo, a sight that was nothing short of distressing at the time, debilitating. She had missed her opportunity for escape, and it was one unlikely to present itself again.

But then the snows began to melt—rapidly—and the roaming white devils quickly turned to rotting white corpses, dying as a result of either the atmosphere around them or the gnarled fingers and teeth of their brothers and sisters in battle. Danielle had watched in horror as the white savages ran tormentedly about the streets, fighting amongst themselves and yawning in desperation toward the sky. They had looked to be in unimaginable pain, as if they were burning from the inside. She still sometimes woke to the sounds of their muted screams of dying.

By day four, every crab Danielle saw was a dead one, and by the end of the week, her spirits began to lift incrementally. Was it possible that all the monsters were dead? She didn't know for sure, but the idea had wedged itself in Danielle's mind, giving her faith, growing her optimism. Her quest to survive would still be difficult, of course, but with no crabs hunting her, it was no longer impossible. She had been lucky. That was all there was to it. She was alone and stranded in the cordon (so not exactly a lottery winner!), but the melting had killed off her predators. She had a chance now, hope, and, considering the situation, hope was about all she could have asked for.

And then, over breakfast on the eighth day, her hope shattered like a Faberge egg.

She had been sitting at a window booth in the Riverside Diner, a nice spot really, a Father's Day kind of place with a view of the bridge and a clear sightline over to Warren County. The location made Tom's strip mall spot look like Baghdad, and even under the circumstances, Danielle hadn't been able to help but do a little math, calculating how many more tips she would have gotten working in this part of town.

Still though, on the inside, diners were mostly the same, with red puffy booths and chrome swivel stools, and a menu of omelettes and burgers and chicken nuggets for the kiddos.

And frozen lasagna.

Perhaps the Italian delicacy wasn't a staple of American diners, but Danielle had found a pre-made frozen version in the Riverside's freezer, a modern number with a tight seal and several more days of sustainability.

The lasagna had been fully cooked but would take several hours to thaw, and in the meantime, Danielle had grabbed a handful of crackers and cozied up in the booth, taking a breather, basking in the updated familiarity of the joint. She was relaxing, if only for a moment, gazing out at the river. Maybe the place could even be her base for the next few days, she had thought. Food and high ground, two of the more important qualities in any fort.

And perhaps escape—or even rescue—was imminent, she had thought. With the crabs all dead, it was simply a matter of biding her time. There had been no way of knowing what was happening on the outside, of course, but if the crabs were dead, extinguished for good, there would be no need for the cordon any longer.

And then she saw movement near the bridge.

She had been staring out across the river, waiting for the lasagna to thaw, reflecting on the first days of the crisis, and then later when Dominic arrived at Tom's. She had placed a cracker in her mouth, resting it upon her tongue, lost in a stray memory of her parents, wondering what had become of them.

The movement was just a flash at first, a shuttering of what appeared to be light off the fender of a Dodge Charger. It was morning and a light fog was settling, and the cloud cover triggered a warning in Danielle that the flash she had seen wasn't the sun.

Danielle had propped herself to her knees first, and then to her feet, standing atop the booth and pressing her face to the glass like a toddler in the ape house at the zoo, her eyes as wide as the brim of the coffee cup on the table below her.

She saw nothing at first, so she moved off the booth and walked to the door, not taking her eyes off the place where the light had originated. When she reached the glass entrance, she had stood there staring, waiting for the movement again, keeping a small space in her mind for hope, optimistic that the flash of light had originated from an ambulance or fire truck, or perhaps a county cop or state trooper, armed and uncorrupted, poised for rescue.

But that hope had dissolved like a cube of sugar in hot tea.

From her new perspective, Danielle could see them, a pair of crabs, standing at the base of the bridge in such a way that their bodies had blended seamlessly with the gray of the concrete, making them invisible. But she could see them with perfect clarity now, hunched like monkeys, their backs facing Danielle so that they looked like two melting snowmen. Except their whiteness had changed, no longer the chalk white that had been characteristic of the crabs from the early days. Their color was a dirty white now, as if they had been damaged by smoke, the hue of snow found on the curb of a hardware store two days after a storm.

Danielle had kept her stare fixed on the two figures, watching them as they gawked toward the water, their bodies wavering slightly, their heads twitching up and down, left and right, as if uncontrollable, like nervous hens in a barnyard.

And then, for reasons Danielle would never quite be able to explain, she opened the door and stepped out to the sloshy snow on the diner stoop, compelled to get an unfettered look at the beasts.

With the first crunchy step, both crabs froze in place; on the second, they spun toward Danielle like a pair of mongooses.

They were fifty yards away, perhaps a bit more, but even from that distance, Danielle could see the aggression in their attentive expressions, the wrinkle of their heads, the cocking down of their necks, measuring. They stood that way for only a beat, however; within seconds, they were sprinting toward her.

Danielle immediately retreated through the diner door, closing it slowly and locking it, the whole time watching the undead albinos rushing at her like torpedos until they collapsed against the door, splashing against the glass panes like a pair of exploding snowballs.

Danielle recalled that they had lingered there for hours, their bodies pressed against the two doors of the entrance like leeches, staring and watching Danielle's movements inside, occasionally opening their mouths wide in silent, horrifying gapes.

She had seen the same type of violence from the crabs before, of course, at the diner with Tom's son, Greg, and later in the Thai restaurant with Alvaro.

And then on the water during her group's attempted escape from Warren County, when the fiends had dropped from the bridge like icicles and built a link of bodies to their cruiser boat.

But the reaction of the beasts that day at the Riverside Diner had felt different to Danielle. It wasn't curiosity that had drawn them to her, and they hadn't been provoked by her proximity or felt trapped like the crab inside Thai Palace. The monsters at the Riverside that day seemed not just defensive or hungry. They seemed angry. Rabid.

By nightfall, the pair of crabs at the door had vanished, but Danielle had remained at the diner for another two days, barely sleeping as she kept watch from behind the counter, quivering with each gust of wind or scurrying squirrel on the doorstep. Perhaps the next attack would come from a different angle, she had thought, from the roof or the delivery area out back.

As she stood guard throughout the next two nights, she had considered that perhaps it was only a few of the stronger ones that had survived the melting, and it was just a matter of time until they, too, died off. Maybe the cold had kept them alive in the beginning, their ferocity at bay, preserving both their bodies and tempers like meat in a freezer. And when the world began to warm again, the weaker of the species had spoiled quickly, leaving only the desperate strong to survive, if only for a few more days.

It was only a theory, of course, and though it may have proven partly true, the last bit, the portion about the strong having only days to live, was quickly dispelled. As the days turned to weeks, and later a month, Danielle knew the crabs that had survived weren't dying at all.

On the contrary; they were getting stronger.

Danielle had left the Riverside Diner on the third day after the attack, searching for a location with more security. The diner, though ideal from the standpoint of food and comfort, was a freestanding, glass-fronted restaurant on the water. It was simply too exposed. It would be only a matter of time before every window was blanketed in white crabs, their bodies clinging to the glass like giant white frogs on the panes of a lake-cabin porch.

And glass wasn't steel, or even wood; eventually the wave of crabs would crash in on her like an avalanche.

Danielle had set out on her trek toward downtown Maripo like an assassin, traveling the roads that led away from the river, slowly, methodically, hiding out in deserted homes and stores along the route, expecting to see the spidery beasts at the end of every blink.

But her journey to the county hub had been without in-cident. She saw not a single crab, in fact, and once she had reached the cluster of buildings that formed the downtown area, Raise the Flagon quickly became her new home.

The city-center of Maripo was small by most standards, but the eclectic architecture and numerous doorways and al-leys gave it a sense of security that the suburban and rural sections of the county did not. And the group of buildings by Raise the Flagon was perfect. Not only did Danielle get the below-ground feature of the bar, on the opposite side of the alley was the C.M. Jones Realty building, which was five-stories high and offered an above-the-world perspective of the cordoned off area.

By the third day in her new home, Danielle had begun watching for crabs from this new high ground across the al-ley, and only a day later, she observed a second pair of the new off-white breed of crabs emerge from the parking garage next to the courthouse, three blocks from the building.

The pair had moved slowly, lumbering, nearly staggering as they exited the garage onto the street, so unlike what Danielle had seen at the diner. One stood upright and hunched, nearly dragging its knuckles; the second was on all fours, bounding like a chimp. Their heads bobbed down for moments at a time before twitching sideways, as if they'd heard some distant sound or caught a smell on the breeze.

Danielle began to stagger the times for when she would observe the streets of downtown Maripo, hoping to acquire some piece of datum that might keep her alive, assist in her escape. She always sat well back from the window during these stakeouts, never quite sure when a group would suddenly appear around a corner and stride up the sidewalk on Franklin. To this point, the caution had been largely unnecessary, as none of the crabs had raised their heads to look up, but she assumed that day would come, and there was no point taking a risk.

What became obvious within that first week, however, was that there were far fewer crabs than before—probably by as much as two-thirds or more. But what they lacked in numbers, they made up for in randomness, unpredictability. They moved in pairs and threesomes—that seemed a constant—but beyond that, the details of how they lived and when they came out were a mystery.

By the end of the second week, Danielle had begun to observe them at least once a day, but she still hadn't established any routine or pattern to their movements. And though Raise the Flagon was stocked with booze, its nonperishable food was limited, and eventually the time came when she had to venture beyond the corner at Huntington and Poplar and further into the city for provisions.

Danielle closed her eyes and came back to the present, not ready to dive into the next part of her recent history, those first treacherous days when she had hunted the city for food and supplies. She had made it out alive; that was all that mattered now.

No more reflection tonight.

She leaned over the bar and grabbed the fifth of whiskey which was now down to about a tenth. Dewar's. Blended. Not too shabby. *Never could have afforded this a year ago*, she thought.

Bright sides and all that.

She poured a careful shot and dumped it into a tumbler, and then took a sip, swirling the warm liquid across her tongue and gums. She took a deep breath, enjoying the prickly burn of the scotch, and then she tipped the glass again, this time shooting what remained.

Done for the night.

She allowed herself one shot a day, just to take the edge off. Gotta keep it together.

Tomorrow would be better. She would rise early. There were goals to achieve.

Find a Rifle.

2.

Danielle kicked the bottom of the front door with her foot, an informal knock, just a tap really, as if casually testing the tires on a new car. She turned back toward the street and paused, scanning the vacant cul-de-sac for any sign of being watched. Nothing. With her eyes still on the road, she then placed her hand on the knob and turned.

Locked.

She stepped off the porch and quickly headed toward the back of the ranch-style home, a sprawling house that was as big as the first three Danielle grew up in combined.

She had made the decision to continue her search for a rifle west of downtown, beginning with the upper-middle-class neighborhood in which she was now. Her hopes were low that she would find the coveted prize there, but she hadn't explored this part of town yet, and before she simply set off toward the country where rifles were almost certainly more plentiful, she wanted to cover the nearer bases first. If she could accomplish her goals without having to roam miles into the countryside, that was obviously preferable, and if nothing turned up in this posh part of town, she would continue west toward the perimeter.

Therein lay the dilemma, however. Although she was far more likely to score a Remington and a box of shells in one of the homes near the blockade, she was also putting herself at risk being so close to the fortified edges. And she'd already developed enough gray hairs mapping the cordon,

18

so she kept her fingers crossed that she could avoid a return there until it was time to escape.

The sun had just begun to climb above the rooftops of the neighborhood homes, and the house she was attempting to raid was only her third of the day, the first two bearing nothing deadlier than a butcher's knife and a Louisville Slugger.

But this place looked more promising.

There was a flagpole in the yard and a Chevy Silverado in the drive, and Danielle estimated (based strictly on knee-jerk stereotyping) she was more likely to find a gun here than in the houses beside it. The one on the left had a Honda Odyssey in the drive, the other a Suburban and Land Rover paired neatly in the open garage. It was pop psychology at its best, of course, but Danielle figured screw it: in her own little mini-apocalypse, she was allowed to be politically incorrect.

She stepped quietly around the side of the house until she reached the beginning of a six-foot-high privacy fence that stretched maybe twenty yards out. She followed the wood planks to the corner and turned left, tracing it down the long side of the rectangle, walking until she came to a gate at the back.

The top of the fence was dog-eared and a good six inches over Danielle's head, but the lock had been installed near the top of the gate, and she was tall enough that she could reach over and release it.

She stood on her tiptoes and felt over the top for the iron hardware, and as she pulled up on the hinge and drew the gate open toward her, she immediately heard the sound of trickling water coming from somewhere inside the yard.

Danielle held her breath, listening. A burst pipe? Perhaps some final runoff from the snow that had covered this sliver of earth only weeks ago?

Danielle pulled the gate fully open and stepped inside, and there, standing with his back toward her, in the far corner of the fence where it buttressed the house, was a boy, urinating against the base of the enclosure.

Danielle threw a hand to her mouth and gasped, instinctively easing the gate steady so as not to evoke any further squeals from the hinges or pops from the wood. The boy hadn't heard her, not yet, not over the sound of his splashing pee, and in an instant, Danielle weighed her options.

From behind, the boy appeared to be African-American, maybe mixed race, perhaps twelve or thirteen, old enough that if Danielle could get his attention without severely startling him, she could introduce herself calmly, reason with him, find out who he was and how he had survived for this long inside.

Or else she could retreat. There was still that window of opportunity. Now that she knew for sure there were more survivors inside the barrier—at least one anyway—she could go back to her base and develop a plan on how to deal with him, and then return later under more stable circumstances.

And armed, of course. Just in case. She had left the shotgun at the Flagon, not wanting the extra baggage in case she found a rifle. Who could have known?

"Who are you?" a voice boomed from somewhere in the house, and Danielle immediately threw her hands out in front of her, her fingers splayed, showing she was unarmed, suddenly grateful for her decision regarding the shotgun.

She didn't so much as wiggle her toes as she waited for some type of command from the voice, which was male, deep, but also calm and measured. Danielle assumed the father.

The boy spun toward Danielle, whizzing the last of his bladder's load in a wild spray, and Danielle reflexively averted her eyes to avoid espying the boy's private parts.

"It's okay," she said, staring at the sky as she spoke to both the boy and the voice behind her. "I'm alone. I thought your house was empty. I thought they were all empty. I'll just leave. I'll leave you alone."

This time Danielle heard the shifting of a round into a chamber, and she knew now there was a rifle pointed at her.

Looks like I came to the right place, she thought.

"Don't take a step. In any direction."

"Okay."

The boy looked toward a spot just to the left and behind Danielle, and she turned slightly to get a glimpse, keeping her feet flat to the ground. She could see a window there, cracked open but shrouded in curtains, and sticking through it, resting on the sill, was the barrel of the rifle.

"I asked you a question. Who are you?"

"My name is Danielle," she called, staring up to the sky again. "I'm trapped in here just like you. I've been inside since the beginning. Since the snow started falling."

"Us too!" the boy cried.

"Quiet, Michael!"

Danielle looked at the teenager and nodded, smiling. She judged the boy to be a little older than her original estimate, fourteen probably, though short for his age.

"Hi, Michael," she said, almost seeing the cringe of the boy's father behind the drapes at having unwittingly revealed his son's name. "It's nice to meet you."

Michael said nothing, and within seconds, the glass door of the walkout basement slid open and the metal barrel that was in the window moments ago now emerged through the doorway.

"Whoa, whoa, whoa!" Danielle yelped, raising her arms higher.

The man holding the gun stepped out to the stoop, staring at Danielle through the sight as he came. Almost instantly, however, he lowered the gun to his hip and lifted his chin high, chest out, keeping his narrow glare on the trespasser standing before him.

The man was black, well-built, mid-forties, maybe older; his posture and tenor—not to mention the assault rifle in his hands—suggested military.

"Get inside, Michael," he said, not taking his eyes off Danielle.

There was a pause in Michael's obedience, but it was short-lived, and without another word, the boy followed his father's command and sheepishly ducked back into the house.

"Where are you staying?" the man asked.

It was the question of a soldier, Danielle thought, reinforcing her military assessment. "Not far from here. Two miles maybe. Franklin and Poplar."

"Downtown? You're living downtown?"

"I am now." Danielle had questions of her own and she quickly turned the interview. "How about you guys? Are you alone here? Is this your house or...or are you squatting here?"

"Why do you ask that?"

Danielle shrugged. "I don't know. I'm not living in *my* house."

"You think a black man can't be a patriot and drive a pick-up truck, is that it?"

"What? No! I—"

The man grinned and cocked his head up, letting Danielle in on the joke.

Danielle smiled, squinting in mock amusement.

The man's expression grew serious again. "It is my house. And we don't leave it often. Michael almost never."

Danielle took this as a threat, that if she had plans on staking them out and doubling back later, she'd be wise to think better of it. It was a good sign, she thought. It meant he had no intent on harming her as long as she kept cool.

"Still though, nature doesn't care that the plumbing's out, so...well...I'm sure you know the deal as well as we do."

Danielle grinned and nodded.

"You need food, I assume? That's what you're here for? I've got a little. No water though. Can't part with that."

"That's kind of you. Really, thank you for the offer. But I'm here for another reason, actually."

The man cocked his head, curious.

"I'm looking for a rifle. Kind of like the one in your hand there. But I guess you're using yours."

The man gave a full grin this time, nodding. "I am using this one, Danielle, but why don't you step inside. I might have one to spare."

3.

Danielle had never actually been inside a gun shop, but the storage room in Scott Jenkins' basement looked exactly like ones she had seen portrayed on television shows and in movies. The rifles were lined along the wall in their slotted stands, neatly at attention like the soldiers for whom they'd been crafted. Danielle's father had been a hunter, and she'd gone with him a handful of times, so rifles weren't quite a mystery to her; but the arsenal before her was stunning.

"Just a collector, really," Scott stated flatly, pulling the key from the huge bolt lock above the door. "Guess my hobby comes in handier than baseball cards, huh?"

"That it does." Danielle pulled her stare away from the weapons and looked at her new cordon neighbor. "Have you had to use one yet?"

"Kuwait. November 1990."

That wasn't what Danielle meant, and she knew Scott knew it too, so she kept quiet, allowing him a moment to arrive at the answer she was after.

"Killed probably twenty of them. Maybe twenty-five." He closed his eyes and took a deep breath. "Still can't believe it." Scott lingered for a moment and then snapped his eyes wide; they were full of confusion now, terror. "How long has it been?"

"I think about four months."

The man kept his eyes locked on Danielle as if waiting for more from her, and when she said nothing, he simply nodded.

And then he began his story.

"They were outside when I heard the blast. My twins. Right in the side yard between the sandbox and the playground." He smiled at Danielle. "Never used the sandbox though. Even when they were little."

Danielle smiled back sadly.

"Of course, I rushed to the window, terrified, expecting to see...I don't know, a plane going down or something. Rockets in the air. I don't know." He shrugged. "But there was nothing. Just the two most beautiful eight-year-old girls you ever saw." He paused and swallowed, staring at a spot low on the wall. "Except..."

Danielle could see the tension growing in his neck, and she tried to relax her own muscles, hoping unconsciously to bring Scott down a notch or two.

"Except a few seconds later the snow started to fall, and within minutes, they were throwing it at each other, laughing like fools." He looked up at Danielle again. "It was May, and they were having a snowball fight. And sticking their tongues out to catch the falling flakes." He frowned and shook his head ruefully. "I knew there was something wrong. Didn't know what, of course, but I knew. Just let 'em play right on through though. Stood right at the sink and watched my girls splash that death powder all over each other."

Danielle listened with her heart in her throat, the tears already forming behind her eyes as she imagined the children Scott had described, frolicking in their final moments.

She had never seen the change occur in anyone she had loved. She was at the diner that day, working a double shift as usual, and once it became obvious the spring snow was a signal of catastrophe, and that the world—or at least Warren and Maripo Counties—had changed forever, there was no leaving. Danielle's parents still lived in the area, just outside the cordon (she couldn't imagine the struggle they were dealing with not knowing their daughter's fate), and her two sisters had moved away years ago, one to Europe with her husband who was in the Army.

What was the story they were being told right now? Danielle thought absently, though not for the first time. *Who on the outside was able to keep this huge tract of land shrouded in mystery?*

Danielle shook away the questions, re-focusing. Finding the responsible parties was a goal further down on her list.

"It happened quick, you know?" Scott Jenkins used the knuckle of his thumb to wipe a tear from the corner of his eye. "The girls finally came inside and started complaining that they were hot. Then that they were tired and needed to lay down. Both of 'em, same thing. So I sent them to their room and...couldn't have been five minutes 'til I heard the screams."

"Dad?"

Michael appeared at the top of the basement stairs.

"Go back to the kitchen, Michael!" Scott barked.

Michael bowed his head and walked out of the doorway.

"It's okay, Mr. Jenkins, you don't have to—"

"I want to," Scott replied softly, nodding his head. "I've never spoken about it. I mean, to who, right?" He shrugged. "And I need to. I do. It's true what they say about going to therapy. Talking out your shit. Or at least talking out the shit that traumatized you. Doesn't have to be with a doctor, but you gotta get it out. The people I shot in the Gulf, what that did to me, I don't know what I'd have been like if I didn't have my buddies to talk to about it." He paused. "But not with this."

Scott scoffed, his eyes wide and pleading, trying to impart the injustice of his situation.

"I ran up to Jay and Izzy's room, and when I opened the door..." Scott stopped and put his hand to his mouth, as if preparing to vomit, and then he bent over at the waist and began to cry.

"It's okay, Mr. Jenkins."

Scott fell to his knees and then sat back in a heap against the wall, his hands across his face as he sobbed.

Danielle stood helpless at the doorway to the armory, unsure of how to console the man on the floor beneath her. But she figured this was what he needed, to let out the pain that had been eating him from the inside, and her mere presence was all that was necessary.

A minute or so passed when Scott finally wiped the last of his tears away, concluding the session with several deep breaths. He continued. "Izzy had changed. Her body was as white as the snow outside. She looked like a...a alien, like the images they show you in those abduction stories. Except her eyes weren't huge like that, but they were...so black. And the features of her body were like...like they'd been erased. Erased and then bleached."

He paused as his face bled into an expression of helpless terror, and then he looked up toward the ceiling, recollecting.

"Not Jaycee though. She was...still in the process. But...Izzy had already turned on her. Had already begun—"

"Dad!"

Michael was at the top of the stairs again, listening to the story from the landing above, and Danielle realized he was hearing the events for the first time and had now heard enough.

Scott closed his eyes and shook off the rest of the story. "Michael's mother was at the store. She never came home. For all I know, she's one of the ones I killed."

Danielle continued to stand in awkward silence, not sure whether to console the man or allow his emotions to run their course. She decided on the latter, and after several more minutes passed, the man stood and walked past her and up the stairs.

At the top of the landing, just before he exited the basement, he turned back to Danielle and said, "Take whichever gun you want. The rounds are stacked beside them. And please, if you don't mind, limit yourself to five boxes."

Kill a Crab

1.

The next morning, Danielle stood atop the bar and used a fine point Sharpie to cross the second goal off her list.

Goal 2. ~~Find a Rifle~~

The moment Scott Jenkins climbed the last stair and was out of Danielle's view, she had chosen her weapon quickly and then fled like a burglar through the sliding door and out the back gate. And once she reached the tree-lined street of the cul-de-sac, she ran the entire way back to the Flagon, sprinting at times when her lungs allowed it.

Danielle had made it back to the bar sans issues, and though she hadn't suspected any elaborate traps to have been laid along her route, she was living in a different world now, and she took nothing for granted.

But there had been no encounters, no sightings, and at an hour no later than noon, Danielle had already accomplished the second of eight goals on her list.

But she had carried something else back from the Jenkins' residence, and it was a feeling that began tugging at her mind before she was even a block away from the upscale home.

Guilt.

She had left a child behind, and though Danielle didn't get the impression that Scott Jenkins was violent or abusive—on the contrary, it seemed he had done everything a father should to keep his son alive under the circum-

stances—there was an instability in the man, a rupture in his psyche, and that wasn't likely to get better in the solitude of his bunkered house.

But Danielle didn't have the luxury of assuaging her guilt, at least not yet. She had a process to work through, and if she did it properly, she would find the Jenkins again, and, if possible, help bring them out of this world of death and fear. The boy and his father were new motivations in Danielle's arsenal now, new purposes driving her to accomplish the remaining six objectives on her list.

Next things next though.

Goal 3: Kill a Crab

She had killed crabs before of course—several of them, in fact—but not since the days following the Maripo river crossing, when she had guided James, Tom and Stella to the relative safety of the bank. There, Danielle had killed several of the monsters, and there was no doubt that without her, all three of her companions would have been killed more than once over.

And she had learned something deeper about herself during those days: she was a survivor. A killer. Capable of both mercy and cruelty. She had felt no remorse for the white beasts as she slaughtered them, and had even enjoyed watching the crimson explosions from their heads and chest dye their chalky bodies like a Pollack.

It wasn't the violence she'd enjoyed, though—she wasn't psychotic—it was the feeling of satisfaction each time one was destroyed, a buoying of hope that with the thinning of her enemies, the prospects of survival and escape grew stronger.

But that was months ago, and the monsters she had taken out by the bank of the river had all been close-range killings, shotgun blasts, and even one fatal takedown with a piece of stray lumber. The latter slaying had occurred during the night, when Danielle had saved James from one of the silent killers as he slept through his watch.

The killings hadn't been easy, of course—the horror of their proximity in this new, open world had been enough to reduce her companions to defenseless cowerers—but the experience they provided did little to prepare her for her latest goal. Her goal now was to kill a crab with skill, not with the sloppy rampaging methods she'd used on the riverbank. And for this she needed practice from range, reps with her new rifle, to learn how to kill with one clean shot from distance.

And only then would she draw a line through Goal 3 on her list. Only then would she be ready for the larger mission before her.

Danielle sat at the bar and stared up through the recess window that looked out onto the dirty street of the alley. She had become somewhat obsessed with the window lately, anticipating the day when a pair of white shins and calves would enter the frame of the glass, pausing for just a moment before finally turning its toes toward the window.

But the view had remained clear to this point, and, in fact, Danielle had never witnessed a crab in the alley at all. With every tour of duty atop the realty building, she always expected one to turn down the side street, shifting its focus on a dime as it caught a strange scent on a passing breeze, or else heard the scurry of a rat or a rummaging raccoon.

They always just passed by, however, luckily, as if the alley repelled them or existed in a blind spot.

But it was just a matter of time. The odds almost guaranteed it. And when it finally did happen, when one or two brave souls eventually ventured off the path of the main thoroughfare and headed into the narrow side street, the end of Danielle's barroom paradise would follow soon after. She had learned many of their patterns, and she knew by now that where one pair went, others tended to follow.

And when that day arrived, the day the first one ambled into the dark toward Raise the Flagon, she would plan to be gone by the following morning.

Danielle poured a half can of ginger ale into a plastic cup and hopped off the bar stool, and then she crossed the dance floor to one of the tables on the opposite side of the bar. She placed the soda on the tabletop and lit the candle in the center, and then picked up the rifle that had been gifted to her earlier that morning. She curled it up and down several times like a barbell, allowing the bulk of it to weigh heavy in her hands. She raised the sight to her eye now and looked through it from a few inches away before placing it flush to her socket, shrugging her shoulders up to get the proper feel. She stared through to the stage, focusing first on the center of the kick drum and then up to the top of a mic stand. Further up now to the spotlights, tapping her index finger against the metal trigger, pretending to pop a round in each bulb as she moved across the row and then down again, homing in now on the buttons of a floor amp.

She had selected a Remington 700 from Scott Jenkins' armory, and though there had been more effective looking guns along the wall—assault rifles with rapid fire capability—Danielle had never used those types before and they intimidated her; she didn't want to spend the next week on a learning curve, and when she fired her first round, it needed to be intended to kill.

The Remington 700 she knew, though. It was her father's gun of choice, and holding one again in the dark shelter brought the memory of him to her like a punch. She took the gun away from her face and lowered her head, allowing the memory of her beloved dad to run its course. She held her lids tightly to keep the tears at bay and then put the sight back to her eye, taking in a large breath as she did. Anger had replaced sorrow now, and she felt a driving urge to fire off a round and take out the neon Coors Light sign above the door. She wouldn't dare, of course, as it was not only destructive of her own home, it was likely to draw crabs her way.

But holding the gun now, her finger resting with dead weight on the trigger, Danielle also knew something else: Tomorrow was too far away. She couldn't wait until then to get to the roof of the car dealership. She had to begin her new mission today.

she stared at the sea of mint-new Mazda 6s and
that separated her from the showroom, similar im-
attack emerged in her mind. The cars were eight deep,
crab could be lurking behind any one of the bumpers,
ide any fender or quarter-panel or tire. She had consid-
walking the perimeter until she reached the back where
ervice entrance was; but the rear of the dealership had as
y obstacles as the front, dumpsters and service bays that
ked rife with treachery.

Danielle took a deep breath, stepped off the sidewalk,
d then took a slow step forward between the first pair of
rs, keeping her eyes peeled and her head on a swivel. She
eld the rifle high in order to clear the side-view mirror of
the car on her right, the weapon proving to be more of a bur-
den than a benefit. But she figured that wouldn't be the case
for long. She could almost smell the danger on the breeze.

She was halfway through the lot, with three rows of cars
still to go until she reached the showroom, when movement
to her right snared her attention.

Danielle shifted her eyes in the direction of the flicker,
but she kept her neck and head straight toward the door.

Two rows to go. Almost there.

The movement again, this time clearer, obvious, no mis-
taking its existence. A flash of white to the right and just
ahead of where Danielle stood frozen now. It came from in
front of the last row where the pavement met the hedges that
bordered the building.

Danielle stopped walking, stopped breathing, anticipating the movement again, her eyes a pair of narrow slits,
watching the location with a suspicious glare, silently praying

2.

The roof of Maripo Mazda was a fe\
the top-floor window of the C.M. Jo\
and wasn't likely to offer the same outw\
County. But the car dealership had other \
alty building didn't. It was a freestanding\
rooftop that offered a three-sixty view of dov\
large footprint meant there were fewer buildi\
the monsters from sight.

And, as important, it was several blocks from\
If her gunfire produced only the shattering of glass\
and concrete—and not the bones of wandering cra\
wouldn't risk drawing the beasts to her base. Of cou\
hadn't quite mapped her escape from the dealership\
whole scene went to hell, but that was a problem she de\
not to ponder. She'd made it out of tight spots before, an\
she thought too much about the potential one that lay ahe\
of her, she feared she might not follow through.

Danielle stood on the perimeter of the dealership, having walked the seven blocks from the Flagon at a pace just
below a trot. She had kept to the street proper during her
march, and though the road meant she was more exposed,
more visible to any stray beasts who might be wandering by,
the dark doorways of the businesses and town homes along
the sidewalk spooked her. She couldn't help but envision a
dormant crab exploding from one of the façades, hopping at
her with its mouth wide, fingers curled in grasping death.

the flash was nothing more than a white take-out bag, or perhaps a disposable service mat which had been caught up in a stray gust of wind.

But the air on the lot was as still as outer space, and Danielle knew in her heart it was something more.

The showroom was so close now, and the urge to make a dash over those final seven or eight steps was strong. *It could be like a firewalk*, she thought—*just do it and get it over with.*

But her instincts and intellect guided her differently. She knew better. Succumbing to urges was a character trait that no longer existed in the cordon. Anyone still inside who wasn't dead or a crab could thank prudence for their continued existence, pragmatism. Those who panicked or gave into impatience had been naturally selected for extinction.

Danielle slowly placed the rifle on the roof of a Mazda 3 to her left, absently wishing she now had the shotgun instead. But that would defeat the point, she knew. She was here for long-range target practice; if she had brought the shotgun with her, she wouldn't have put herself in this position to begin with.

She cleared her thoughts and focused back to the present, beginning to feel the fear growing inside her, alarm that at any moment one of the monsters would rise up beside her, or dash toward her from the front of the hood and snatch her before she could move into position.

With a move resembling a gymnast mounting a balance beam, Danielle pushed herself up to a sitting position on the hood of the 3 and then swung her legs up so that they were parallel with the engine cover, feet facing the grill. She then stood quickly and scuttled up to the roof, grabbing the rifle she had set there earlier. From there, she stood tall on the crown of the car, now with a clear view of the sprawling lot.

She took a deep breath and then brought the sight of the gun to her eye, focusing on the direction of the original movement, anticipating the black eyes of the crabs to come into view, staring back at her.

But there was only the white of the pavement, the glistening of chrome and glass. Danielle shifted her aim left now, her finger crooked and twitching, silently hoping a crab would appear. She figured if she couldn't make it to the roof, the practice offered by a crab scurrying across the lot would suffice for now.

Still nothing though, and she rotated her torso to the right, glaring toward the service entrance and the used car trailer that sat in the far corner of the property. A squirrel appeared from the bushes of a tree and ran toward the main building. With the gun, Danielle followed the animal, which stopped on its haunches for a moment, sniffing the air, and then galloped ahead down one of the aisles, sure of its stride and purpose. Danielle kept the squirrel locked in her scope, maintaining the center of the crosshairs on the rodent's torso.

And then, as quickly as the animal had appeared, it was gone, snatched from the road like a cricket into the mouth of a chameleon.

Danielle lowered the weapon and stared at the spot with her naked eyes, not exactly sure how it had vanished. Did she see a white hand? Or did the squirrel suddenly dash beneath a car, erratically changing directions as they often did, hastily hopping off to some new destination.

But Danielle suspected otherwise. It was the crab she'd seen flash in her periphery moments before. She was almost certain of it.

And now she had a bead on it.

She lowered herself down to a sitting position on the roof, and then, in one motion, Danielle slid down the glass of the windshield and dismounted the car, landing lightly on the pavement, never taking her eyes from the spot where the squirrel had been only seconds ago. She listened closely for any sounds of scampering, and then for the crunching of bones or tearing of hide, holding her chin up as she did, hoping to better receive auditory signals that matched those actions.

But there was only silence on the wind, so Danielle took a step forward toward the site of the squirrel, then another, lightly touching the ground with her toes like a Special Forces soldier, craning her neck around the bumper of each car she approached.

She stepped into the wide aisle of asphalt that separated the new and used cars, exposed now, staring at the empty spot where the squirrel had just been. She engaged the rifle and stepped to the rear of the car nearest the spot and then spun the barrel to the opposite side.

Nothing.

Danielle released a sigh and closed her eyes for a moment, and when she opened them and turned toward the showroom of Maripo Mazda, ready to make her final journey toward her goal of the main building and eventually the roof, she shrieked at the sight of two crabs hopping from the sidewalk, now moving toward her, dashing with speed, their arms akimbo like a pair of deranged chimpanzees.

Danielle couldn't believe the vision at first, and a low, horrified chuckle rumbled deep in her throat. But the truth of the moment quickly lodged in her mind, as did the primal instinct to run.

The used car trailer was closest; she would head toward that and pray the door would open when she arrived. But as she prepared for the desperate sprint, an even more profound force of nature took hold.

The one to kill.

Danielle knew on a baser level that running was a move of death in this situation. Even if the door to the trailer had been left unlocked, it was too far away, and though she could hold her own in a foot race, the crabs already had a head of steam while she'd be starting from still.

Danielle snapped the butt of the rifle to the pocket of her shoulder and steadied it with her left hand. She let out a breath and relaxed her neck, focusing her aim, harnessing the lessons she'd learned as a girl from her father. She exhaled fully and then squeezed the trigger in one fluid motion.

The report was deafening, but she held the position of the gun, resisting the urge to jerk her head up to witness the result of her shot.

And the technique paid off. She struck the crab coming at her from the left squarely in the face, directly between the eyes at the base of its nose, shattering its skull in a mask of red and cream. It fell to the ground in a heap, leaving its partner to carry on alone, which it did without hesitation.

The second white monster was maybe ten yards from Danielle now, and she calmly pivoted the gun to her right, calibrating the beast in her sights before squeezing the trigger again, hitting it in the chest just above the solar plexus.

This time the crab didn't fall instantly; instead, it stopped in place and looked down at its torso as if shocked to have been hit. It lingered in place for several seconds and then dropped to its knees, its arms hanging limply at its sides. Finally, the beast toppled forward, its face smacking the ground with a dull slap.

Danielle raised her eye from the sight and stared at the two killings with her bare eyes, feeling the power of death surge through her like electricity. She then scanned the lot for any more enemies, almost wishing more would appear—perhaps three this time—anxious for their prey, yet blissfully unaware of the violent deaths they would soon meet. With the rifle now fired, warm and heavy in her hands, Danielle had a new feeling of invincibility, as well as a burgeoning sense of pride, both in her demeanor and acumen.

She waited nearly a minute without stepping from her spot, swiveling her neck slowly back and forth, listening, sensing. Finally, when it was obvious no more crabs would appear, she continued with her target goal and jogged through the lot to the door of the showroom.

She placed her hand on the rectangular metal door handle, and then tugged on it gently, just testing the lock's engagement.

As expected, it was unlocked.

Danielle didn't rush straight in, however, hesitating on the sidewalk instead, recognizing that the potential for trouble still existed inside. To this point in her nightmare, Danielle hadn't seen a crab that could work a door, so anyone inside the dealership who had turned after the snow and didn't have a way to exit would have likely remained trapped inside, at least until a door had been opened for it. Or, if there were other survivors inside, people who hadn't turned and were armed and willing to give their turned fellow citizens the mercy of death, they may have quelled any danger by eliminating the white beasts themselves. She could hope.

The front of the dealership was a panorama of glass, and the showroom itself was a mostly white room consisting of thousands of square feet of wide-open space; so, if there was life inside, Danielle figured she would have seen it from her position at the door.

Still, there was no need to rush, and she waited several beats before tapping lightly on the glass to draw forward any lurking life. The report of gunfire from outside would likely have been enough to bring them to the surface, but one could never be too safe.

There was only stillness, however, so, finally, Danielle pulled opened the door and stepped inside, raising the rifle again to her shoulder, prepared to pick off any aggressors as they approached.

With the gun still raised, Danielle headed toward a narrow stairway that rose just to her left and which surely led to offices. She ascended the steps two at a time until she came to the top landing where a mezzanine area circled above the showroom, giving management and ownership a bird's eye view of the daily operations below. She went left, passing the office of the general manager and, beside it, the owner. She continued walking to the far wall where the track of the mezzanine began to curve, and there, rising up next to a utility room, was another set of stairs, this one metal and painted industrial-white. She walked to the top and came to a door with the words 'Roof – Employees Only' painted conspicuously at the top. Danielle grabbed the knob and turned, receiving only the frustrating snag of an unyielding handle.

"Dammit! Of course."

Don't get pessimistic, she scolded herself. *At least the front door was open.*

Danielle descended the stairs and headed back down the mezzanine until she came to the GM's office again. She pushed the door open and stood in the doorway, staring into a large room that had a long white desk and a view facing downtown. Just above her, she thought, on the roof over this office, that was where she needed to be. That was the direction to begin perfecting her shot. She had already killed two crabs, that was true, so, technically, she had achieved her next goal on the list. Again, though, killing them wasn't really the point. She needed to pop one from a couple hundred yards out, if possible. That was the skill she would need to move on to the next goal.

Danielle walked over to the general manager's desk and stood at the edge, studying the contents on top. Other than the usual computer and various papers and folders, there was a variety of personal things: wallet, phone, an unopened granola bar, the last of which Danielle instinctively grabbed and pushed into her pocket.

And a set of keys.

She eyed the set of twelve or so keys, instantly skeptical that any of them would fit the door that led to the roof of Maripo Mazda. *But maybe*, she thought. *Just maybe.* This guy was the GM after all, so it wasn't a stretch to imagine him comingling his house and car keys with the doors of his workplace. After all, Danielle had looped a key to Tom's Diner onto her personal ring a thousand years ago, only six months or so after starting work there.

She reached forward for the set, and as her fingertips were about to touch the leather of the keychain, a shifting sound like the scurry of a dog rumbled from behind her.

She froze like a mannequin in her extended position, listening, waiting for the sound to repeat. She held the pose for several beats, then, without turning toward the noise, Danielle pressed the front of her thighs against the edge of the desk and moved around the perimeter until she reached the chair that was pushed under the desk at the head. She lifted her eyes now and stared toward the door she had just entered, searching for the source of the sound.

And she found it quickly, at least a segment of it.

She could see only one white limb of the creature—its lower leg—while the rest of the crab was covered by the door that had been swung to the wall when she entered.

She raised the rifle, locking the exposed leg into the sight, and then continued around the desk until she was at the opposite corner from where she'd started, having now circumnavigated the full length of the bureau.

The back half of the crab was in full view now; the monster was in a prone position, face down, its head somewhere in the crevice where the open door met the jamb. Its left arm hung limply by its side, its hand unmoving. If Danielle hadn't heard the scuffle from that area earlier, she would have assumed it dead.

"Hey!" she called, touching the trigger with the side of her finger, waiting for the beast to snap to life and explode toward her.

Not a move.

Danielle repeated the lure and again got no reaction, so she moved a step forward, away from the desk and toward the entryway to the office. She took another step, then another, and was now only a yard of so from the door. She kept the gun high, pointed at the back of the crab, and when she was finally close enough, she nudged the door closed with the barrel of the gun, exposing the crab fully.

The monster was facing the wall, its left cheek flat to the floor, but the moment the door swung away, it snapped its neck around and stared up at Danielle, its teeth bared in silence, its jaws snapping up and down like a mechanical nutcracker. The creature's black eyes were as desolate as the world in which Danielle now lived, and it sported a dent in its head that ran from the top of its left orbital socket to the middle of its skull. The depression was the width of a pool cue, and a river of blood had dried in a cascade from the indentation down to the middle of its neck.

Danielle gasped at the horror of the sight, and, as if the sound of her catching breath activated something in the crab's brain, the beast made a lunging move upwards, grasping its fingers as it did, scrambling its feet beneath it in a cartoonish attempt to rise.

But before it could even get to the plateau of its knees, and before Danielle could snap of the round that would have brought an end to the thing's living damnation, the beast recoiled back to the floor, flailing in frustration and torture.

Danielle moved with pace now, backwards toward the far wall of the office, the aim of the rifle still pure, only breaking its mark when she slammed her back against a bookshelf. She lowered the gun now, breathing frantically as she continued to stare at the agitated creature, still weighing whether to bring the gun back to position and let a round fly into its rotted brain.

But she refrained from killing it for the moment, and instead locked her eyes on the body of the thing, trying to find the reason for its continued occupation of the floor, for why it hadn't rushed at her the way several dozen of its brethren had over the last few months.

And then she saw it. Its right hand was bound at the wrist by what appeared to be a thick piece of leather—a belt, she assumed—which had been wrapped onto itself and secured to a large couch that ran along the wall opposite where Danielle stood currently.

Danielle stared at the creature for a moment longer, weighing her options, trying to understand who had restrained the creature and why. *Had the beast done this to itself? Before the change when it was still a man? Had he seen the result of the others in his dealership who had been out in the snow and, not knowing for sure if he was to be next, tied himself up so that he couldn't harm anyone if he did change?*

It seemed the most likely scenario, and this made Danielle feel sympathy towards the creature, an emotion she rarely wasted on them.

She decided there was no real upside to wasting a bullet on the crab—not yet anyway—and she wasn't in the mood for blunt force murder. Maybe on her way out, after she'd achieved her goal for the day, if she had a couple of rounds remaining, she could stop back in and put the thing out of its misery.

She held the keys tightly and walked slowly back to the office door, edging sideways as she exited the room, pushing the door open onto the cornered beast again, keeping the danger of its continued thrashing at bay. Once outside on the mezzanine, she caught another glimpse of the creature, and its flailing now appeared more painful in the silence of distance. Danielle now promised herself to revisit the office before she left. The crabs were dangerous, that part was without question, but they were also suffering, and it was her duty as a human to end that suffering if she was able.

For now, however, she trotted back to the stairway that rose to the roof and then scaled the stairs two at a time until she was facing the door again. There was no point sifting through the set of keys, she figured; trying to find one that looked appropriate for the door was a fool's errand. So, she started with the first on the ring and tried them one at a time.

The task was cumbersome with the rifle in hand, so Danielle placed the gun on the top step to speed up the process, placing the second key in the hole and turning. Nothing. Third key. Again nothing. There were maybe ten still to go, and as she put the fourth key in the lock, she heard a sound behind her.

She turned on her heels, and as she did, her toes clipped the butt of the rifle, sending it over the edge of the landing and down the metal stairway. It skimmed like a toboggan as it descended on the lips of the steps, and then, as it reached the bottom, it nearly slid through the lower railing of the mezzanine down to the showroom below. Luckily, it stopped just short, the butt peeking several inches over the rim, threatening to plummet.

Danielle descended the first two steps on her way to retrieve the gun, but as she did, she saw a glimmer of white in the top line of her vision.

Danielle stood tall in a panic, and as she did, she immediately saw the source. Coming toward her down the length of the mezzanine was the crab from the general manager's office.

Danielle blinked several times as her brain attempted to fight off the reality of what her eyes were displaying. The crab continued bounding toward her, however, hopping on the balls of its feet, clicking its knuckles on the floor with each bounce like a rabid baboon. It then stood erect for a few paces, manlike, before dropping again to its more natural crab/chimp form.

Danielle's heart and jaw dropped simultaneously, and her eyes watered to the point of blurring her vision. She knew instantly there was no time to retrieve the rifle; even if she was able to secure it before the crab reached her, she would never be able to aim and shoot before the crab was on top of her.

Yet, although she was now weaponless, there was something different about this crab that would give her a chance at surviving. This beast was slower than the others, handicapped somehow; any of the others she had encountered over the months would have been within a few yards of her by now. This crab still had a ways to go, however, struggling to push off from the floor, not able to achieve the typical spring and acceleration as it tipped awkwardly to its right, nearly toppling over before needing to recalibrate its proper posture and re-start its attack.

Danielle was momentarily mesmerized by the movement, and she stared squinting at the beast, curious.

The crab toppled again, and this time, as it attempted to push itself up straight, Danielle spotted the disadvantage in its gait. It was missing its right hand. The arm that had been tethered to the belt and sofa was now free of any restricting thumb or fingers, having apparently been ripped from its wrist in a desperate need to escape. *Well*, Danielle thought, *at least I won't have to go back to grant it mercy.*

She turned back to the door that led to the roof now and, for no other reason than to break a pattern that had been unsuccessful to that point, she pinched the last key on the chain and slid it calmly into the lock, turning it to the right as she gripped the handle with her left hand.

The key rotated in the lock as if through butter, and, as Danielle turned the knob and pushed the door open onto the sunlight of the outside, from the corner of her eye she saw the attacking crab at the bottom of the stairs. It had made its way to the second step, sliding on the metal, unable to grip the floor with its injured hand. But it was progressing, and it seemed to be catching its stride. It was like a gargoyle come to life, she thought, learning the basics of human existence slowly but relentlessly.

Danielle pushed through to the roof and instantly spun to her left, ducking behind the ajar door, holding it open as if she were a butler inviting an emissary into a country manor.

Danielle counted the steps in her mind, trying to calculate when the crab would arrive, and then, as if on cue, the beast emerged through the door, barreling clumsily onto the gravelly, unfamiliar ground of the rooftop. Danielle couldn't see the creature, but she could hear its feet and hands scurrying several yards past the opening, and she peeked around the corner of the door just as it stopped suddenly at the parapet at the edge of the roof.

Danielle held her breath as she watched the crab stare out at the cityscape beyond the building, peering once to its left, lifting its head as if chasing the scent of Danielle, or perhaps searching for it, knowing instinctively that she must be close.

But Danielle wouldn't wait for the monster to find her. Instead, she spun quickly around to the interior side of the door and pulled it closed, resisting the urge to raise her eyes and observe the attack, which she knew from the sound of the ghost's scurrying feet was in progress.

The door latched closed with a thud, and Danielle was back on the landing of the interior stairway again, her back against the door as if keeping out the danger. She slowed her breathing, finally sighing with finality at having exorcised the beast to the roof. Within seconds, however, her heart was jolted to panic again as the crab hurled itself against the door from the outside.

Danielle shrieked and backed away, staring at the closed door suspiciously, waiting for the next crash which arrived seconds later.

They can't work doors, she reminded herself, though she couldn't imagine that skill deficiency would last forever. She considered locking the door again, just in case, but she planned to stay inside for only a moment. She still had a goal to achieve, and she wasn't going to let a single crab discourage that effort.

Danielle focused now and descended the stairs quickly, and then she carefully gripped the barrel of the strewn rifle and pulled it from the precipice with care. She held the weapon tightly to her body like a toddler with a security blanket and then turned and walked back to the top of the stairs, with purpose now, hoping along the short route to manufacture the confidence she would need to open the door again.

She reached the top and listened as the barrage against the metal barrier continued outside. She listened for a pattern now, a sequence or span of time between attacks, something she could record to gauge when to push the door open.

After two or three minutes, Danielle hadn't cracked any code, but she did note the delay between crashes was no less than eight seconds, and up to sixteen seconds on the high end. And they were beginning to diminish in ferocity as well, the thuds not rattling the door in the way they had in the beginning.

Danielle stopped on the third step from the top, and with the next slam, she gripped the doorknob and took a giant breath. Her palms were a sweaty mess, so she removed her hand from the knob and rubbed both palms down the thighs of her pants several times.

Another thudding crash and she re-gripped the door handle. That was it. One more and it was go time.

Bwum!

Danielle had figured eight seconds would be the right delay, gauging that the crab would linger on the door for a second or two after its assault and then turn and walk back toward the edge of the roof to begin another attempt. At that point, its back would be turned from the door, yet still close enough so as not to leave any question about the quality of Danielle's shot.

Six. Seven. Eight.

Danielle took a breath, allowing one more second to elapse, just to be sure, and then she pushed open the door firmly (though not so quickly that it would recoil closed) and immediately put the rifle to her shoulder, aiming.

And there it was, a bit farther across the roof than Danielle had estimated, but its advancement had put it in the perfect spot for Danielle, just at the edge of the roof, its back still facing the rooftop door.

Danielle put the rifle sight to her eye, aligning the back of the monster's head between the crosshairs, allowing her finger to rest limply against the trigger, ready to squeeze the crescent-shaped metal once she felt the aim was perfect.

Danielle let out a breath as the creature turned its head slowly toward her, the exhaustion and pain in the simple movement obvious. Its full torso followed next, displaying to Danielle the full carnage of blood and bruising that the beast had inflicted upon itself smashing against the heavy door.

They were so different now, she thought to herself (for what must have been the hundredth time since the melting). *They were so much more violent than before.*

She again reminisced about those first days outside the diner, when the snow on the ground still looked as white as talc and the creatures—'Ghosts,' the diner crowd had labeled them—first began to approach. Those beasts were reticent, docile even, and only after some unknown perimeter around them had been broken did they become violent, as when Greg had gotten so close to one he could have hugged it and was ripped apart.

But when the melting began, they began to change. And this new breed—the survivors—were nothing short of savage.

The crab ('ghost,' she remembered again. 'Crab' was Dominic's name for the damned, not hers, so, at least for the moment, she decided to revert to their original moniker.) stood on two feet and took a step forward, hunched aggressively, its mouth open in a yawning gape.

Without hesitation, Danielle fired a shot to the middle of its chest.

The ghost recoiled several paces toward the thigh-high parapet that fortified the ledge of the roof, crashing against the wall just below its buttocks. It maintained its balance and stood tall, however, its eyes a mixture of confusion and fury.

Without dropping her eye from the sight, Danielle chambered another round and fired again, this time striking the ghost in the middle of the forehead.

As if yoked from behind by some invisible string, the ghost toppled backwards over the edge, its toes pointing straight to the sky for just a blink before it disappeared from the building.

For a second or two, the air was as silent as the ocean's bottom, and then the unmistakable sound of shattering glass and bending metal rang out through the lot of the dealership below as the lifeless body of the ghost crashed atop the inventory.

And then came the blaring screech of a car alarm.

The police should be here soon, Danielle thought and then chortled aloud at the notion, knowing police response to a car alarm was an absurd idea even before the annihilation of Maripo and Warren Counties.

There would be no police, of course, but with the blaring screech of the alarm, Danielle assumed the ghosts would be on their way soon.

Danielle walked to the ledge and peered over, gawking at her dead victim's crumpled torso below, which had landed draped across the frame of the windshield, its right leg wedged between the broken glass, keeping the corpse from slinking to the ground.

She looked up toward the street now and scanned the width of the city, not knowing what to expect exactly, but fearing the worst. The ghosts had the ability to hear, that much Danielle knew, but there was no indication they were attracted to loud sounds or sirens. In fact, Danielle imagined the noise currently being made by the alarm would be particularly unattractive to them, as it would be to most animals.

She contemplated once more firing at the hood of the car, to quiet the beacon, but then decided she would put the hypothesis of the noise lure to the test. If the alarm was indeed a draw, that would be new data, material to analyze, information that may come in handy one day.

Of course, there was a downside to acquiring that knowledge; if the ghosts emerged from the shadows like rats from a ship and came toward the dealership by the dozens, she would be in serious trouble, especially if this new breed could form the ladder of bodies and climb the way Dominic had once described a lifetime ago in Tom's Diner.

Danielle walked to the western side of the roof, her thoughts wracking her nerves, and she suddenly had serious doubts about her decision to let the sound of the alarm continue to ring. She barely blinked as she scanned the distant streets for any hordes of ghosts, ready to turn with the rifle and take out the blaring siren behind her if she saw any mass movements. It may be too late by then, she knew—if the crabs discovered her location and waged an attack—and in that case, she would have no choice but to fight. She had killed three crabs already today—which wasn't nothing—and she was more than impressed by how quickly she reunited with a rifle.

But she also possessed a limited amount of ammo, and as her mind continued to race, she was beginning to develop a phobia of the roof. If they arrived en masse and surrounded the dealership, Danielle feared they would never leave. And then she would be stuck. And once the bullets were spent, she would be forced—somehow—to work her way back through the showroom and escape through the throngs. And then, even if she did make it out and through the hordes, she would still have to get home, unmolested and unseen.

Suddenly, the images Danielle conjured in her mind made the whole task seem impossible, and death now appeared the most likely outcome for the day. But a half hour passed with no sightings, and when the end of the first hour arrived without even the whisper of danger, Danielle's anxiety began to wane. There were no packs coming for her—not on this day anyway—and almost another full hour passed before she saw the first movement of ghosts, a trio of creatures that had emerged from the rear parking lot of a Wendy's three blocks down from the dealership.

It was a perfect scenario, exactly how she had envisioned the goal playing out when she'd first added the task to her list, with a small group of ghosts wandering alone, not too far from the sniper's nest, yet far enough away to give her meaningful training.

Danielle ducked low and studied the group through the rifle sight, trying to control her breathing. Her palms quickly slickened with sweat again, and despite her earlier acumen in the parking lot, she was suddenly worried about the effect the perspiration would have on her shot. She stayed low behind the roof wall, though it was a move that was likely unnecessary; in her experience atop the realty building, she hadn't once seen a ghost look up. Still though, no point taking a chance at this stage.

The three ghosts walked at a slow but even pace, their positions staggered by about ten feet or so, the middle ghost farthest behind. They moved along on all fours, resting on their haunches periodically, swiveling their heads back and forth in a spastic, anxious motion.

And though they were advancing toward the dealership, it didn't appear that they were drawn specifically to the sound of the car alarm. Still, though, they were meandering in the direction of Maripo Mazda, getting closer with every step.

No point in letting them get too close, Danielle thought. *This is as good as it's likely to get.*

She took a deep breath, freeing her lungs of the polluted air of anxiety, clearing her mind for the shot. Her whole purpose for being there was to develop the skill of killing from distance, and this was the opportunity she had been waiting for.

She steeled her body now as she took aim at the middle ghost, the one in the back and farthest away. She gauged it to be the slowest of the three, as well as the one moving least erratically.

Danielle licked her lips once and swallowed, and then she squeezed the trigger.

The ghost hit the ground instantly, but its head flailed in anger and pain, and Danielle knew immediately that it wasn't dead. The way it had fallen flat to its chest, she had likely struck it in the thigh, or perhaps the right hip; she had crippled it for sure, but it wasn't a kill.

The other two crabs moved away quickly, not exactly terrified by the sound of the report and their newly fallen companion, but agitated for sure.

Danielle quickly aligned the crosshairs over the head of the fallen middle ghost and fired again. This time, however, she missed the beast entirely and instead struck the pavement behind the ghost, summoning from the pewter ground an explosion of dirt and asphalt.

And then it happened.

For the first time since Danielle had begun studying the ghosts from atop the C.M. Jones Realty building, one of the creatures looked up toward the roof and directly toward Danielle.

She ducked below the parapet and sat with her back to the wall, scrunching her shoulders and neck low. *Had it seen her?* Perhaps not her face or even the rifle, but certainly it had seen movement, and that's all that really mattered. Danielle didn't know the extent of the ghosts' intelligence, but she had seen enough of them to know they weren't the mindless monsters of zombie films.

A sound had rung and a ghost had fallen, and its brother had then seen movement from a rooftop in the distance. There was no question they would be coming.

Danielle wasted no more time thinking and again positioned herself atop the parapet, crouched as far down as possible now so that her head barely rose above the rifle sight. She was in the posture of a true sniper, keenly aware of her position and vulnerability. She shot a third time and again missed everything but the street, and this time both unharmed beasts looked up toward her, the one on her left twitching its head like a curious beagle, its eyes like tiny black holes drilled into a white star.

That one had seen her. Or, Danielle considered, it had at least seen where the shot originated. She hid again behind the low wall of the roof, barely breathing, hoping that in the short time it would take for them to arrive, her position on the roof would wane in the minds of the creatures.

Just be still for a few seconds and they'll eventually move on, she thought, knowing in her heart it was a lie.

Danielle counted to twenty in her head and then turned back to the ledge, lifting her eyes slowly over the wall in the direction of the crabs.

Gone.

At the pace they were moving, by now they would have been somewhere in the middle of the block where the dealership sat, though the injured ghost was likely dragging farther behind. Danielle rose to a stooping position and walked to the ledge ninety degrees to her left, searching for the troupe.

Nothing.

It was possible they had already passed the building and were at the next cross street, though it would have meant a pretty fast pace. But maybe they were scared, she considered, and had upped the pace to flee the danger.

Danielle suddenly feared the failure of her goal. If this group passed and another didn't come again soon, she would have to leave, which meant she would have to make the trek back to Maripo Mazda tomorrow. Her nerves wouldn't allow it, she thought, not after the encounters with the other ghosts in the lot.

She stood tall now and searched the main avenue past the dealership, still seeing nothing.

A clanging sound suddenly erupted from the ground in the area of the lot where the ghost had plummeted and was harmonizing with the car alarm.

Danielle, now on the opposite side of the roof from where the ghost had landed, spun in the direction of the sound. She put a fist to her mouth in fear, and then, as if spooked that she had taken her hand from the rifle, gripped the butt and put it to her shoulder and walked slowly toward the edge of the roof where the ghost had gone over.

She was halfway to the parapet when the alarm suddenly stopped, and the tinny banging sound that had accompanied it ceased a second later. Danielle froze in place, staring at the ledge, her throat tight, suddenly gripped with thirst. She waited for several seconds, listening, hearing only the lightest of scraping sounds below, so soft they would have gone unnoticed in any other circumstance.

She took another step toward the ledge. Then another. Now maybe fifteen feet away, trying to look over the ledge, craning her neck, standing tippy toe. But the place where the crab from inside the dealership had fallen was directly down from the ledge; she would need to get closer.

Danielle took an additional step, and as she lifted her foot to take another, the tips of four white fingers slapped atop the parapet, followed by a second set three feet apart.

Danielle screamed and raised the rifle, and as she did, the face of the ghost appeared in her sight, its eyes black and relaxed, its mouth a thin line of apathy. She shot and missed again, though the bullet seemed maybe to have clipped the thing's ear.

The direct threat of Danielle seemed to trigger a new strength in the beast, and it lunged its torso quickly up over the parapet, followed by the swing of its legs. In seconds, it was on the roof, staring at Danielle, its body crouched and crooked, its eyes ebony beads.

Crabs, Danielle thought absently. *That's what Dominic saw.*

Danielle didn't move her feet, but instead followed the white monster in her sight as it hopped nimbly around the perimeter. She rotated the barrel in a half turn and suddenly a second ghost appeared in the sight, near the ledge where Danielle was standing only seconds earlier.

"Shit!" she cried, firing off another round and missing badly. Reflexively, Danielle reached in her pocket for a replacement magazine

The first ghost that had scaled the building was now gone from Danielle's view, having disappeared behind one of the HVAC units that rose from the roof like short tin soldiers. But the second ghost stayed crouched before Danielle, exposed, almost daring her to shoot. She stared at it for several beats, trying to measure its intent, and then she lifted the gun slowly and placed the sight against her socket. She was sure of her shot this time, unmissable. Danielle rested her finger against the trigger, crooking the top of the digit around the metal crescent. But before she could squeeze off another round, the beast finally reacted to the danger Danielle posed and hopped forward like a spider, brushing past her and scrambling toward a long tunnel of air conditioning vents.

Danielle shrieked and lowered the gun, watching the chalky menace disappear around the metal corridor. She drifted again toward the edge of the roof and began to quickly walk the perimeter, searching for the third ghost in the trio now, wondering if it, too, had scaled the wall somehow.

She cleared the first two sides of the rectangle, and then the second two, nearly sprinting as she went around, constantly glancing toward the ventilation system which shrouded the first two white adversaries.

The final sides of the dealership's perimeter showed no signs of danger, which made sense in Danielle's mind, since the last ghost was wounded, probably badly, and it wouldn't have been able to scale the walls of the building with a shattered leg.

Danielle kept the backs of her thighs to the parapet and did a slow skulk now, taking the role of the hunter. She had the gun. She had the advantage.

Cwung!

The sound was low, like a timpani, originating from the far end of the air duct where the tubing entered the roof of the dealership. Danielle snapped her head toward it in time to see the ripple in the sheet metal where the ghost had unwittingly bumped against it. She held her breath and cocked her head toward the area, trying to align her eyes and ears to give her the perfect location of the sound.

The ghost had become still as well, but as Danielle looked to the ground of the rooftop, she could see three white sticks protruding from behind the metal duct, as if pieces of used chalk had been laid out on display.

Toes.

The ghost had stopped just short of exposing its body, but it had failed to pull its feet back fully.

Danielle raised the gun again, now aiming at the open area just in front of the metal tubing, waiting for the ghost to poke its head forward, which it would have to eventually.

But for several minutes it remained committed to its position, unmoving, and Danielle lowered the rifle, giving her arms a rest.

She closed her eyes a moment and cleared her thoughts, and when she opened them again seconds later and re-pointed the gun, her aim had moved six inches to the left of her previous target. The barrel was now pointing at the metal duct where, on the opposite side, she gauged the ghost's torso to be.

The hint of a smile formed on Danielle's mouth now as she squinted at the metal box. This was the shot, she knew, and without hesitation, she squeezed the trigger.

The bullet entered the steel tunnel with a pop, and a second later, the ghost collapsed forward into view, a single red hole pouring blood from just above its ribcage.

One down.

She rushed to the spot of the fallen crab, making the snap assumption that it was the safest place to be at the moment, since the other crab wasn't likely to be in the same spot. Instinctively, she pulled herself on top the metal tubing, just above the place where the bullet had entered. There she stood tall and quiet, chasing the sounds in the air, trying to locate her prey.

And her technique paid off.

The second ghost was as still as a brick wall, but it couldn't hide its breathing, and Danielle could hear the winded respiration of the beast coming from the HVAC unit just beside the roof door.

Danielle made no attempt at stealth now, and she followed the metal tunnel around to a raised, second story of the roof. There, she climbed up five feet or so and then walked over toward the door to the roof. She was now looking down on the ghost from above.

She pointed the rifle down at the ghost, which was completely unaware of its imminent death. It twitched its head back and forth, appearing to listen for Danielle somewhere in the distance. But once she had stepped off the steel tunnel and onto the solid upper roof, she became as quiet as a quail.

She didn't need the sight from this distance, and instead held the rifle low by her chest.

"Psst," she hissed, just for fun, mimicking the deed of some action hero she'd seen once in a film.

The ghost threw its head backwards and stared straight up, as if looking at a constellation of stars just above, its eyes squinted, its teeth bared in a cross between grimace and smile. It caught Danielle's eyes just as the bullet exploded from the weapon, and then it crumpled to the ground of the roof as the metal missile ripped through its skull.

Two down.

Well, two plus the general manager of the dealership and the other two out front. That was five kills total. Still though, none of them had occurred in the way she had hoped and planned. Killing ghosts in general wasn't the goal. Killing from distance was the point. Perhaps she should have been more specific with her list, she thought.

Danielle retraced her steps back across the upper roof, and as she was about to step back down onto the air duct and then again to the main roof, she heard a scraping sound coming from the street below. She stepped to the edge of the top tier of the roof and looked to the pavement, and there, the third ghost appeared in full view, dragging its way forward, its right leg wobbling grotesquely with each pace. It had no intention of attacking, and there was something rather pathetic in its gait. It was just surviving now, and the distress in its movements was obvious.

Danielle lowered herself to one knee and put the rifle atop her shoulder. The upper roof had no parapet on which to rest the barrel, so Danielle had to steady the gun with her left hand alone. This was the shot. This was why she was here. It wasn't this *specific* shot that mattered, of course, it was the preparation it would give her for later, when she moved on to Goal 4.

Suddenly, memories of the people Danielle had lost over the last few months, both through death and absence, began to drift to her mind. It wasn't an unusual practice, this reminiscence, but it was one she normally saved for the quieter moments, late in the evening in the basement of Raise the Flagon.

But the faces appeared unconsciously to Danielle now, in the throes of battle, and yet they brought with them a calming element. She felt her breathing and hands steady with each face that passed, and when her thoughts came upon Dominic, she fired.

The wounded crab went down in a slow melting motion, and Danielle knew she had struck it pure. Head shot. Dead before the sensation of pain could be felt. She couldn't know that last part for sure, of course, but she believed it anyway.

She held the pose of the shot for several seconds, hoping to imprint the success of the connection, to memorize the exact placement of her hands and eyes and thoughts at the time of the shot.

She placed the rifle at her feet and exhaled and then stood tall at the edge of the roof and stared down at her kill. She closed her eyes and replayed the shot in her mind, understanding that she would need that level of precision at some point in the near future.

She stared off to the distance now, finding the location of the cordon where the attack would finally come. She had been there only days earlier, and after several nights of meditation and planning, she believed it the only place possible to cross. Even so, the chance at success was as unlikely as her survival at that moment, and yet there she stood, marksman, killer, queen of her cold, desolate province.

Goal 4 would be her most ambitious yet, but everything from this point on was icing, and this understanding instilled a level of excitement and invincibility in Danielle's thoughts.

She walked to the door of the roof and back down to the mezzanine of the dealership. She thought of exploring the remaining offices for supplies, but she decided she'd had enough of the place for the day. Forever.

She pulled the granola bar from her pocket and tore the top of the wrapper, and then a thought struck her. She reached her hand back into the opposite pocket and pulled out the ring of keys. She ran quickly down the flight of steps that led down to the showroom and dashed to the door and out to the lot. There she stood in front of the first parking spot which had a sign that rose above it which read, "Reserved – General Manager." The spot was taken by a sporty number, a MX-5 Miata.

"That looks like a slicked back GM's car," she said aloud.

Danielle fumbled the key ring in her hands until her fingers came upon a key fob, and with her thumb, she covered the START button and pressed it.

Danielle shrieked as the car purred to life, and she looked around the lot one last time, instinctively, ensuring there were no other ghosts running at her, attracted by the sound of the engine.

But the lot was quiet now, and she knew that was the end of her adventure for the day. She took a bite of the granola bar and opened the door, and as she sat down in the bucket seat of the sports car and closed the door, she began to cry.

Kill a Soldier

1.

Danielle sat with her legs draped over the inside of the bar as she stared at the fourth goal on her list. She took a second sip of the whiskey, carefully, trying to leave enough in the glass for a final, satisfying third gulp. She could have used three more shots really, but discipline was one of the few things she still had left, and if she relinquished that to the temptation of the bottle, her hopes of survival would be all but dashed.

> Goal 1. ~~Map the Cordon~~
> Goal 2. ~~Find a Rifle~~
>
> Goal 3. ~~Kill a Crab~~
>
> Goal 4. Kill a Soldier

There was such finality to the strikethroughs of the first three goals, almost a violence in the way the marks split the letters in half, and Danielle suddenly felt the desire to fire off another round of the rifle, or thrust one of the establishment's steak knives into the bar, imagining it was the face of a squirming ghost.

But that goal was complete; she'd killed a crab—ghost—and now it was time to turn her focus toward the perimeter of the cordon and the humans keeping her inside.

She had the weapon she needed to kill a man, and now, with the afternoon at Maripo Mazda behind her, she knew she had the strength and acumen to kill as well. She had accomplished the third goal on her own, and it was important to capitalize on the momentum.

Except that wasn't entirely true.

A stranger had helped her. Scott. He could have killed her if he'd wanted to, and with the justification of protecting his son from someone who was on his property uninvited. But instead he had offered his aid, and Danielle couldn't erase the thought of what remained of the isolated family. She decided she would make a final visit to the house before she headed to the cordon, just to make sure they were okay, and to tell them her plans and that she would get them help once she was on the outside. She would promise to bring the mass of the world down on whoever was behind their nightmare, and, more importantly, she would arrange for their freedom.

But that visit wouldn't come for another few days. Right now, Danielle needed to rest. To sleep. And then tomorrow, with the sun up and her mind refreshed, she would begin working out the details of Goal 4. She knew the place where she would take the shot—that part had been worked out over a week ago—and with her sniper practice atop the dealership now behind her, she felt a new confidence about her accuracy.

It was the goal that followed, however—Goal 5: Escape the Cordon—that still loomed large in Danielle's mind, and she didn't know exactly what her move would be once the soldier hit the ground. Even if the watchtower by the fence was unmanned, she still couldn't quite imagine the escape. She had a car now, and that seemed like it should at least be part of the solution, but there would be other soldiers roaming the area, and smashing a car through a barrier wall didn't make much sense in her mind. She would get a half-mile at the most before the chase began, or worse, before tank mortars started flying in her direction.

Danielle closed her eyes and took a deep breath, clearing her mind. She couldn't think it all through tonight. That wasn't how her list was designed. She had to bask in the successes, if only for the day, and then figure out the details of the next mission once the new one arrived. Four and Five were concepts for tomorrow. Tonight, she would celebrate, mostly in her mind, but also with a final taste of Dewar's.

She took down the final swig as if putting the final exclamation point on a drinking contest, and then, for no other reason than she felt an urgent need to release the adrenaline that had clogged up inside her, she launched the dram glass toward the back wall of the bar, side-arming it as if skipping a large stone across a pond, smashing it against one of the wooden beams that rose beside the men's room like the entrance to a tiki hut.

She felt the additional impulse to scream as she hurled the jigger, but she restrained herself, and instead swung her feet up to the bar and reclined, stretching her legs straight with her feet together as if lying in a coffin.

She rested only a moment, however, before a shout echoed from outside.

"What the hell was that!?"

The words entered the bar muffled but loud, as if someone had shouted them through a pillow directly outside the recess window.

Danielle's eyes shot wide, but she stayed still, her throat seizing with fear.

Someone was in the alley—a man—and his question was in response to the sound of the shattering glass.

Danielle shot up from the bar top and quickly jumped to the floor, and then, like a cat burglar exiting a bedroom, ran to the table where the candle flickered frantically. She pressed her finger and thumb on either side of her tongue and then crushed the flame with a sizzle. Then, with the same hand, she reached blindly for the shotgun that was resting on the stool beside her.

She gripped the weapon and waited.

There was still no reply to the question outside, at least not one Danielle could hear, but a few seconds later, the same voice—the one which had sourced the original question—boomed again, and now that Danielle was on her feet and standing in the dark anticipating, he sounded closer than before, like he was standing beside her in the room.

"What the hell *was* that, McCormick?"

"I don't know," a second man answered, now as close as the first. His voice wasn't panicked exactly, but it sounded more agitated than the one that had posed the question, nervous.

"It sounded like it came from down there."

"Shit!" Danielle mouthed the word silently as she made her way toward the stage, shotgun poised as she climbed the riser like a panther on the hunt. She walked to the back wall and stood below the window, listening. She was hidden there, at least for the moment. If anyone looked in through the window now, with the candle extinguished, he would see only the dim outline of the back area of the bar.

But she had given up her hideaway the moment she'd pitched the shotglass, about that there was little doubt, and her only hope was that the men would wait a while and then move on, deciding to chalk the noise up to scurrying rats or some starving Maine coon on the prowl for scraps.

Or even to crabs, Danielle thought, though she figured that assumption would likely warrant an investigation. She knew these men were looking for people—and maybe even her, specifically—but she figured they would take the opportunity to kill as many ghosts along the way as they could.

But even if they weren't looking for ghosts, Danielle had had the candle going, and if they had seen the light extinguish the moment they arrived, that would have piqued a different kind of interest.

"What do you say?" It was the first man again. "You want it?"

There was no reply from the second soldier, and a couple of beats later the first one began to laugh. It was the masculine cover that Danielle knew so well, macho men responding with insouciance to situations that, to others, appeared serious and fraught. It was a quality she remembered appreciating at certain times in her life, particularly as a child and young adult, with her father and a few boyfriends, when they had made her feel safe with a chuckle or scrunch of the face as they walked a dark street or anticipated news in the waiting room of a doctor's office.

But she was older now, certainly wiser, and she knew the danger that such an attitude could bring. The soldiers were in a situation where levity would be costly. If they didn't leave soon, Danielle would see to that.

"Alright, McCormick. Since you're the virgin amongst us, I'll grease the skids for you, and then you come in behind. Watch the alley until I signal you. I'll break out this window and—"

"Look!"

Again, there was no image attached to the word, and Danielle could only infer what was happening above.

"What is that?"

"I think it's a stairwell. With a board over it, covering it."

"Well, shit, how did that get there?"

"Someone put it there. Looks like they wanted to hide the entrance."

The flimsy particle board had worked to keep the ghosts away, but it was a lazy effort all and all. Danielle always knew it would be the downfall of Raise the Flagon, but she usually figured it would be when some stray crab walked down the alley and stepped on it, sending it crashing into the well. She thought about replacing it almost daily with something stronger, more camouflaged, but there was so much else to do, so much else to prepare for, and she'd never come across the perfect substitute.

Within seconds, the handle on the door, which was now maybe six feet from Danielle, began to jostle.

And then the banging began.

Danielle checked the last round in her gun and stepped to the edge of the stage, rotating a quarter turn so that the barrel was aiming directly at the middle of the door, ready to send a blast into the chest of whichever man came through first.

The fact that these men were here meant they were beginning to close ranks, to bring the barren wasteland of Warren and Maripo counties to an end. The presence of soldiers downtown couldn't mean anything else. Danielle had never seen a soldier this far from the border—and she had been watching for them daily from the realty building—but she always knew it was just a matter of time. The military—no matter how shadowy and corrupt—couldn't keep a world of lies and containment alive forever, and the only way to keep the secret buried was to finish off whoever remained from the ravaging snows of May.

And, Danielle, they knew, was still alive. Whether they had placed her as the woman who'd escaped from Stella and the colonel, she couldn't know, but it mattered little, really. They were there to capture her. Kill her. She was a loose end, and thus almost certainly at the top of their Most Wanted list.

Well that was fine. Danielle had her own list, and though she didn't know the exact name of the soldier who was coming through the door, he was on it.

The wood around the latch exploded in a splintered burst, and a half-second later, the door banged open, bouncing off the jamb before swinging back closed for an instant. But the lock was gone, and a moment later, the door fluttered open again, and this time a flashlight moved slowly into the entrance, swiveling from left to right, searching.

Danielle couldn't see the man's body, but she could easily decipher his location; besides, with a shotgun, it would have been nearly impossible to miss her target.

She felt the twitch of her finger, but she let it fall to the side. She couldn't do it. Not like this. Killing in this way wasn't the purpose of the fourth goal, just like killing the crabs in the parking lot hadn't served the purpose of the third. She would have been in her right to shoot him, of course—the soldier was almost certainly there to kill her—but it didn't feel authorized, appropriate.

Besides, her instincts told her there was something to be gained by keeping this man alive.

"McCormick, get down here!"

Danielle had momentarily forgotten about the second soldier, and her heart skipped a pulse. One soldier she could manage; two were a problem.

She moved again toward the back of the stage, pressing her body against the black velvet wall that formed the backdrop for the live bands, and from there she watched the first soldier continue further into the bar. If he turned around now and pointed his light toward the stage, she'd be caught in the beam and the shootout would begin. It was a fight she was likely to lose, but she wasn't leaving Raise the Flagon with these men. About that she had already decided.

"What is it?" McCormick answered.

"Just get down here. You're not gonna believe this. The place looks pristine."

Danielle crept further down the stage until she was only a foot or two from the entranceway to the door. She stood on the edge of stage left which rose about three feet off the floor, waist-high to anyone entering the bar. She turned the shotgun in her hands, holding it high on the barrel with her right hand, her left by the port, positioning the butt of the gun down, pointing it straight like the business-end of a pitchfork.

"Davies?"

McCormick whispered the name of his companion just as he took his first—and only—step into the building, and, as the apprehensive soldier turned the light atop his rifle in the direction of the stage, Danielle could see only the glare off his helmet as she thrust the triangle stock of her shotgun into the center of the man's face.

There was a sickening crunch of cartilage and bone, as well as a dull "ugh" from McCormick, followed by the instant crumbling of the man's body to the floor. The light from his rifle splayed wildly and then settled on a random spot low on the entry wall.

For a moment, Danielle considered going for the scattered gun, but her instincts directed her instead toward the freedom of the alley where the rise of the stairwell awaited. She didn't look back for the soldier who'd first entered—Davies—and instead dashed up the concrete flight of steps and into the alley.

Danielle reached the intersection where the alley met the street, and then she glanced quickly over her shoulder.

And there was Davies, already in the alley and closing quickly.

Danielle turned left on Franklin and headed in the direction of her car, but she was still more than two blocks away, and at the rate the soldier was moving—combined with the benefit he had of a guiding light on his rifle—she would never outpace him to the Mazda.

So, Danielle made the snap decision to duck into the entranceway that led to Bigg's, a neighborhood jewelry store about three doors down from the entrance to the realty building.

The shopfront was a concave tunnel of windows that led naturally to the door, about five paces or so off the sidewalk. Danielle reached the glass door and stopped, closing her eyes for just a beat before pulling gently on the door, almost caressing it, hoping her consideration would somehow factor in its opening, but knowing in the depths of her soul that it was locked.

She prayed for a miracle, and when the door opened without a sound, she silently thanked God for supplying one.

But there was no time to bask; the soldier was only steps behind her now, and she could hear the quickening of his feet as he neared the shop. Danielle slipped across the threshold and eased the door closed, and then she pulled the shotgun tightly to her chest, crouching a few paces inside, off to the side of the entrance and out of sight.

Had the soldier glimpsed the door, seen that last little movement just before it squeezed shut? Had he heard it?

Danielle couldn't be sure of the answer to either question, so, as a precaution, she moved further back into the shop, tiptoeing as she strode across the thin carpeting, gliding nimbly past the displays of earrings and necklaces that stared up at her, the green and red and yellow gems glistening at her subtly in the darkness, as if trying to entrance Danielle to free them from their enclosures.

But the golden metal strands and delicately cut stones were worthless now, simple elements of the earth for which Danielle could find little utility. *How precarious the world was*, she pondered. *How teetering.* It had always been that way, she knew, Life, wobbling like a battleship on the tip of a sword; but seeing the bleak incongruity of the treasures in this space of death and abandonment made the point suddenly visible. The store was filled with what would have been treasures only a few months ago, and in a moment, they had been rendered insignificant.

Danielle blinked herself from the trance of the jewels and focused back on the door, where the dim outline of the soldier had paused at the storefront. He hovered there, investigating the shop for evidence, and it seemed certain that he would turn into the wide corridor that led to the shop and ultimately through the door.

At that point, there would be no more room for mercy. Danielle would have no choice but to kill him.

But after ten seconds or so of browsing the glass, the soldier's shadow disappeared, presumably to continue his search further down the sidewalk, and Danielle took a full breath for the first time in what seemed like an hour.

"Thank god," she whispered and then lay her forehead flat on the glass countertop. She stared down on the rows of small diamond earrings that were lined precisely under the glass and then closed her eyes. The cold press on her forehead felt pleasant, curative, and a wave of exhaustion suddenly flooded her. If only she could sleep. In that moment, she would have given any of her possessions for just an hour of sleep.

But rest was a distant goal now. Even if she made it out of this predicament, she would have to make plans to flee her base for good. Not only Raise the Flagon, but the city proper as well. She could see no other choice. More soldiers would be back with reinforcements tomorrow, kicking down every storefront until they dug her out.

But she had to get back to the bar for just a few minutes. She had supplies there. Food and water and whiskey. Her rifle.

Her list.

This latter item was hardly a necessity—she had committed her goals to memory the first day she had written them—but there was a symbolism in the thick, black words that gave Danielle strength whenever she viewed them, a constant re-centering that had kept her strong and stoical until now. She needed food and her gun for survival—plus, to 'Kill a Soldier,' she would definitely need her rifle—but she needed her list for something just as precious: Purpose.

Suddenly Danielle's neurons began to fire again, organizing strategies and routes back to the bar. She could double back now, she thought. It wasn't too late. In fact, the present moment seemed the perfect opportunity. McCormick was down and would be for a while (perhaps forever if she had struck him just right, though she didn't think the blow had been fatal, despite the purity of the strike) and Davies had moved on and was likely more than a block away by now. There was a window here, a chance to duck back into Raise the Flagon, if only for a few minutes, and gather up the essentials. And then she would move on and not look back, likely in the direction of the north cordon, the spot where she would kill the soldier.

Right now, though, her focus was the bar. It was the only choice; she had to go back.

Danielle lifted her head from the glass and gripped the shotgun that she had set beside her, and then she moved quickly toward the front door, a smirk of determination across her face.

But she barely reached the edge of the rear display case before the figure at the door stopped her mid-stride, causing Danielle to shriek. Instinctively, she brought her left hand onto the shotgun, but dropped it immediately at the sound of the chambering rifle that was pointed at her chest.

"I'm not going to hurt you," the soldier said, his voice quick and certain, trying to stave off any sudden reflex of panic from his newly won prisoner. "But I'll need you to put that gun down. Lay it on the glass top beside you, just like it was a second ago."

It was Davies; he hadn't wandered away after all. He probably *had* seen the door, Danielle assumed, and then pretended to move on down the road so that she would let her guard down, take a beat to relax, and eventually wind up in the exact spot she was now.

She placed the gun on the counter as instructed, not daring to test the calm and steadiness of the barrel pointed at her. Her time would come, she still believed that, but it wasn't this moment.

"What's your name?" Davies asked. His face was shadowed, but his voice had a steady and clear resonance, almost comforting if not for the semi-automatic weapon in his hands.

Danielle's first instinct was to stay completely silent, refuse to speak, like she'd seen from captured enemies in the movies. But on a deeper level, she knew that wasn't the play here. What was the benefit?

"What difference does that make?" she asked.

Davies shrugged. "Just makes conversation easier, that's all."

The soldier kept his gun raised as he spoke, his eye to the sight, knowing if he lowered it for even a second and Danielle bolted, even with the light on the gun, it would be difficult to regain the advantage he had currently.

"I'm here to help you. *We* were here to help you. My partner is going to have a nasty bruise and a bad headache when he wakes up. There was no need for that."

With this last sentence, Danielle heard the first hint of anger in Davies' voice. But what was more important was that he had checked on McCormick before chasing her from the bar, and apparently the man was only unconscious and not dead. That meant her window was even tighter to make it back to the Flagon, if, somehow, she could find a way to make it out of her current predicament inside Bigg's. The prospect seemed highly unlikely at the moment, but she was still breathing, and she could only go from there. And for a reason Danielle hadn't yet figured, the soldier was keeping her alive.

"There's no reason not to trust me."

If this had been her first encounter with a soldier, perhaps she would have been more open to the possibility of trust; but since Danielle hadn't brought up the subject, the soldier's mention of the abstract quality suggested to her he was protesting a bit too much. Besides, she knew the story of the blast and the snow, at least the broad strokes, and she had witnessed the actions of other soldiers for several weeks now. They weren't there to assist. They were there to hunt. To guard. To kill. And unless Danielle made a move soon, she would never know freedom again.

"Where are your companions?" Davies asked. "I'm sure you're not alone in here, right?"

And there it was. Companions. He hadn't killed Danielle yet because he figured she could lead him to a larger stash. If he arrived back at base having captured or killed one cordon survivor, that was commendable, but if he captured or killed a group of them, it was career-making.

"They've gone out for the night," she lied. "Reconnoitring."

"Reconnoitring?"

"Is that the word? Maybe not. Exploring? I don't know. Anyway, it's the system we devised to keep our supplies fresh and our area safe. Twice a week, we go out at night, it's the only time we do, and on those bi-weekly excursions, one of us always stays behind. I was the lucky one tonight, I guess. Then we..." Danielle suddenly felt as if she were rambling, and that all of the 'information' she was so freely giving would quickly be spotted for the lies that they were.

"Then you what?"

Danielle dropped her eyes for a beat before glaring back at the soldier. "Why are you still pointing that gun at me?"

Davies didn't answer, and Danielle presumed it was because he didn't have one.

"I know you're not here to help us, Davies," Danielle said, using the man's name aggressively, as if to intimidate him, inform him that she knew who he was, though what good such information did in the moment she couldn't have said.

She took a step forward now, her chest and chin jutting forward, daring the man to act.

"That's far enough," Davies' said, taking a synchronized step backward toward the front door. His voice was still calm and low, which emboldened Danielle further, figuring that if the man were going to shoot her, it would be a measured kill and not one born from a twitchy trigger finger.

"You're gonna kill me like you did my other friends then? Is that about the size of it? How many do you have notched on your belt at this point?"

"If I was going to kill you, I'd have done it already." He paused. "And I don't know who you're refer—"

"You don't? Are you sure? You and that colonel of yours? And the rest of the maniacs that caused all of this to happen? You don't know who I'm referring to?"

Davies went silent and took another step back, keeping the proper distance, maintaining a clear shot on Danielle for when the time came to take it.

"The experiment that caused all of this, soldier. You're the reason behind it. Or at least you're a part of it."

"How...how do you know about that? The experiment? If you've been inside this whole time? How could you?"

"How I know matters even less than my name. I just wanted you to know that I know. And my new friends know too."

Davies cocked his head and removed his firing finger from the trigger, using it now to point at Danielle. He wagged it twice in her direction. "You were part of them, weren't you?" Davies' voice had the air of fascination. "The Internals who escaped on that helicopter."

Dominic. And Tom and James. They had *gotten out. Or at least two of them had.* What happened to them afterwards she couldn't have known, but it had been them on the helicopter, just as she'd prayed. *Were they still fugitives? Or had they been captured and killed?*

"So, I'm right then," Davies continued. "I can tell by your silence that it's true."

"Did they make it?"

Davies paused. "What do you think?

Danielle didn't answer.

"How far do you think they could have gotten? Do you think this army would allow an unauthorized helicopter to simply fly out of the cordoned area?" His voice sounded genuinely interested in the answer, baffled that someone could hold such a belief.

Danielle's mouth went dry, as if it were filled with sand. She didn't believe the soldier, not necessarily, but she also didn't want to hear the answer to his question, so she preempted his intimidation from going any further.

"Well, I'm sure the helicopter wasn't authorized to be taken in the first place, and that's a thing that happened. So maybe you're not as organized as you want me to believe. I mean, let's face it, your buddy McCormick is face down right now in a pool of his own blood and snot. And that probably wasn't authorized either."

Davies shook his head slowly, as if he felt sorry for Danielle. "You had better hope we're organized, and you'd be wise to be on the side of civilization, because if it spreads out there..." He paused, swallowing... "And it's already happened. More than once. Nothing's going to matter anywhere if that happens."

"Spreads? What are you talking about? It doesn't spread. It's not a virus. I already know about the experiment, soldier. I was in here when the snows came. Only if you were touched by the falling snow. That's when you became..." Danielle cut herself off, realizing she didn't actually know any of the science behind what happened, other than what little Stella had revealed.

Stella.

She was a name on the list, of course, and Danielle had plans to look into her eyes at the moment of her death. Dominic had been right about her all along. She had been the driving force behind the whole catastrophe. But it wasn't until the day the soldiers arrived and took Tom and James that Danielle knew it for herself.

The memory of the camp flooded back in an instant, the night Stella had been on watch. The fire had been low when Danielle had finally turned in, blazing just enough to give off a small perimeter of warmth. But when she'd awakened to pee, she could see through the tent that the fire was raging, much larger than what they had agreed should ever be the capacity. Danielle's hand was on the flap of the tent, ready to exit and scold, when she'd heard the footsteps approaching.

Danielle had watched Stella rise to her feet quickly, motioning toward the sleeping quarters, pointing at the three tents where she and Tom and James had been sleeping. Danielle had a decision to make in that moment: to warn Tom and James and likely be captured with them, or to close the flap and sneak out the back of the tent and sprint to safety.

She'd chosen the latter, of course, which had allowed her to fight another day, and though she hadn't once doubted the wisdom of her decision, she could never quite shake the guilt of leaving. Or for trusting Stella.

Danielle had made it to the top of a ridge by the camp that night, just in time to see the end of the capture. There had been no bullets fired, and no struggle at all, really, which meant Tom and James had likely been taken prisoner. Danielle couldn't know for what reason—it seemed that killing them would have been the obvious play, just as it seemed so now—but she assumed if they were kept alive, it was for something other than humanitarian reasons.

"Maybe you don't know as much as you think you do," Davies said. His tone was flat, with no hint of smugness. "I can tell you all about it, though. But I need to know where your friends are first. Once were all together, I'll tell you everything you're authorized to know. Which is more than you might think. About the snow. About the experiment and what went wrong. And about the spread."

Danielle doubted Davies knew any details about the experiment itself or what happened exactly—in fact, Danielle probably knew more than he did.

But the *spread*. That rang true. All the ghosts hadn't died in the melting, which meant whatever turned them was still alive inside them.

But contagious? Had whatever killed the others become infectious in this new breed?

"If we don't take the necessary measures, it won't be long until what happened in here will be everywhere."

"That's what you're here for then? To round up the rest of us inside and execute us? Just in case we have the infection too. To keep the spread from continuing?"

There was a beat of silence, just a second or two longer than Danielle would have wanted from someone on the verge of the truth, and the pause created a rumble of dread inside her belly.

"Of course not," Davies replied. "Like I said, I would have killed you already if that was the goal. I'm going to take you out of here, but it's important we find your friends too. And soon. As soon as possible. When are you expecting them? Tonight?"

Danielle hadn't trusted Davies, of course, and she had assumed he was going to murder her at some point. But she was still alive, speaking freely, and that had left a lingering grain of hope inside her.

But Davies had paused conspicuously before answering her question about her execution, and that was all Danielle needed to hear. He *was* there to kill her. Maybe not with the bullet chambered in his rifle—perhaps it would be in some underground laboratory in Montana or Utah—but that she would never know liberty again if she surrendered to Davies was certain.

Danielle felt the sting of tears in her eyes as she thought of Tom and James and Dominic, and she now figured—whether Davies was lying or not—that there was a strong possibility they were dead.

And what of the world outside? Was it truly on the verge of cataclysm? Would Warren and Maripo County be forever known—to some rebuilt society thousands of years from now—as the epicentre of the destruction of civilization? It was an overwhelming thought, and one capable of opening up the path of nihilism and submission. What difference did this moment make if the rest of her life was destined for bleakness and death anyway?

And as that thought passed through her brain and into the heavens, she saw the flicker of light by the door, directly behind the armed soldier.

It was a shudder of moonlight, a passing shadow by the door, and Danielle's first thought was of the Grim Reaper, that he had arrived just at her moment of pessimism, a timely arrival to pay off her thoughts in real time.

But there was no grand entrance from the smoky manifestation of Death, only the erratic bouncing of black and gray on the sidewalk that led to the entrance of the jewelry store. The shadows were low on the door, just below the Bigg's name, and Danielle had to move just a fraction to her right to get a better view. But she kept her eyes on Davies as she shifted, not wanting to give away this potential advantage by casting her eyes toward the door.

"No," Danielle said, finally answering Davies' question about the return of her imaginary group of survivors. "They're not coming back tonight. We have an outpost where we stay during these hunts."

Danielle averted her eyes on the last sentence, signaling to Davies that it was an obvious lie. But the glance was purposeful, since it now allowed her to look toward the door where she could see the shape of two mutant ghost-crabs, twitching behind the glass like demons trying to fathom a way to re-enter hell.

"You're lying. I can see that even in this light."

Danielle knew the moment in front of her was the only one she would get; if she was going to make it out of the store alive and free, she was going to have to take a risk.

"And what if I am lying?" she answered, taking in a frantic gasp, and then following it with the sniffling back of manufactured tears. "What do you want from us anyway? We didn't do anything to you! We're just trying to survive!"

Her voice came in a steady crescendo, and by the last few words, she was screaming. And with every word, Danielle barked her way forward and was now within a few feet of Davies, who continued his gradual retreat to the front of the shop, his back now only a few feet from the front door.

"I told you I'm not here to hurt you," Davies replied, still cool and measured. "But if you're not able to calm down, I will. That is the last time I'm going to warn you." He cocked his neck and shifted his firing shoulder, positioning the rifle properly once again, preparing to fire, if necessary.

"So why did you do it then, huh?" Danielle's eyes were wide with indignation, madness. "What benefit did you get from the crab...snow monsters? There's been a lot of military around here lately..." She chuckled and scanned the soldier from boots to helmet. "...so I guess it's safe to assume you were...I don't know...weaponizing them. Weaponizing us. Is that getting warmer? You wanted mutant soldiers, right? And you figured Warren and Maripo were as good a place as any to pool from."

Danielle took another step toward the soldier, and from this vantage point she could see the ghosts at the door more clearly, though they were still only gray outlines in the darkness. They watched silently over Davies' left shoulder, staring like mute ghouls in the throes of some catatonic rapture, barely moving as their eyes remained fixed on the scene beyond the door, their heads angling just a tic every second or two, cocking back and forth like an obedient lab awaiting its next command.

"We weren't responsible for the damage—we never are—we're just here to make sure it doesn't get worse."

"I *saw* you!"

"Saw who?"

"Not you, specifically, but others. Soldiers. I've been seeing them since the day we first left the diner. We were almost killed by your army that first day. You *are* responsible! You're as responsible as anyone!"

At that moment, Danielle took the leap of faith that would decide whether she lived or died in Bigg's Jewelry store, and she lunged her chest and chin toward Davies on the word 'anyone,' as if to put a physical emphasis on the remark.

She prepared herself for the pain of the bullet, praying that if it did come, it would enter through her skull and kill her instantaneously.

But Davies only retreated further, two more small steps, just far enough that his back touched the glass and nudged the door open a crack, exposing Bigg's Jewelry to the awaiting ghosts, still unseen by him.

Two sets of hands were upon him instantly, reaching through the gap in the door as if it were their genetic destiny, the way a Venus flytrap snaps down without thought on a beetle that's absently trekked onto its deadly leaves.

The ghosts had a grasp of Davies' cargo trousers around his left ankle and knee, and Danielle could hear the tearing of the fabric mixing with Davies' screams.

But Davies reacted quickly to the assault, and though he couldn't position the gun to shoot the creatures, he was able to get enough leverage to slam the butt of the rifle down on the ghosts' arms and bat them back outside while simultaneously trying to get the door closed fully, essentially locking them out.

Danielle didn't wait for the struggle to end before she scrambled toward the back room of the store, where she began searching for the rear exit that certainly must have existed. And exist it did, but it wasn't the traditional kind of emergency exit, the type that locked on the outside but was always accessible from inside to out. The door she found had an exit sign above it, but it wasn't built for emergencies. It was merely a back entrance to the store and had been key locked from the inside. Not up to code today, probably, but the building had been constructed long before such exits were mandated and had perhaps been grandfathered in.

"Shit!"

Danielle suddenly thought of the shotgun in the front of the store and raced back toward it, but just as she was about to exit through the employee entrance and into the front room, she heard a groan of agony followed by the words, "No. Oh god, no."

She stopped a few feet from the passage and listened, and within seconds, the soft-spoken words of denial turned to howls of pain and distress.

Danielle's first thought was that the beasts had found their way inside and were now tearing the soldier apart, which also meant that without an escape route in the rear, Danielle was trapped. Her only hope was to reach the shotgun before they spotted her, and then take the ghosts out before they disappeared somewhere behind the closely arranged display cases.

She took a breath and walked back to the employee entranceway that led to the front of Biggs, and there she stopped again, pausing in the shadows, peeking out through the entrance, trying to gauge the difficulty.

But there were no ghosts, only the outline of Davies, alive and seemingly unharmed, though his helmet was off, displaying a silhouetted muss of hair. Danielle could see the crabs outside at the door, behaving as they were only minutes earlier.

He'd done it. He'd kept them at bay.

Danielle continued to study Davies from the shadows, waiting for him to regain his composure and begin his exploration of the rest of the store, presumably beginning with the back where she stood currently. It wasn't a great scenario, but it was better than where she had been five minutes ago, and certainly better than one involving the white killers hopping around the store.

And she'd be ready for Davies this time. The second he walked past the threshold of the employee section of the store, she would hit him with a knee-shot to his groin.

But Davies wasn't moving. He was just standing in place, his neck dipped low as if examining something on the floor below him, shaking his head ruefully.

"No!" he finally bellowed, sounding exactly as he had only moments earlier. "Goddamit, no!"

Danielle dared not move, keeping open the possibility that this was some type of performance, a trick.

Finally, Davies rubbed his hands across his face and stood tall, and then projected his voice up to the ceiling. "I don't know if you're still in here," he called, "but if you are, I...I need you to come out." He lowered his head and spoke in a more conversational manner. "I need you to do something for me. I've been cut by them. It's broken the skin and I'm bleeding. There's nothing to be done about it now. I'm going to...I just need you to come out. Please. You need to end this for me before..."

Danielle listened in terror, bewilderment, immediately calculating all of the times she had encountered the creatures and whether she had ever made physical contact with them. She couldn't recall, but even if one had brushed against her at some point—like during that day following the landing at Maripo—it had been so cold most days and she was constantly bundled in layers, it certainly hadn't cut her.

Which meant Davies could be telling the truth.

"It's the chemicals they used," Davies continued, his voice now defeated, though containing a mild hint of persuasion. "I don't know exactly. But it comes through their skin like oil. If it gets into the bloodstream, it spreads. Quickly. That's what I was talking about earlier. That's how it's spreading."

Danielle waited, not ready to fully believe.

"So I need you to shoot me. This gun is too long or I would do it myself. And besides, this is mostly your fault, so it has to be you."

Davies lifted the gun and walked to the display case at the back of the store. He laid the weapon on the glass surface before turning with his hands held high and walking back to the front. He paused for a moment at the sight of the crabs outside the door, and Danielle could almost feel his frustration, his fury at not securing his prisoner. He turned back toward where Danielle stood. "Are you still here?"

Danielle still believed a trap was possible, but she decided to take the chance, and without fully weighing the consequences, she stepped from the darkness of the employee section of Bigg's and immediately grabbed the gun. She pointed it at Davies. "Don't move again."

Davies snickered. "I will if it means you'll shoot me. Didn't you hear me?"

Danielle shook her head in denial. "I don't believe you." And then, "Where did they cut you? I don't see anything."

Davies lifted his left leg and rested it on one of the counter stools next to a display case. They tore my pants and had their hands all over me. They don't have nails, but their hands are strong. They ripped out a good chunk of my lower leg."

Danielle clicked on the light atop the rifle and pointed it below the soldier's knee. His shin and calf were streaked with blood.

Danielle raised the rifle and found Davies' face with the light. His eyes were wide, sad.

And his cheeks were turning white.

"I'm dead. There's nothing to be done about it. I've seen the change. I've seen it more times than I care to count."

"Who have you seen? When?"

"Like you said earlier, I *am* responsible for this. Just know that I'm telling you the truth. I wasn't earlier, when I said I was here to rescue you. I would have killed you once I found the others."

"There are no others."

Davies gave a weak smile and nodded, acknowledging Danielle's well-played charade, and then his face turned grim. "Please, do it now. Before the pain starts."

Danielle took a deep breath and then shook her head. "It might not happen to you as quickly as you've seen in others. Maybe we can get a doctor or—"

"Do you think I would have given you my weapon if I thought there was a cha—" Davies slammed the heel of his right hand to his forehead and began pressing, as if trying to drive his hand into his brain. He then gave a staccato *Ahhh!*, the scream one gives to ward off an approaching evil.

"What's...happening?" Danielle knew this was no act now; Davies' fear and pain were real. "What do...what do I do?"

Davies rose tall now and stared at Danielle, and she followed his movements with the light on the rifle. He pulled his hand away and flashed his eyes at her. His pupils were massively dilated, filling their sockets with pools of black, and his face had turned (a whiter shade of) pale, as if the first layer of Dracula makeup had been applied for a Halloween party he'd be attending later that night.

Tufts of hair had begun to fall to the floor around him, and his face was flaked black from the hair of his eyebrows that had begun to scatter.

"Oh, my Jesus."

"Do it!"

Davies' voice was barely a whisper, and as he spoke, his body began to shiver as if overcome with chill. And then the contortions began, wild, flailing gestures, as if his body were collapsing in on itself. His shoulders snapped dramatically inward, toward his chest, and his back arched like a startled cat's.

"Do it!" He hissed again, and Danielle knew these would be the last words he ever spoke.

Davies' neck twisted upwards now, so that his face was pointing to the ceiling. He screamed again, but this time there were no words, only a gaping white mouth of silent, gnashing teeth. The last of his hair fell to the floor of Bigg's in a clump.

He began to tear at his clothes now like they were on fire, and Danielle couldn't help but think of a werewolf in an old fifties horror movie, painfully transforming, clawing his shirt apart at the sight of the full moon. Within seconds, the top half of Davies' uniform was in a shredded heap on the floor, his hairless white chest now resembling those of the ghosts outside and not the former man whom she'd been speaking with less than two minutes earlier.

Danielle put the sight of the rifle to her eye now and held the man's face in the crosshairs. She rested her finger on the trigger, and as she was about to squeeze, she saw Davies—or what little of the man who still remained—thrust his head forward and smash it on the glass top of the display case, shattering it into large, jagged chunks.

Danielle lowered the gun and took in the scene with her naked eyes. She was mesmerized by the changing soldier before her, an image that was at once both grotesque and fascinating. Grains of glass which had lodged in the slices on Davies' forehead glistened in the ambient light as the blood from the wounds flowed absently over his eyelids and across the bridge of his nose.

Then, as if to display one final act of humanity, Davies—a soldier only minutes ago but now as crablike as any she'd ever seen—grabbed a large shard of glass from inside the display case and lifted it to his neck. He closed his white eyelids, turning his face to a blank white canvas, and then carved a valley of red across his throat.

Danielle watched in silence as Davies' ghost body crumpled below the case of exposed diamond necklaces. He coughed and hacked so quietly it was as if he were a mime imitating the actions, but it was as real and violent as any scene Danielle had ever witnessed, the blood from the thing's jugular spewing out in a fountain.

She considered for a moment firing a bullet into its brain for good measure, to ensure Davies' death was complete before he could suffer any longer. But there was danger still on the perimeter, and there was no sense alerting any other hunters who may have been outside. After all, McCormick wasn't dead, and he could very well have been conscious by now and searching for her.

The Flagon.

If she could return to the bar before McCormick awakened, before he could alert his command of his and Davies' troubles in the cordon, she might have a chance at salvaging her home.

She checked the status of Davies one last time and then flung the rifle across her back. She walked over to where the shotgun lay and picked it up, chambering a round before stepping forward to the protective glass of the front door. The crabs were still there, hovering like hyenas outside the boundary of a lion pride's kill.

I guess I'll have to make some noise, after all, she thought. *And if anyone else is out there, I suppose we're gonna have ourselves a firefight tonight.*

Danielle took several steps back from the door and then pointed the shotgun low at the glass and fired twice, turning her head on the first shot as buckshot and glass exploded everywhere, including into the bodies of the ghosts outside.

She turned back to the door and saw that the ghost on the right was clearly dead; Danielle could tell by the twist of his body and the giant hole that had been created in the middle of his chest. The second ghost, the one to the left, had also been badly damaged, but he was still moving, trying to turn his body away from the store and pull his tattered torso out to the street. But he wouldn't get far. The blast had destroyed its legs from the knees down, and it had barely moved a few inches, its fingers gripping pathetically at the pavement.

Danielle gave no thought on what to do this time, and she immediately shot the ghost again, this time from point blank in the back of its head.

She lifted her eyes to scan the scene around her, but from her place on the sidewalk, she was blind. She walked slowly into the middle of the street and stopped, resting the shotgun on the ground at her feet and arming herself with the rifle. Using the night scope, she searched the darkness of the downtown streets, turning back and forth several times, waiting for a squad of soldiers to appear, or perhaps a trio of mutated ghosts.

But there was only the darkness and the low brush of wind through the streets, and Danielle noted the nip of chill in the air. It reminded her of the first cool morning of fall, which then prompted thoughts of the brutal winter that surely lay ahead.

2.

Energized with the instinct to survive, Danielle picked up the shotgun and ran quickly down Franklin in the direction of Raise the Flagon. Within minutes, she was through the alley entrance to the bar, the shotgun leading the way in.

McCormick was still on the floor where Danielle had seen him last, and, by all accounts, still unconscious. His rifle was missing, but she assumed Davies had grabbed it on his way out the door and tossed it, a precaution in the event Danielle gave him the slip and found her way back to the bar.

She moved in close to the motionless soldier now, studying his face for any sign of life. She placed two fingers against the side of his neck and knew instantly by the warmth of his skin—and then the beat of his pulse—that he was only asleep. She walked quickly to the bar and reached across it, fishing a half-empty bottle from the shelf behind. She then walked back to the knocked-out soldier and splashed a few tablespoons of water into the soldier's face.

He stirred.

Danielle immediately put the twin barrels of the shotgun to the man's forehead, and when he opened his eyes, he clutched them closed almost immediately. The pain of the blow he'd taken was surely acute, as was his current predicament as a prisoner.

"Davies is dead," Danielle announced. "I want you to know that up front. I didn't kill him, but I would have. And I'll kill you too. Unless you want to help me."

McCormick opened his eyes, squinting them in confusion as he shook his head once in either direction. "Help you? Why would I do that? I came here to capture you. To kill you, if necessary. And even if *I* didn't end up doing it—or Davies—you would never have been allowed to leave. It's not a personal thing against you or anyone in here—we have no idea who is still alive—but whoever is, they can never be allowed to leave."

"I appreciate your honesty, Mr. McCormick, I really do, but the situation has changed a bit, so we're going to see what else we can work out." Danielle flipped the barrel of the shotgun up. "Get up."

Gingerly, McCormick rose as instructed, pinching his forehead with his thumb and forefinger. His eyes were bloodshot and badly bruised.

Danielle took a few steps backward, holding the gun low at her prisoner's torso. "How's your vision, soldier?"

McCormick removed his hand from his face and blinked several times, testing. "A little blurry still, but it'll be alright, I think."

"Can you see that?" Danielle pointed to the list tacked above the bar. "Can you see that piece of paper pinned up top there?"

McCormick searched in the direction of the finger for a few seconds and then found it. He nodded.

"I want you to go over there and take a good look at it. You'll need to hop up on the bar to read it."

"Why?"

Danielle's voice fell flat. "Because I told you to."

McCormick didn't debate the issue further, and within a few seconds he was standing on the bar top in front of Danielle's list. "Ok."

"Number four. That's the one I want to bring to your attention. Read it."

"Kill a Soldier," he read. He then turned back to Danielle. "That doesn't sound too promising."

"No, I wouldn't think so either if I were you."

"So, since you said you didn't kill Davies, I guess that leaves me. Is that the point?"

McCormick sighed and swallowed hard, and for the first time since his awakening, Danielle could see a trace of fear in the man's face. It was of the same variety that she had heard in his voice when he first arrived outside the bar. He didn't want to be here. He didn't want to be part of this. Davies may not have either, but Danielle could tell that Davies was too far in to be turned. She held out hope for McCormick though.

"I would be thinking the same thing if I were in your shoes. No question. And, if push comes to shove, it will mean that yet. But that goal is not one of revenge, Mr. Mc-Cormick. You carrying out your duties isn't personal, and neither are my goals. Well, at least not that one."

Danielle thought of two of the goals further down the list, where things *did* get a little more personal.

"That particular goal is there for one reason and one reason only."

McCormick awaited the answer without asking.

"Because killing one of you is the only way I'm going to get out of here."

McCormick swallowed nervously. "Okay."

"But...I would be willing to forego that particular item if there were another way." This time Danielle waited for McCormick to speak before continuing.

Finally, the soldier shook his head and asked, "What way is that?"

"Well, I don't know exactly, soldier. That's where I'm looking to you for some answers. Being as you work around these parts and all. I was thinking you might know the ins and outs a bit. Capiche?"

He shrugged. "Even if I did, I can't help you. What would I say when I get back? *If* I make it back? Sergeant Davies is my partner. I can't just announce he's dead. Or that he disappeared inside. How would I be able to explain that? I would be questioned for days, relentlessly, until I couldn't speak anymore. Lie detectors. The whole thing. And if I tell them the truth, that Davies...whatever it is that happened to him, I still—"

"Stop, soldier!" Danielle shouted. "For Christ's sake, shut up!" She lowered her voice and, through habit, peeked up at the recess window. "You're not going back. Ever. Your days as a soldier—if you have any days left after tonight—are over. But you are going to help me get out of this county. Out of the cordon."

"How am I supposed to do that?"

"I don't know exactly—your clearance or connections or whatever—but you have knowledge of the cordon that I don't, and you're going to help me figure this out."

"And what if I say 'no?'"

Danielle shrugged. "Nothing lost then. I hadn't expected any help to begin with, so that leaves me right where I planned to be. You know, the place I was before I encountered you charming gentlemen." She paused. "Except maybe that's not quite true. I'm maybe a little better off knowing there are two less soldiers to deal with."

McCormick scoffed. "You think they won't miss us? That they won't come looking for us? They knew exactly our search location; they'll be here within a few hours if we're not back."

Danielle scrunched her face dubiously. "Will they? I don't know. I would think the risk inside here is known to be pretty high. Especially by the top of the food chain. So, you'd be missed, I'm sure that's true, but I can't imagine there would be any emergency measures taken right away. You're in unknown territory now. You know, now that you and your team has unleashed monsters into the world. I would think the masterminds behind this containment effort would expect there to be a few broken eggs along the way."

Danielle was conjecturing, but the drop of McCormick's eyes implied she wasn't too far off.

"I am going to escape this place one way or the other. With your help or not. So, if you don't help me, if you decide that evil is the path you'd rather take—"

"I never signed up for this. These are my orders; I have to follow them."

Danielle dropped her head slowly and shook it with disappointment. "Wow," she scoffed, "I can't believe soldiers still say that. After all we know from history."

McCormick stared up toward the ceiling now and covered his face with his hands, as if the exhaustion of his life was just now collapsing down on him.

"As I was saying, if you'd rather take the path of evil, then I'll simply follow through with goal four and be done with it. It won't bother me in the least. It's kind of satisfying crossing the words off, you know?"

The soldier looked back to the list and then eased himself down to the bar top and hopped to the floor. Danielle kept the shotgun level.

"Well, if you like that feeling, you can go ahead and cross off the one second from the bottom too, because that's already been taken care of."

"What?"

"Stella, that second name of your list up there. I assume that's Stella Wyeth?"

Danielle tensed at the name, though she now realized she had never known the woman's last name. She felt the grit of her teeth as she spoke. "Probably. Do you know her? And what do you mean 'it's been taken care of?'"

The soldier nodded, studying Danielle curiously. "I guess that makes sense that you wouldn't know—why would you, right?—but Stella's dead."

"What?" Danielle felt the blood rush from her face in a euphoric combination of delight and disappointment, a feeling which ultimately converged in her chest. Her legs weakened, and she moved to one of the tables and sat, keeping the gun on McCormick.

"They found her body—or what was left of it—in the lab. D&W? That giant hangar complex off the interstate?"

Danielle knew of the building vaguely, though not its purpose. "What happened?"

"What always seems to happen with people like her. Destroyed by her own invention. I don't know."

"What does that mean?"

"The story is that the corrupted got her, but no one knows for sure exactly how any of it happened. Not really. There was some kind of mutiny inside they think, or maybe a hostage situation. And apparently some of the workers assisted a couple of the Internals and they escaped the cordon. Internals is what we call—"

"Yeah, I know."

"Anyway, it seems they got the drop on Stella and the colonel and flew the hell out of there."

Danielle was bursting with excitement and anticipation, but she kept it tempered, assuming that the story was going to end badly for her friends. Still, she was compelled to ask, "What happened to them? The ones who escaped? Did they ever find them?"

McCormick shook his head and shrugged. "Not that I've heard. The pilots and the girls who worked at the place eventually made it back to base, but not the Internals. The pilots gave the location where they'd dropped them, but by the time the brass sent a team out to find them, they were gone. No one has seen them since. And it was particularly hard because no one really knew who they were to begin with. Most of the people in this county are...gone. The people running this disaster had no idea who was who. It could have been anyone flying out of there."

"But the pilots must have seen them. The women who worked there."

McCormick shrugged again. "I don't know. Some think they had military assistance. That that's the only way they could have pulled it off."

"Assistance from who?"

"Like you said, it's not unusual to lose people inside. We lost a lot of people over these few months."

Danielle let all of the information sink in and then felt a tear form at the side of her eyelid. It was an unspecified sadness, about her friends, her family, her life. She blinked it back and lifted her chin high, steeling her voice for the question to follow. "So what do you say McCormick, are you ready to be a hero?"

The soldier closed his eyes and then squinted them open. "Tonight?" he replied sheepishly.

"I was thinking tomorrow."

"Good, because I've still got a hell of a headache."

Danielle smiled; she considered apologizing but refrained.

"Have you got a plan?" he asked, his voice and face subdued.

"Not really. Like I said, I hadn't factored you into this plan until ten minutes ago."

McCormick looked to the ground just off to his right, as if pondering some question with deep consideration. "Well, do you have a car?" he asked finally.

Danielle smiled. "As a matter of fact, I do."

3.

The following morning, Danielle was up before the sun, which meant she'd probably gotten fewer than four hours of sleep. But it was enough; her adrenaline was flowing like a river. Besides, with McCormick sharing her living quarters for the evening, restful sleep wasn't in the cards anyway.

She had no reason to trust the soldier, of course, other than her gut instinct, which, to this point in her life, probably had about a fifty-fifty success rate. Danielle knew most people considered their instincts to be great, and then they ended up committing themselves to a string of abusive relationships or bad business deals. But Danielle was honest about her own intuition, and she knew it was below average at best.

Still, though, there was something—or someone—in McCormick who she recognized and believed in, and as much as she hated to admit it, that person was Dominic.

No one has seen them.

McCormick's words were as good as any she could have hoped to hear regarding the survival of her friends. If they'd made it out alive and had yet to be captured, it was almost a guarantee that they were still safe and in hiding. How Danielle would ever find them if *she* ever made it out, she couldn't know in that moment, but that was a problem for later.

That was Goal 6.

Danielle walked to the stage where she found Mc-Cormick still asleep, his face flat against the dusty floor. Before she had finally gone to sleep the night before, she had draped a tablecloth across the man's back, a twinge of pity for the soldier finding its way into her heart. But that act had been a farce, as the makeshift blanket had crept up and was now almost completely around his neck.

McCormick's hands were still bound behind his back, loosely, sloppily, and Danielle knew that if he had really wanted to escape, he could have freed himself from the binds over the course of the night and then removed the duct tape around his ankles. The latter binding—the duct tape on the ankles—Danielle had forced McCormick to apply himself. It was the first step in his detention, and it kept him relatively immobilized while she did the wrists. But the truth was, even with his legs rendered useless, Danielle knew McCormick could have overpowered her as she tied his hands behind the chair, turning the tables on her in seconds.

But he hadn't moved a muscle as she bound him with rope she'd secured from the Flagon's storage room. He had simply allowed it to happen, and Danielle felt confident that he was all in on the plan to help her escape.

Well, seventy-five percent anyway.

Danielle stepped softly over to the bar, not wanting to wake McCormick yet, and then grabbed the keys to the Mazda which she'd placed next to the bottle of Dewar's (a luxury she'd foregone the previous night, despite needing it more than ever). From there, she headed out the door and up to the alley, and then to Franklin Street where she made her way south towards the car. Within minutes, she was sitting behind the steering wheel with the keys in the ignition.

She took a deep breath and turned the key, and the car started easily, purring to life the way only new cars do.

The headlights came to life automatically, and Danielle fumbled around for the controls, trying to find the manual shut-off knob. She found it, but just before she turned the knob left to kill the beams, she glanced up through the windshield and saw a dull mass rising up in the distance, just over the horizon where Franklin began to crest down toward the river.

It wasn't quite dawn yet, and what little sunlight there was had been consumed by a thick layer of clouds across the sky.

Fog, Danielle assumed. *That's all it is.*

She turned the headlights off and shifted the car into drive, and then she began slowly forward toward the alley and the Flagon.

She was a block from the intersection at Huntington and Poplar, and still, even in the darkness, she could see the mass on the horizon. It was growing larger, in fact, closer, like a storm cloud ballooning over a distant plain.

Her belly rumbled with anxiety, and a pain fulgurated through her chest.

It wasn't fog. The only question now was how bad it was going to be.

The first crab exploded out of the whiteness as if it had been thrust through a portal in time, the features of its body pixelating from blurry to crystal clarity in the blink of an eye. Its dead, white face was a thing of repulsion, appearing at once to be both modern and prehistoric.

It came at the car with ferocity, a white spasm of speed and determination, galloping toward the vehicle like a wild boar. There was no expression in its face, only the cold stare of focus that Danielle had come to know so well over these few nightmarish months.

A dozen more followed behind the first, entering into view one after the other, streaming at her now like a blizzard and then fanning out several feet before they reached the car, alternating directions in what seemed to be some coordinated, instinctive pattern. It was the move of hunters, Danielle thought, like a pack of wild dogs, and she was suddenly reminded of the Maripo River Bridge and how the crabs had plunged into the water one-by-one and then proceeded to form their own bridge of bodies toward their boat.

The torrent of white beasts finally ended, and by the time it did, the ghosts had formed a circle of bodies around the car. There were at least twenty of them in a perfectly dispersed perimeter.

Danielle could only stare in frightened disbelief over the steering wheel, fearful not only of her current predicament, but of how much she still didn't understand about this enemy with whom she shared a world. She had yet to witness this exact behavior, despite her almost daily study of them.

The Mazda was still in drive, and Danielle slowly felt the car begin to drift. The movement snapped her back to the moment, and she quickly moved her foot to the brake, pressing on the pedal as if she were trying to push it through to the street below.

She turned and looked frantically over her left shoulder, then her right. The ghosts were everywhere, about eight feet apart from each other, perhaps twenty feet or so from the car.

The crabs were crouched in their familiar way, subtly bouncing and swaying as they studied their target, their disconnected eyes never shifting an inch.

"Screw it," Danielle said aloud. "I've got four thousand pounds under me. That's enough to crush all you fuckers five times over."

She lifted her foot up from the brake and eased the car forward, testing the reaction of the crabs in front of her. Nothing at first, so she continued drifting further until she was maybe nine feet or less from the ghost directly on path, the one that would first feel the front of the car's grill if it didn't move.

Another yard and the ghost finally hopped a step back, though not to the side; it was a motion that seemed almost a taunting gesture, Danielle thought, as if it were leading her like a matador. Danielle already knew the creatures had at least a primitive instinct for self-preservation—she'd seen it on the roof of the dealership and the previous night at the jewelry store—but their behavior here was something else. Danielle would have expected them to fear the car, or at the least be suspicious of the large rumbling machine. But they seemed neither.

"This is why I don't come out at night," Danielle scolded herself.

That was a mantra she'd stuck to since her arrival at the bar. Don't come out at night. There was plenty of time during the day to do whatever task was on the agenda. There was too much that could go wrong at night. And this night was a case in point.

Had they been waiting for her? she thought. *Maybe the arrival of Davies and McCormick had led the creatures to her location. Lord knew the soldiers had been loud enough.*

Or maybe it was the two that had tracked her and Davies down to Bigg's Jewelry. And then, once she killed the last one with the shotgun, the blast alerted a horde of them and they simply awaited her return to the area. Patiently. All night. Relentlessly.

Danielle lowered her foot on the accelerator for just a half-second, revving the engine so that the RPM gauge shot to the right, and as the car lurched forward, the ghosts in front scattered, with Danielle nearly clipping the legs of the crab by the right fender. It wasn't her goal to hit them—she didn't want to start damaging the car for no reason—but if she was forced to run a couple of these bastards over, she was perfectly willing to do that.

She checked her mirrors again and could now see that the ghosts behind the car were following, and Danielle thought for sure now that they were tracking her, hoping she would lead them to her home.

No chance, bitches.

Danielle gave a firm press on the accelerator now, and, in a matter of seconds, the car was past the front crabs and cruising steadily away at forty miles an hour. Another few seconds and the crabs were out of sight and Danielle was on the edge of the small downtown area.

She turned left at Dimon Avenue, the last cross street before Franklin turned to Frederick and the row of commercial buildings began to transform into residential homes.

Once on Dimon, she drove at a jogging pace, winding up and then back down the small city streets, taking each one to its dead end before snaking back and then reversing the route. She did this for several minutes, hoping the crabs had continued to follow her, not comprehending that they could never keep up with the car on foot, yet still unable to resist the compulsion to chase.

After ten minutes or so of doubling back several times, all the while marking a few of the shops she thought worthy of further investigation, potential sources of supplies, just in case the whole escape plan fell through, she turned back toward the Flagon, taking Annandale around to the east end of the alley.

She parked the car so that it was blocking the side street and then did a quick scan of the area, the sunlight of dawn finally making its presence felt on the day, penetrating the clouds which had begun to thin. The streets were clear, and Danielle quickly exited the Mazda, easing the door closed, and then sprinted toward Raise the Flagon.

At the top of the stairwell, she checked the landscape one last time and then lifted the particle board and descended the steps to the bar. She opened the door and backed in, and when she turned around, she shrieked at the voice that broke through the darkness.

"Thought you'd abandoned me."

It was McCormick. He was sitting at the bar drinking what appeared to be a glass of dark soda; it could have been whiskey or rum, Danielle supposed, but she doubted it. His legs and arms were free of the restraints, and the rifle and shotgun were still resting in their respective spots, yards away from McCormick, right where Danielle had left them.

Danielle's eyes flickered toward the weapons, and the soldier noticed.

"I'm going to help you, okay. Or at least I'll do the best I can." McCormick shrugged, indicating that was the only thing he could think of to say. He looked at his ankles. "But it'll be a lot harder with my ankles taped together."

"Yeah, sorry about that," Danielle quipped, "I'm sure you understand."

McCormick rested his drink on the bar top and hopped to the floor. He looked at Danielle sheepishly and gave a sad grin. "Actually, I *don't* understand. Not really. If it had been me, and you were one of the people who'd been keeping me captive in this hellhole for the past...what, four or five months? I would've pumped a shot right into the middle of your chest before you had a chance to blink and then taken my chances going it alone."

McCormick turned and pointed at the list above the bar.

"And then I would've made a nice thick mark across goal Number 4." He smiled brightly and then dropped his eyes in shame. "So, please, don't apologize. It only makes me seem like more of a villain."

Danielle nodded several times, considering how to respond. "Okay, I won't then." She then contorted her face to a squinted grin and shook her head in a quiver. "I was just saying it to be polite anyway."

McCormick chuckled and nodded. "Good." He held Danielle's eyes for several seconds, studying her face. "You look like you've seen a ghost."

"Really? That's strange because...oh, wait, that's because I *did* see a ghost. Almost literally. A couple dozen of them, in fact."

"Jesus. Where?"

Danielle took a deep breath and rolled her eyes in exhaustion, and then she walked past McCormick to the bar. She reached over the counter and, with one trained hand, grabbed the bottle of Dewar's and a shot glass. She then ambled to the table where the shotgun lay and sat.

"I think you might have drawn them out," she said, pouring the Dewar's, not bothering to measure the perfect shot, erring on the heavy end. "And in our direction. You and...Davies." The memory of Davies slicing his neck open flashed in her mind, and she frowned. "By the way, I *am* sorry about him. I don't know if you two were friends or not, but—"

"Don't be. He was going to—"

"I know. I understand what was going to happen. Still, he was a person and probably not a bad one in most areas of his life. I'm sure he had a family and friends who will miss him. Anyway, I could tell he was conflicted about what's happening in here—and it sounds like maybe out there too—the same way you are."

McCormick nodded. "Maybe not the same way, but yeah, you're probably right. But what gives you reason to think that? Did he say something to you?"

Danielle locked eyes with the soldier and then considered for a moment retelling the events in Bigg's Jewelry, about the way he had changed so quickly after being injured by the crabs. And about his subsequent suicide, a gesture Danielle would always believe was done to protect her.

But the story was a little much for her to speak about in the moment, especially considering the attack she'd just escaped, and it was probably too much for McCormick to hear.

"Maybe another time," she said.

McCormick nodded again, seeming to understand that the magnitude of whatever was on Danielle's mind required the subject to be put off for the night.

"So then is it true?" Danielle asked. "Is this...event happening everywhere? Davies said there have been other cases. That crabs had shown up outside the cordon."

McCormick's eyebrows twitched up reflexively. "That's the report, yes. And apparently, it's been confirmed. I haven't seen it with my own eyes, but yeah, let's just say there's concern. And, due to that concern, they've begun ramping up efforts to clear the last of the Internals."

"And thus, why you're here right now."

McCormick closed his eyes in a long, rueful blink. "Yes."

"How many of us are still inside?"

McCormick shook his head. "Not many. A handful, we think. But we really have no way of knowing."

Neither spoke for a few minutes as Danielle relished her drink. Finally, McCormick said, "Crabs, huh? That's an interesting term for them."

Danielle chortled. "Yeah, but it's not mine. And I go back and forth between that one and 'ghosts.' Not mine either. But both seem to fit."

"I like it. The military calls them 'corrupted.'"

"Of course they do."

McCormick smiled.

Danielle shot the last of the Dewar's and held the bottle up as an offering to McCormick, who held up his palms, declining.

"You might want to reconsider. It could be the last drink you ever have. Come this afternoon, if you're still coming with me, we're heading toward the cordon. And if things go well, outside of it. With what you've said, about ramping up efforts to clear us out, I don't think I can wait any longer."

McCormick nodded. "I agree. And leaving that soon might even give us an additional advantage."

"How's that?"

McCormick gave a nonchalant shrug of the shoulder. "Now that the contamination has spread beyond the cordon, even though it's only been a couple of cases and they've managed to extinguish them quickly, the brass is starting to reconsider their tactics. They've been able to keep the press under control for the most part, but that can't last forever. Leaks are beginning to occur. People—soldiers and others on the inside of this thing—are starting to feel the pressure of their consciences. Anyway, let's just say those in charge are getting concerned."

"So how does that help us?"

"For one, they're having to expand the cordon to account for the spread, which means a wider perimeter and fewer resources at any one spot. And second, we don't have the time or resources to debrief every soldier that shows up at the cordon. It's battlefield promotions out there. So when you and I approach the gates, there won't be a whole lot of questioning about where I'm coming from or what I'm doing."

"Approach the gates? Is that what you think the plan should be? That might be true about not interrogating you, but don't you think they might have a question or two for me, some random woman rolling shotgun?"

"They won't see you. You'll be in the trunk of that car you mentioned."

"There won't be questions if you come out in a Mazda?" Danielle asked.

McCormick shook her off. "It's not unprecedented. It's a good way to transport the dead ones out without risking infection of our own vehicles."

Danielle nodded slowly, suspicion creeping into her eyes. "Well, it was a few blocks away, but now it's parked down at the end of the alley."

"Perfect."

"But before we leave, we have to make a stop first."

McCormick lifted his eyebrows. "A stop? Like to pick up a gallon of milk?"

"No." Danielle didn't crack a grin at the joke.

"Well...that's probably not the best idea. They already have eyes on this place and—"

"I thought you were the eyes."

"Yeah, well, they have eyes on the eyes. At least I think so. But here, in this bar, at this time of the morning, this is as hidden as we're gonna get. They wouldn't have sent another team in yet. Plus, you moved the car when it was still dark, so even if there were other soldiers surveying the area, it's not likely they would have noticed until later in the day. The time is now. It's not going to get better than this." And then, as if he were the one in charge, McCormick snapped, "No stops."

Danielle cocked her head quizzically at the soldier, as if suddenly realizing some misjudgement she'd made about the man. She didn't appreciate the way he'd flopped the command onto the end of his opinion, and she was now a bit wary again.

"You can go back alone then soldier," she stated coldly. "Like I said, I have a stop to make, and I'm going to make it."

McCormick held up his hands defensively and gave a conciliatory nod. "Okay, I was just trying to give us the best chance. But if this errand of yours is a must, then I understand."

Danielle gave the soldier another leer as she brushed by him. "So glad you do."

4.

Danielle and McCormick walked quickly to the top of the Flagon steps and stood watching the dark alley for several seconds, each scanning the length of the narrow road, allowing their eyes to adjust to the day.

Nothing.

They looked at each other and nodded and then sprinted to the car.

Danielle took the driver's seat and the instant the passenger door closed, she shifted the car in gear and sped toward the Jenkins' residence. Within minutes, she was parking the Mazda next to Scott Jenkin's pickup truck, which appeared not to have moved since her last visit.

"Please be here," Danielle whispered; they were the first words spoken by either person since they'd left the bar.

"What are you hoping to find here?" McCormick asked.

"Not what? Who?"

McCormick's eyes grew wide and he tilted his head, confused. "Wait...we can't bring anyone else out with us. You know that, right. There's no way."

"We're going to try."

McCormick put his hands over his face. "Is that what we're doing here? You think I can get two people out? You're kidding? Getting you out is going to be hard enough."

"Why? The trunk is big enough for more than one person."

McCormick scoffed loudly and seemed ready to throw a fit.

Danielle gave the soldier another cold stare. "Like I said back at the bar, Mr. McCormick, you don't have to be a part of this. Just give me a head start, that's all I ask of you."

"You won't make it by yourself."

"I guess I'll have to hope the resources are spread out like you said, and that my marksmanship is up to snuff."

"Marksmanship? So now you're ready to shoot someone again? I thought that wasn't a goal of yours anymore."

"Didn't say that. I said I wouldn't if I didn't have to."

McCormick stayed quiet for a few beats and then asked, "What makes you think the guy is here anyway. Or that he would come with us?"

"What guy?"

"What?" McCormick wrinkled his brow, bemused.

"You said, 'the guy.' How do you know there's a guy here?"

McCormick cocked his head and glared. "Really? Look at the size of that truck." He pointed to the pickup rising above the Mazda, the bottom of the passenger door nearly as tall as the Mazda's roof. "I don't mean to come across as sexist, but that truck belongs to a man."

The inference about the truck was sound, but if it were Danielle inquiring, she wouldn't have asked about 'the guy.' She would have asked about 'the people;' that seemed the more natural phrasing. Her antennae vibrated just a bit more.

But she didn't continue with the line of questioning; if McCormick was lying and knew more than he was saying, and then Danielle boxed him into a corner with her interrogation, she wasn't in the perfect position to fend him off.

She turned to the back and grabbed the shotgun off the seat, and as she did, McCormick reached for the rifle resting beside it.

Danielle snatched the shotgun up like a gunfighter and held it on the soldier, leaning back against the door as she did, her eyes wide and taunting. "What the hell do you think you're doing?" she asked breathlessly.

McCormick stared at Danielle for a few seconds and then, slowly, he tilted his head back and put his hands toward the roof. He then shook his head slowly, exasperated.

"You still don't trust me?" he asked. "Are you kidding? If I'd wanted to kill you, I could have shot you the second you walked through the bar entrance. Christ, lady, you're going to have to give me a break."

Kill a Soldier. She hadn't done it yet, but that goal was still on the table.

"The rifle stays here. You don't need it. Just stay near me and you'll be fine. No need to go in like the Marines. I know this house. I know who's inside."

Danielle was careful not to reveal too much more, but she saw a flicker again in McCormick's eyes, one she couldn't quite decipher. Might just be bad instincts again, she realized, but she catalogued the look just the same.

Danielle waited for McCormick to exit the passenger side of the Mazda first, and once he did, she followed, keeping her distance from the soldier as she directed him to the side of the building and around to the back.

"Why are you going down here? Why not through the front?"

Danielle ignored the questions, and when they reached the back gate, Danielle opened it from the inside and then stepped into the yard. She held the shotgun high in the air with her right hand, a demonstration that she was coming in peace. She thought back on Scott Jenkins' temperament when she'd left him last—not exactly the model of stability—and considered the possibility that, by now, he had lost it entirely.

There was still Michael, though, and in the depths of her heart, Danielle knew he was the real reason she had insisted on returning.

"Mr. Jenkins," she called, directing her voice upward in the direction of the house. "It's Danielle. Do you remember me? You gave me the rifle. It's come in handy since, so thank you for that."

She listened and waited for a reply, and when none came after several seconds, she moved toward the sliding glass door that led into the basement. She gripped the faux wooden handle and pulled.

Locked.

"Dammit!"

"Maybe he left," McCormick offered.

Danielle turned to the soldier, who was standing at the threshold of the open gate, his arms folded as if waiting for her to finish trying on outfits in a dressing room.

Danielle walked the length of the house to the window where Scott Jenkin's had anchored the barrel of his rifle and aimed it at her during the first visit. She pushed in on the glass and then up, and instantly heard the suction of the seal followed by the slide of the window upward. It budged just an inch or so, but it was wide enough that Danielle could get her fingers between the frame and sill. She lifted with a heave and opened it fully.

She looked back at McCormick. "I'm going to go unlock the door."

McCormick sighed and then made a motion of his head as if to protest, a move that signaled to Danielle he was hoping the house would have been impenetrable and they would be forced to leave. Instead, he only replied, "Sure."

Danielle was inside the house and at the door within seconds, sliding it open and finding McCormick waiting on the stoop.

"Now what?" he asked, the ring of irritation still present in his tone.

"Isn't this what you do for a living, soldier? What do you mean 'now what?'"

"I just meant that if he didn't respond to you—this Jenkins person—what makes you think he's just going to be waiting for you in his recliner, ready to saunter out on your command? I mean, how well do you know him? Do you know him at all? He could be violent."

Danielle stared at McCormick for a few beats, studying the questions in her mind, feeling there was something a bit off about them, steering her.

He did have a point though: if Scott Jenkins had, in fact, lost his grip on reality, as he seemed on the verge of doing only a few days ago, he could be dangerous. But it was a chance she was willing to take, especially considering that if that were the case, there was a child that needed rescuing.

"I guess we're going to find out," she said, and then turned and walked toward the armory room and the stairs that led up to the first floor. McCormick followed, keeping a step behind. "I just have the feeling they're here," Danielle added, as if needing to bring the thought to life.

Danielle could hear McCormick stop immediately, now a few paces behind her.

"They?" he uttered.

"What?" Danielle continued down the hall, but she could sense the bubbling of dread rising in her gut. She turned slowly toward McCormick, and as she did, she saw only the blur of the soldier's hand as it snatched the barrel of the shotgun and ripped it from her grip.

"What are you—?"

McCormick thrust the bottom of his foot forward, crashing the sole against Danielle's left hip, sending her sprawling against the wall beside the armory door. The back of her head smashed against a studded area of sheetrock and a flash of white exploded across her vision.

And then she waited for the blast of buckshot to follow.

Instead, McCormick's voice cut through the basement air like a sword, quiet and annoyed.

"This could have been very easy," he said. "We could have just driven out of here like we'd planned, you in the trunk, and then cruised right up to the lab like fucking UPS. No issues, no violence." He paused. "Of course, you would have been pissed at me once you realized what had happened, but at least you'd be alive. For a while." He then nodded toward Danielle. "And without the headache."

Danielle blinked several times, clearing the cobwebs from her head, and when she had a clear view again, she glared up at the traitorous soldier, processing his words slowly, trying to make sense of them in a brain that was almost certainly concussed.

"Why didn't you just take me prisoner when I came back from the car?" she asked. "You were free. You had the guns right beside you."

He shrugged. "I guess I pegged you as someone who might not allow herself to be taken alive. Thought maybe you'd made a pact with yourself or something. Could have had a cyanide pill in your pocket, maybe. Or a .22 in your boot for just such an event. So, I figured if I could prove to you I wasn't a threat, that I was actually on your side, you'd be apt to go along with the escape plan. Especially if I made it seem like it was your idea to begin with."

"It was mine."

Danielle thought back on the idea of escaping in the trunk of the Mazda, using McCormick's rank as the cover. Some of the plan was hers, she supposed, but as she reflected on it groggily, maybe not the more important elements.

McCormick smirked and shrugged, finding no point in debating what was now a frivolous issue. "Who else is here?"

Danielle had been right to be suspicious in the driveway—a point that was obvious now—McCormick had been to the house before. And she understood now that they had found Scott. That was why he referred to the household in the singular.

The guy.

But that also meant they hadn't found Michael.

She thought of Scott again. *Was he dead? Did he fight them? Or had they taken him to 'the lab?'* Danielle assumed the former, based on the stockpile of weapons that sat behind the door less than six feet away and the man's anger at losing his daughters. She couldn't imagine him going quietly.

She looked over at the large steel door that protected the armory and the adorning lock that was the size of a softball. It was intact.

"I don't know," Danielle finally answered, "I was only here once. There was a man here, Scott, he's the only person I met."

"I don't think so. '*They're* here. I just have the feeling *they're* here.' That's what you said. You wouldn't have phrased it like that if you thought only one person lived in this house."

Danielle shrugged and closed her eyes. Her brain was still foggy from the smack to the back of her skull, and she couldn't invent whatever lie was needed to throw the soldier off the trail. "I just assumed there were others. I don't know. Anyway, you've obviously been here. You searched the house. Did *you* find anyone else?"

"No, but that doesn't mean anything. Not necessarily. They could have been out at the time we were here. Scavenging and such."

"Well, let's say there was someone else living here. Do you really think they would be still? After knowing you already came by and took...where did you take him? Where is Scott?"

McCormick ignored the last part of the question. "Maybe not, but that doesn't change the fact that there may be others in the cordon who are uncorrupted. We need to find them and bring them to safety."

Danielle laughed heartily at this last line and then looked up at the liar standing above her, the shotgun in his hands still aimed low, positioned toward her chest.

The weapon didn't matter now, though, not unless it was in her hands; McCormick outweighed her by eighty pounds, at least.

"Are you really still doing that thing, McCormick? Trying to play the part of good guy? Jesus Christ, soldier, at least own that you're a monster and let that shit go."

McCormick clenched his jaws. "This is what I do. It's what I'm trained and paid to do. I know it isn't fair. None of this was your fault or anyone else's that was in here when this all happened. But it happened, and all we can do now is try to prevent it from spreading further."

"Then why not just hunt the ghosts? The corrupted? Why not *help* the survivors? What a concept that would be! To rescue us when you have the chance—like now, for instance. That's what a human being would do."

McCormick shook off Danielle's notions as if they were the silly suggestions of a child. "We can't be sure there's no corruption in you. Lying dormant. Incubating. We have to quarantine everyone who was inside at the time until we know for sure."

"Yeah, and how long does that last, this quarantine?"

McCormick looked away. "I don't know. That's classified."

Danielle chuckled. "That sounds like another way of saying 'forever.' Have you ever seen someone come out of quarantine?"

"Like I said, its—"

"That's because they don't." Danielle shook her head in disgust. "Nobody is worried about 'corruption.' Not the physical kind anyway. They're worried about the more common type. The kind committed by your commanding officer and his commanding officer and god knows who else. God knows who's a part of this whole genocide."

"Call it whatever you want. We're trying to keep an accident—a terrible accident—from turning into the end of civilization."

"It was no accident!"

McCormick didn't respond.

"And what do you call this? Soldiers imprisoning innocent people. Ultimately killing them. Does that sound like civilization to you?"

McCormick had nothing else to say on the matter, and he simply flipped the shotgun up, compelling Danielle to stand.

She put her head back against the wall and closed her eyes again, and then Danielle recalled how Scott Jenkins had been in that exact position, his eyes glistening with tears as he re-told the story of his daughters and their turn toward abomination. She wanted to cry herself now as she remembered him, imagining the terror he was feeling at that moment—if he was still alive—agonizing over the state of his son.

Where was Michael?

"Get up!" McCormick commanded.

Danielle stood slowly, testing her balance, which was a little wobbly, and then she took a step forward, lurching, nearly bumping against the barrel of the shotgun.

McCormick stepped back quickly and pumped the weapon once. "If you want to die now, on the floor of this basement, then do that again. Let's go."

Danielle walked toward the back door, her mind racing, desperate to focus on some solution to her current capture. But her head was swimming, finding only disjointed memories and panic.

She was about three paces from the door when she heard a *Wump!* sound rush through the room. It had come from the bottom of the stairs, at the place she'd been only seconds earlier.

"The hell was that?"

McCormick turned toward the stairs for an instant and then snapped his head back to Danielle, holding the gun steady, assuring her that he had her covered if she was thinking about making a move.

A creaking sound squealed into the room now, the opening of a door.

"Let's go," McCormick instructed, nodding in the direction of the noise. His voice was leery, urgent. "Get in front of me."

"Why thank you; such a gentleman."

Danielle shuffled back down the hall and, as she turned the corner, she could see instantly into the armory.

The steel door was now wide open.

"Look!" she said.

"What the hell? How the..."

McCormick turned on his heels, holding the gun out as he spun three-sixty, trying to find the person responsible for this impossibility.

"Maybe he's inside," Danielle said, offering what she thought was the least likely scenario.

McCormick pushed Danielle into the room and then pulled out a flashlight, shining the beam across the walls of rifles and ammo and a variety of other weaponry. "Holy shit," he whispered. "This is why we couldn't get in this room. We figured it was something valuable, but damn, look at this place."

Then, as if suddenly remembering why he was there to begin with, McCormick jerked his neck quickly to his left. Then his right. But the room wasn't very large, maybe 12x15, and there weren't a whole lot of hiding options.

"Nobody's in here," he stated, not quite confidently, and then he nodded Danielle back to the main basement area.

Danielle was first through the door, McCormick a step behind, and as the man cleared the door frame to the armory, a voice boomed down from the top of the stairwell.

"Hey!"

Instinctively, Danielle dropped to the ground like a bag of wet laundry, covering her head and ears, muffling the sound of the *Pop! Pop! Pop!* that rang through the air. The shots were followed by a wail from McCormick that lasted only seconds before sputtering to silence.

Danielle stayed crouched for several beats, and when she finally glanced up the flight of stairs, she could see Michael on the landing, crouched on one knee with a rifle on his shoulder, his eye still pressed to the sight.

She looked back to McCormick who was flat on his back, his eyes bulging, a hole the size of a cherry and just as a red glowing in the middle of his throat. He was choking on his blood.

Danielle stood quickly and pointed to the boy on the stairs. "Get outside, Michael!" she barked. "Wait by the car parked next to your dad's truck. I'll be out there in a minute."

Michael stood and stared down at the man who lay dying on the ground at the bottom of the steps. He blinked several times in disbelief.

"Now, Michael! Go!"

"I need my bag. Dad said never leave for good without the bag."

"Where is it?"

"It's right inside the door. On the right. I need it."

Danielle softened her tone now, almost whispering. "Okay, I'll get it. Now go."

Michael finally met Danielle's eyes and nodded once, and then he turned and dashed through the doorway leading up from the basement.

Danielle waited for the sound of the front door to open and close, and then she picked up the shotgun.

She looked down at the fallen soldier and felt a wave of sympathy flood her. He'd never wanted to be this person, she thought. Certainly not as a child, and probably not a minute prior to joining whatever deranged company of men and women to which he had belonged.

But he *was* this person now, if only for a few seconds longer.

Danielle set the shotgun down and then walked into the armory and picked up one of the two dozen handguns that were set neatly on display in a cushioned velvet case. She slammed the accompanying magazine into the well and released the slide, locking the round in place. She then picked up Michael's bag, took a deep breath, and stepped outside the armory, back to the spot where McCormick was anguishing.

His whole body was quivering now, his head convulsing as if he were possessed, his eyes pleading for Danielle to help him.

With a squeeze of the trigger, she did.

Escape the Cordon

1.

"Michael!"

Danielle burst through the front door with a Santa-sized satchel on her back; she hadn't cleared out the armory, not by a long shot, but she took enough to be trouble for anyone that came looking for it.

She ran past the pickup—which, from the front of the house, covered up the view of the Mazda entirely—and then stopped at the car where she'd told Michael to wait for her.

He wasn't there.

"No!" Danielle uttered, spinning a quarter turn at a time, searching for the boy. "No! Michael!"

A mechanical whir buzzed behind her and she spun on her heels, the shotgun pointed, seeking the sound. As she turned, she knocked the duffel full of arms into the Mazda's mirror, and for a moment, she expected the bag to explode. But there was only the rattle of metal, and Danielle took a breath, trying to calm herself.

"Maybe we should take the truck instead."

Danielle looked up to the truck's passenger window, and there was Michael, the window now fully open. He stared distantly through the front windshield, as if rapt by some figure floating out over the hood.

Take the truck.

Danielle looked back to the Mazda, assessing the two choices. She was familiar with the Mazda at this point and

135

felt comfortable driving it, and she didn't have experience driving such a giant 4x4 as the Silverado beside her. But it *was* a four-wheel drive, which could come in handy, and since the enemy already knew about the Mazda and the car was now likely on a radar somewhere, they might just be expecting it to show up at the border eventually.

"It's got a full tank," Michael added.

The Mazda was just under a half. She was sold. "Okay."

She gave a thought to grabbing the rifle that remained in the backseat of the sedan, but with her raid of the armory, she had more than she would ever be able to use in her bag already. If she had planned on staying another month or two, she would have taken the extra ten seconds to grab it, but at that moment, she wasn't planning on staying another day.

Danielle walked quickly to the driver's side of the truck and hopped in. Michael had turned the truck's power on already, so Danielle turned the key another quarter turn and started the engine, rumbling it to life with a growl. She threw the truck into reverse and backed it out quickly, with authority, squealing the tires and nearly clipping the Jenkins' mailbox, missing it with her mirror by an inch. She then headed southwest toward the Flagon

"Are you okay," Danielle asked, keeping her eyes fixed on the road, expecting to see a convoy of army jeeps at any moment, or perhaps the flock of crabs that had ambushed her earlier. To that point, however, the road remained clear.

Michael turned toward Danielle, his face pained, puzzled. "He wouldn't let me help."

"Your dad?"

Michael nodded. "When they knocked on the door, he made me go to the safe room and promise that I wouldn't come out. No matter what."

Danielle gave the boy's recollection a moment to resonate and then softly she asked, "What happened?"

A tear began to stream down Michael's face; he made no motion to clear it. "They came at night. I don't know, two nights ago, maybe. Or the night before that. I don't know anymore."

"And they knocked on the door. Then what?"

Michael swallowed and took a breath. "The sensors kicked on but...by the time we could see what was happening, who it was on the property, they were already at the door. I told my dad we should both go to the safe room. I pleaded with him! I still don't know why he opened it."

Danielle waited a few seconds, allowing the boy to steady his emotions a bit, and then she asked, "Why did he? Why do you think?"

Michael shrugged. "I could see it in his face that he knew it was the wrong decision, but he just looked at me and said, 'We can't stay here forever.' And then he smiled at me. It was the first time I'd seen him smile since all of this happened."

Danielle wanted to cry now also, but a surge of fury blossomed inside her instead, replacing the pangs of sympathy.

"Then he told me to get to the safe room and lock it. There's food and water in there for a month, and it was built so that it would take a bazooka to get it open without the key."

"And you didn't hear anything? There was no fighting or guns or anything?"

Michael just shook his head. "I could hear them trying to force their way into the room, but I didn't hear anything that sounded like fighting. They probably tried to make him open the door, but I know he would have died first." He paused and then looked at Danielle again. "Do you think he's dead?"

Danielle met Michael's eyes, lowering her chin to impart an air of assurance. She then shook her head. "No, I don't."

Michael looked away, down at his lap now, considering the answer. "Then why didn't he come back for me?"

Danielle frowned. "Look, I'm not saying he's not in trouble. He almost certainly is. But I believe he's still alive. At least for now."

"Why do you think that? What do you know? Who was that man back there?"

"I know enough that we don't have much more time in here. And your dad probably has even less. We need to leave. Later today, before it gets dark."

"How? How are we gonna get out?"

"It won't be easy, but I've got a plan. And we have guns now. And a giant truck."

Michael gave the hint of a smile.

"You saved my life today, Michael. And now I want to find your dad and help save his."

Michael nodded, having no real choice but to trust this woman who appeared from nowhere only days ago.

"What's in the bag?" Danielle asked.

Michael shrugged. "My dad has always had it. Said everyone should be ready to go at a moment's notice. Passports. Cash. Things like that."

Danielle nodded, agreeing that was a wise way to live. At least it used to be. She didn't see much use for passports and cash anymore.

"We're gonna go back to my place for a few hours and rest. And then later, a few hours before sundown, we'll head for the cordon."

2.

Goal 1. ~~Map the Cordon~~
Goal 2. ~~Find a Rifle~~

Goal 3. ~~Kill a Crab~~

Goal 4. ~~Kill a Soldier~~

Danielle folded the list and stuffed it back in her pocket and then glanced over at Michael who was slumbering in the far corner of the Flagon, his entire body buried amongst the cushions and blankets that Danielle had amassed over the months and formed into rather comfortable sleeping quarters.

Kill a Soldier.

Technically, it *was* Danielle who had executed McCormick, so she would take credit for the kill, though it wasn't due to any need to feel fulfilled or to satisfy some nagging sense of closure on the fourth item on her list. Mainly, it was to absolve Michael from any guilt or trauma he may have felt for his part in the soldier's death. The boy had delivered the lethal shot, there was no question about that, and had Danielle simply let the wound play out, the soldier would have been dead within minutes.

But it was Danielle who had squeezed off the round that freed McCormick from his pain, and that was the truth. She hadn't told Michael the specifics, of course, only that she had shot the man who tried to kill her and that he was dead. Danielle knew of the potential for Michael to feel remorse about the man's death—though, if he never saw his father again, that would likely dissipate quickly—so in the event there was some residue of blame in his young mind, Danielle wanted to shoulder the responsibility that came with taking another human's life.

Besides, she couldn't have guilt and hesitation clouding the boy's thoughts; she would need his head clear and his finger steady for her next goal. If it came down to killing another of her captors, she now had someone who had demonstrated acumen and composure under pressure. Michael was a child, of course, Danielle could never forget that, and she would do what she could to prevent him from having to put another bullet in someone's neck. But if it came to that, she felt confident he'd be willing. Escape was all that mattered now.

Escape the Cordon.

She had already mapped the perimeter and found the vulnerabilities, and if McCormick had been telling the truth about the army's dwindling resources (which Danielle decided to assume he was; it was the only real choice she had), then escape was a possibility. Perhaps not a fantastic one, but a possibility, nevertheless.

Her second goal of finding a rifle she had accomplished ten times over and was now equipped with enough guns to arm a street gang. She wouldn't come anywhere close to needing them all, but they'd be in the back of the truck just the same. Just in case.

Her stressful day atop the Mazda dealership had ended in the deaths of five crabs—another overachievement of a goal—and her subsequent skirmishes with Davies and Mc-

Cormick gave her a proficiency for battle that would guide her through the challenges that still awaited her.

McCormick.

She'd been wrong to trust the man—that was obvious—and despite an Oscar-worthy effort to convince Danielle he was on her side, she'd always known there was something wrong about the scenario. There was no upside to him helping Danielle, aside from the pretense he'd used to ease his own conscience. It was the same bullshit act Stella and Terry had given, the moment when they finally fessed up to knowing about the experiment.

But Danielle had a trustworthy partner now, a prisoner like herself whom she would protect with her life.

Danielle checked the clock on the wall. Three o'clock. She'd give the boy another half-hour and then they would head toward freedom.

3.

The best chance at escape, as Danielle saw it, was west along the rocky riverbank of the Maripo River tributary, a once-scenic section of waterway that was now unruly and over-grown with trees and shrubbery. Though nearly impassable, the area had still been secured on either side of the shoreline, but instead of the high cement wall that predominated most of the cordon's perimeter, this section of the western border had been reinforced with fencing. Danielle assumed the alteration in material was due to the fact that metal fencing was far quicker and easier to install in such terrain, with the cost of erecting a concrete wall no doubt a factor as well.

When Danielle had first mapped the far western section of the boundary, she thought it unmanned, that it had simply been fenced off and forgotten about, that perhaps the engineers and superior officers had calculated that any crabs who came to the barrier would be sufficiently blocked from escaping, and that any civilians who were still inside—like herself—would never venture into the hostility of the western brush to begin with. And, even if someone did trek that far down the tributary, there was still an eight-foot-high fence that had been reinforced with prison-style barbed wire.

But she had been wrong in that initial assessment; in fact, two guard towers had been constructed amongst a pair of spruces that rose on the opposite side of the fence—one on the north side and one on the south—and had been built into the tree trunks, allowing the guards to maintain their posts mostly camouflaged, essentially hidden from view to anyone who was more than a hundred yards away.

Danielle herself hadn't noticed the towers either, not until she was nearly upon them, and had the guards on duty been carrying out their watch with steadfastness that day, she would have been imprisoned weeks ago and likely dead by now.

But apparently the lack of activity around the perimeter had caused complacency amongst the ranks, and Danielle felt like she was in the same room with the soldier when she had first heard the voice drift down from the canopy above. The soldier was a woman, and she had been talking casually, laughing, engaged in what was clearly a personal conversation with a husband or boyfriend. It was luck that Danielle hadn't been spotted, but it also meant the effort to breakout would be a bit trickier.

Still, though, of all the spots on the perimeter, this was the one where escape showed the most promise. The second tower—the south tower—Danielle had yet to see occupied on any of her scouting missions, and this, she now assumed, was due to the dwindling resources that McCormick had alluded to the night before.

The north tower was never vacant though, and Danielle had kept watch on it for several days in a row, timing the guard changes, listening for the crackle of the radio that would signal when the transitions were to occur. As long as she visited at the end of the day and kept close to the bank, she figured she'd be nearly invisible to the guard above. There was no roaming spotlight across the area or drones flying above, and any noises she made as she walked across the leaf-litter would be dismissed as either fauna or stray crabs.

At the top of the southern bank was a cluster of large rocks—about a hundred and fifty yards east of the guard tower—which appeared to be the perfect position for Danielle to take the shot. It would be a long one, and Danielle—her ghost hunting atop Maripo Mazda notwithstanding—was no deadeye; but the view from the cluster was clear, and she would simply have to step up and make the shot.

From what Danielle had observed, the soldiers worked in six-hour shifts, which was plenty of time to take out the soldier—if she made the kill within a half-hour or less of the transition—and then find her way to the other side of the fence. Five plus hours was a long time, but Danielle knew if she struggled to find a tree to climb over the barrier, the hours would fly like bats from a cave. And if she didn't make it out before the casualty was discovered, another escape would be nearly impossible.

There was a lot that could go wrong with the plan, no doubt about that, but it was the plan she had, and it was solid enough to allow her to cling to hope.

Danielle parked the Silverado in the driveway of an abandoned rambler near the base of a footbridge, and she and Michael sat silently there for several minutes as Danielle reflected on the plan again and again. She visualized the snipe from the top of the riverbank, and then her retrieval of Michael, at which point they would scramble back to the border and the cluster of surrounding tree branches. From there, they would pull themselves up and climb like orang-utans, high enough until they could clear the fence.

At that point, they would be free of the cordon. Danielle didn't know exactly where they would go from there, but that was a problem for a different goal.

Goal 5: Escape the Cordon.

It was all feasible, if not easy, just as long as her shot was pure, and they could stay relatively hidden and quiet as they scaled the trees.

The factor Danielle was dismissing was the second guard tower, that it would be empty, though she had no reason to believe it would be manned on that day. It had been vacant on every occasion prior, and if McCormick had been correct about the pulling back of security, then, if anything, *at least* one tower should have remained vacant, if not both. The latter scenario would have been a giant bonus, of course, so Danielle certainly couldn't go off that assumption.

"Are you ready for this?"

"Why can't I come with you?" Michael asked, not yet convinced of the general plan. "This doesn't seem like it will work."

"It will. And I'll come for you when...when the first part is over. I don't know exactly when the transition will occur—when the guards change—so I need you to stay here."

"What does that have to do with anything? I'll just wait there with you."

Danielle was hoping Michael would accept her illogical explanation on its face, assuming it too complicated for him to understand and thus take it as a given. But the boy was smart, and he listened attentively; he wouldn't be brushed off that easily.

"I'm sorry, Michael, that's the way it has to be. Try to rest in the truck until I get back. You're going to need your energy."

"I already rested back at the bar. I'm not tired."

"I'll only be a few hours at the most."

"It'll be dark by then. I don't want to be here in the dark."

"It might not be, not if the change happens over the next couple of hours." Danielle paused and leaned close. "But even if it is, you'll be fine. You have a sack full of guns in here—which you obviously know how to use—and a tank of a truck that you will keep locked the entire time. Just stay low in the back and wait for me."

Michael's face was full of protest and discouragement, but he seemed to recognize the futility of arguing and simply nodded in agreement.

Danielle nodded back and then hopped from the truck, her new-model rifle slung across her back like a big-game hunter. She wished she had the original gun though, the one Scott had allowed her to take from his stash, and she now believed it had been a mistake not to retrieve it from the Mazda. She didn't need it for the extra firepower, of course, but it was the rifle with which she'd prepared for this moment, and it was a model she'd known her entire life.

Oh well, it was done, and she wasn't risking a trek back to the Jenkins' household for a gun, not when she had a couple dozen in the back of the truck. She would be fine, she thought. Just look through the sight and shoot.

Within minutes, Danielle was crunching across the pebbles that lined the shore of the tributary, heading west toward the perimeter.

She looked over at the steady flow of shallow water, noting the level was as low as she'd ever seen, probably not more than two or three feet high. Another week or two and the riverbed would be completely dry, she thought, though she had no plans to ever see it.

By then she'd be well into Goal 6.

The receding tributary made for an easy passage from the bridge, the firm ground of the riverbed allowing for solid footing and dry feet.

Then, as if the very thought of drought were a trigger to the sky above, or perhaps to the storm divinities who controlled it, a raindrop plunked down and landed at the top of Danielle's forehead, just below her hairline. It then rolled down across her left eye, blurring her vision for just an instant.

She stopped suddenly and wiped the drop away, and then looked up in confusion, squinting at the dark clouds overhead as if seeing such a spectacle for the first time.

"No," she whispered.

She had never factored weather into her plans, and as she stared in dismay at the sky, she couldn't remember the last time it had rained. Perhaps it hadn't since the snows came, she thought, and now considered there was a connection to be made there.

It was strange that she hadn't noticed the lack of precipitation over these several months. She had always been conscious of the temperature, of course—snow in May will do that—but not of the rain or lack thereof.

But perhaps it wasn't so unusual after all. Her world was consumed by survival now—food and shelter and protection—and whether or not she would need an umbrella at the bus stop or to turn on the sprinklers for the lawn over the weekend were luxuries long since forgotten. And since the only water she drank was bottled, which she scavenged from a variety of sources around the cordon, rain, for that purpose, was never considered.

But rain today was not to be ignored. She barely trusted her acumen with the rifle in the best of conditions, and in this drizzle—let alone in a downpour, if that was in the forecast—she trusted it not at all.

Danielle shook the pessimism from her mind and continued her steady trot toward the border, now feeling the pressure to reach it before the clouds opened and released a deluge.

But her hopes of that accomplishment were shattered within another two hundred yards or so as the drops began to fall in large, steady pellets. By the time Danielle reached the ridge across from the north tower and hunched behind the rock that would serve as her sniper's perch, a steady rain was falling.

She flipped the hood of her jacket over her head and pulled the drawstrings tight. The thin windbreaker wasn't completely waterproof, but the material was somewhat resistant and hopefully would keep her dry for a little while.

But if night fell before the soldiers transitioned and the cold set in, her neck and shoulders would become a racket of quivers and shakes, introducing yet another element to an already difficult rifle shot.

But there was another problem. The noise.

She had counted on being able to hear the sound of the radio from her den, but with the air now thick with moisture and the rain splattering in constant rim shots against the thick foliage, the crackle of the radio would be drowned in the commotion. The voices and whirring of the broadcasts that had carried so well before, transmitting clearly from the canopy of the trees down into the valley of the tributary, would be all but lost.

So Danielle would have to rely on her eyes, and with that thought, she pulled the binoculars from her bag and focused on the soldier's nest above, trying to find the shift in movement or the color of skin that didn't quite camo with the lush green and brown of the forest.

And she found it quickly, the figure, just under the awning of a sprawling oak. It was of a man, and he was cloaked in a hood that covered his mouth and nose, hiding his features almost entirely. But he was active in his perusal, leaning over the dark metal rail that surrounded the overlook, giving a steady surveillance of the area. It was more attention than Danielle had ever seen from a guard (a result, perhaps, of the spread of crabs that had occurred, she imagined), and had she continued all the way to the barrier fence as she did that first day of mapping, he would have spotted her easily.

But she was safe in her spot for now, hidden by the large cluster of rocks that rose four feet or so above the banks of the tributary, and far enough from the tower to be nearly imperceptible.

And Danielle soon saw the advantage of this new vigilance by the soldier. If the next guard had the same consideration to detail as this one, standing at attention, spanning the view for survivors, it would make for a relatively easy shot.

Danielle checked the round in the chamber, instinctively trying to muffle the sound with slow, deliberate movements. But her care was unnecessary; the showers around her crashed against the trees like a barrage of cymbals.

And then, through the sound of falling water and the rush of a freshly supplied tributary, another noise erupted, this one from behind her in the forest, past the tree line. It was a sound less pure than that of the rain, violent even, like the crackling of a fire.

Crunching.

Still crouched behind the rocks, Danielle kept her feet and torso motionless as she twisted her neck toward the trees, trying to find the source of the sound. She couldn't see more than a few feet through the thick vegetation, however, and she quickly turned back toward the tower, checking the status of the watch through her binoculars. With no auditory clues with which to work, Danielle was hesitant to take her eyes from the guards for longer than a few seconds, fearing she would miss the transition.

Still though, what was that sound?

Danielle studied the soldier for another thirty seconds and, seeing no visual signs of radio contact, she turned back to the tree line, in full now, squinting through the wet greenery, trying desperately to find the chomping noise beyond.

Then, with her back now to the river and the tower beyond, she walked in a crouching position for several yards until she gained the cover of the trees.

Danielle finally stood tall but remained in place, still searching for the source of the crunching, the rain now coming down in sheets. It was closer now, the sound, that much she could tell, but it was still masked by the falling water, making locating its exact spot nearly impossible.

Then, as Danielle spun to return to the rock cluster, she caught a twinkle of white from somewhere deeper into the woods, thirty yards or so, maybe less, just to the right of her periphery. The sparkle was barely detectable, but she had seen it, and she took a step to her right to clear the sightline further. And there, through the V-shaped opening of a pair of fern fronds, the surreal vision of the crabs fell into view.

There were two of them, wet and shimmering like a pair of mythical forest ghosts, the backs of their canvas white heads glistening with the splatter of rain.

They were hunched, their shoulders and chins tucked close to their chests as their heads shifted and pulled in various directions. They seemed focused, intense, and Danielle squinted, desperate to see what was occurring in front of them.

And then her question was answered almost immediately as one twisted its head upward, turning its profile in Danielle's direction, far enough that she could see the string of sinewy meat hanging from its mouth and the ring of blood that had formed around it.

Danielle froze in place, one foot still in mid-step, and she instinctively placed her left hand against a nearby tree trunk to keep her balance as she lowered her foot to the ground. She swallowed slowly, afraid even the relative silence of that sound could be a trigger, and then she turned and checked her sides in both directions, not quite sure of the next play.

But she couldn't just stand there, that much was certain, so she took another small step to the right, clearing her view of the fern fronds, gaining a clear picture of the crabs and the scene around them, seeing now that they were not alone.

There was perhaps a dozen of the creatures, maybe a few more, bunched tightly like maggots, and Danielle nearly choked on the lump that erupted in her throat, causing her to elicit some ancient version of a cough.

She threw a hand to her mouth, a move that resembled embarrassment, as if she'd accidentally belched at a dinner party. Her eyes were wide with fright, shifting and searching.

But the ghosts hadn't noticed her—not yet—and each of the savage creatures continued to rip away at the corpse of a large brown buck that lay destroyed beneath them, the animal's tongue hanging across its mouth almost comically, its lifeless eyes somehow containing a last glimmer of sadness and pain.

Danielle held her breath and took three steps back until she was again standing in the spot where she'd first seen them, and from there she mentally began working on an exit strategy. There would be no escape from the cordon tonight, that was obvious; the only question now was whether she could leave these woods unnoticed and make it back to the truck alive.

Her reconnaissance had been bad; she hadn't covered all her bases. She had been so worried about the guards in the tower and any soldiers who might be embedded inside that she hadn't considered other dangers, namely the ones currently crouched in front of her, fewer than a hundred feet away, tearing at the flesh of a deer.

Danielle thought of Michael again and how vital it was that she make it back to him. She had been the one who took him away from his house—which she knew was the right thing to do, but still, he was safe there—and now, because of her, he was alone in the truck. Alone in the cordon. And his terror would surely grow with every hour that passed.

And what if another group of ghosts had found him? Perhaps even tracked the truck from the bar? What if they had surrounded the truck and were at this moment banging on the glass, sending spider webs of cracks all around him, their black eyes and gnashing mouths terrorizing him?

She closed her eyes ruefully and took one deep breath, exhaling slowly through her nose as she steadied her breathing, directing her thoughts to the boy she'd left behind, trying to regain her focus and composure.

She continued this meditation for several seconds, repeating the breaths, until soon she could feel the cortisone levels in her body begin to drop as her mind rattled clear.

And then, as she lingered in the foliage with the rain still falling all around her, Danielle noticed that the crunching had stopped. She opened her eyes and looked back to the huddle of crabs, and there, staring back at her, were two pairs of eyes, black pearls of curiosity, locked and unblinking.

Danielle wanted to scream, of course, but her throat was locked tight with fear, and seconds later, another pair of dusky orbs entered her vision, the white head that housed them bobbing slightly left, studying her in the same way as the others.

"Mother shit," she mouthed, and then began to back away slowly, in the direction of the tree line from where she'd come.

And as she did, the crabs crept forward.

Danielle took several more steps, still backpedaling, still slowly, maintaining her sightline on the ghosts the whole way. She tripped over a stray root but was back on her feet in a flash, never losing the vantage. The ghosts were moving more quickly now, seemingly triggered by her fall, and Danielle finally turned her back to the monsters and began to run to the perimeter of the forest.

She was outside the edge of the trees in seconds, and from there she looked up blindly in the direction of the tower. The mission there was lost for now, no sense arguing that fact, so she turned and sprinted in the opposite direction, back up the shoreline and toward the truck. She made no attempt to keep covered from the tower guard as she ran; getting spotted by the soldier on duty would make little difference if she got devoured by the horde of ghosts behind her.

Danielle glanced several times over her shoulder as she ran, and within moments, in her rear, she could see a few of the crabs emerge from the forest.

But only a pair of them had followed her past the tree line, and they had stopped there, apparently deciding not to pursue her. They kept their stares fastened to Danielle as they crouched in place, swaying from side to side as if caught in some swirling breeze.

Danielle gave a silent prayer of thanks that the chase was over, and that the other monsters—those jumbled around the kill in the forest—were apparently too preoccupied with their venison to join the other white predators outside the trees. If they had kept on the hunt, she knew they would have had their prey within a quarter mile.

Danielle had caught a break for the moment.

But her fortune was short lived.

As she maintained her steady pace along the rocky beach, she glanced to her right at the tree line that ran parallel with her current path, and through the brush she could see the other crabs from the kill, which numbered around fourteen or so, galloping at full speed through the brush.

Within seconds, they overtook the progress Danielle had made (reaffirming her theory that she could never outrun them), their ape-like bodies thrusting up and forward like deranged mutant rabbits.

And then, before Danielle could speculate as to the purpose of this strategy, the ghosts began to seep out from the trees, their off-white bodies emerging from the leaves like pus.

Once past the tree line, half of the crabs then fanned out in front of Danielle, spanning across the dry section of the riverbed, blocking her path. The other half of the gang fell in behind her and stopped, sealing off any escape she might have considered back in the direction of the rock cluster.

"Oh god, no!"

Danielle stopped and did a full revolution, her head now spinning with panic. They were everywhere, arced around her like wolves as she stood with her back to the tributary.

The alarm inside her was blaring like the siren of a fire truck, but Danielle fended it off with a growl, and then she lifted the rifle and aimed it on the ghost directly in front of her. She took a step forward, assuring a kill shot. "You gonna go first, shithead?" she shouted through the rain, which was now surging in layers from the sky.

The crab didn't move—which Danielle hadn't expected—and without weighing the options any further, she answered her own question.

"I guess so," she said casually, and then shot the misshapen being through the center of its head.

The figure took two steps back and then collapsed like a bundle of dirty sheets into the puddle below it. Danielle then instantly put her aim on the crab beside it. Her wish was that by shooting the first ghost, the others would scatter, or at least back away, giving her an extra twenty yards or so to work with.

But that wasn't the result. The monsters had shown some level of fear previously, on the streets downtown and earlier at the dealership; but the ones before her now seemed willing to sacrifice themselves for the pack, for the greater good, perhaps for the meal that Danielle had interrupted.

Danielle took the next shot now, killing the beast standing at one o'clock, and then she moved the gun a fraction right and shot the one beside it, continuing with deliberate movements in a clockwise circle, systematically killing each of the crabs like a prison-camp executioner.

And then, as if finally realizing what was happening, and before their numbers could dwindle too much further, the crabs quickly began to close the circle.

Danielle re-positioned herself now, dashing from the center of the ring to the spot in the circle where the corpses of the dead crabs now littered the shoreline.

The crabs were mostly in front of her now—with the forest to her back—and from the corner of her eye she could see the original crabs who had followed her out of the forest begin to move in, trying to close ranks behind her.

Danielle spun toward the encroaching crabs, and as she did, she could hear the patter of feet behind and to the right as the beasts on her blind sides crept forward, shrinking the circle further.

You're going to die here.

The thought erupted in her mind like a volcano, as if preparing her for the inevitable. *Maybe these are the words of Death*, she thought, *the phrase of the Grim Reaper as he arrives at the bedside of a terminally ill hospice resident, or to someone pulling on the ripcord of a defective parachute.*

"No."

She turned back toward the river and raised the rifle high, and then fired off the next round into another crab, striking this one in the shoulder. The crab stumbled back but stayed erect, and Danielle shot it again, pure with her aim this time, killing the creature instantly.

She turned back to the tree line and shot one of the crabs that had moved in as a replacement, squeezing off several rounds into its chest. The one beside it was up next, and she directed her aim there, squeezing the trigger with confidence, steadiness of hand, feeling the flow of killing surge through her body.

But this time nothing happened.

Danielle squeezed again. Twice more. Each time getting the sickening click of the empty magazine.

"No!" she screamed, and then repeated the word in rapid fire, sounding like a needle stuck on a record as she checked the magazine in disbelief.

A full magazine should have had thirty rounds, enough to survive the ambush if she was economical, and she certainly hadn't come close to firing that many shots. Which meant the mag had been used previously, and she had failed to check the load. Live and learn, she thought.

Or maybe not.

She had at least been prudent enough to pack a second magazine, but that one was in her backpack, which she'd abandoned by the rock cluster during her escape.

Danielle's thoughts raced for a solution, and she quickly decided that if she could distract the ghosts for a moment and get off to a good sprint, she might be able to reach the bag before the crabs got to her. At that point, however, she was stuck. She wasn't in a track and field event—there was more to the task than just winning the race. Even if she did manage to reach the rocks, she then had to locate the bag, rummage through it to find the magazine, and then lock the ammo into the rifle and fire off enough rounds to immobilize at least a couple of her attackers.

The effort seemed impossible when she laid it out in her mind, but maybe if she could just make it to the rock cluster without being caught—a longshot on its own—and scoop the bag immediately, she could then climb atop the boulders and out of reach of the deadly hands.

Of course, Danielle already knew the crabs could climb like human ivy, but from her observations, they didn't climb with abandon. They organized first, always methodical in their attacks, and she could gain a few extra seconds to carry out the remaining steps of her plan.

Even adding this climbing element to her plan, though, it didn't seem destined for success. But the crabs were almost at arms distance, and she was out of options.

"Fuck it."

She removed the spent magazine and tossed it over the heads of the crabs that were standing on the shore of the tributary where they had clustered together as if guarding the water from intruders. They spun their heads toward the magazine, following it like dogs to a thrown stick, and in that moment of diversion, Danielle took off toward the rock cluster.

She was maybe six steps into her escape when the first slap of feet came from behind her as the crabs began their squelching pursuit through the muddy bank, a signal that her head start was over. Danielle had always been athletic, and fairly quick in a foot race, but with the weight of the rifle and the sloppy ground beneath her, combined with her general lack of nutrition and conditioning, she felt as slow as a turtle.

Less than halfway to the rocks, she felt the first hand upon her as one of the crabs clipped its fingers across her shin, knocking her right foot across the back of her left, nearly twisting her a hundred and eighty degrees. Miraculously, she stayed on her feet, but the stumble cost her precious distance, and less than a second later, another hand slapped

Danielle's left hip, this time with solid force, pushing her off her current course and sending her in the direction of the tributary.

The crabs that were nearest the water when Danielle began her dash, the ones that had been distracted by Danielle's toss of the used ammo, were still a few steps behind the others, but they were closing fast; and those that had surrounded her from the sides of the bank were now only steps away.

The blow to Danielle's hip had sent her to the shore of the tributary, and the toes of her shoes were now in the surf. She was blocked, with nowhere left to go along the pebbly shoreline. She peeked once at the tributary over her shoulder, and then, without giving herself a moment to reconsider, she backed into the rushing waters. She felt the cold water rush across her thighs and groin, and then she turned in full and waded quickly out to the middle of the shallow Maripo River offshoot.

When she was about thirty feet from the bank, she turned back to the shore and stared at the ogling crabs, which stood like a dazzle of zebras on the Nile, anxiously compelled to make the crocodile-riddled crossing. Except Danielle was the zebra in the simile, and once the crabs began their pursuit into the water, she would be as good as dead.

At her current location, the water level was just below Danielle's chest, and she turned and began walking west with the flow of the river, in the direction of the tower, just trying to get parallel with the rock cluster. There was no real strategy in the decision, and no real scenario where the move paid off; but she went anyway, just trying to buy time.

The monsoon-like rains from less than ten minutes earlier had almost ceased entirely now, and the sounds of the forest and the surrounding area returned, highlighted by a chirping conversation of birds from the trees above just as the late-afternoon sun was beginning to break through the canopy.

But the cheer of those sounds was dwarfed by the low gurgle of light splashes that came from the bank as the crabs began to enter the river.

Danielle turned toward the bank again to see three of the crabs entering the water; the remaining ones—which numbered six or so—had split into two even groups and were headed in opposite directions along the bank.

She watched the group to her left first, following them as they headed upriver twenty yards or so before entering the water. She looked to the right and saw that the other group had done the same, only this time down river. They were surrounding her again, in the water now, and this time, she *really* had nowhere else to run. The only place unguarded was further out into the tributary, but there she'd eventually end up in the open water of the main river and would drown within minutes.

The crabs directly in front of her were only to about the depth of their shins, taking their time with their attack as they often did. Perhaps it was after they fed when they lost the aggression, Danielle thought, still studying the creatures for more data, even under the dire circumstances.

The crabs upriver had also kept themselves in less than knee-deep water, but they were moving quickly in Danielle's direction, and instinctively she moved away from them and further down river. But in that direction, the crabs on that side had moved closer as well, and this group was waist high, almost lateral with Danielle.

She was truly trapped now.

If only she had a gun, she thought, but not for the obvious reason that she could engage in some riverside water battle. She could have used it as a signal now, to alert the guard tower that she was here, a civilian, alive and under duress. The heavy downpour from earlier had certainly masked the rifle shots she'd taken, but now, with the air clear and calm, the sound of a gunshot would rattle to life whatever sleeping guard was above. And that would spark radio calls, reinforcements.

And if soldiers did arrive, Danielle would do her best to keep from being captured, to try and escape in the fracas caused by the soldiers and crabs in battle. And if they did detain her, at least she would still be alive. Whatever situation she found herself in afterwards couldn't be worse than the one she was in currently.

And then, as if she'd just awakened from some hypnotic trance of ignorance, Danielle realized she had another option. It was the most primal of choices, really.

She could scream.

She cupped her hands to her mouth and lifted her chin high and back towards the guard tower. "Help!" she called. "Help me! I'm down here! In the river!"

Now that she had unleashed her calls, they didn't sound quite as loud as she had hoped, which was in part due to her exhaustion and partly to her underestimation of the vastness of nature. She looked up to the trees, waiting for some sign, a spotlight, movement of any sort. But there was only the calm wave of the branches and leaves.

The crabs were undaunted by Danielle's shrieks and continued their steady progress into the water, their white bodies slowly being enveloped by the dark tributary.

It didn't even matter, Danielle thought. *Even if someone heard me, or saw me, what could they do at this late stage?*

As her thoughts began to tumble rapidly toward her demise, a steady rumble suddenly came on the wind, drifting down from upriver. It was just a low vibration to start, but within seconds, it became the roar of a tyrannosaur.

Danielle saw the ghosts turn with alarm toward the noise, and then she followed their stares in time to see the Silverado bounce around the bend of the river, two of the wheels coming off the ground for just a moment before regulating.

The truck splashed into the river like a hunting tiger, and then slammed the bottom of its grill into the heads of three of the crabs, flattening them beneath the surf.

The truck was headed directly toward Danielle now, and she dove further out into the water just as the eight-cylinder beast turned back toward the beach and crashed forward into two more of the hunters.

Danielle quickly plucked her head above the surface, in time to see the truck turn sharply toward the beach, skidding sideways for several feet before getting traction again and accelerating forward.

The remaining crabs in the truck's path began to run now, as if noting this was an enemy they couldn't conquer. But it was too late for them, and the Chevy smashed against the spines of the demons, flinging them face first into the crushed rocks beneath them.

Danielle counted only two of the creatures remaining now, and as quickly as she spied them, they were gone, scurrying like hermits back into the cover of the woods.

The truck slowed for just a moment, and then it lurched forward and slammed into the high sandy bank just below the rock cluster before finally coming to a stop.

Danielle could only stare at the monster vehicle, observing it as if it were being guided by some alien force, waiting for it to levitate perhaps, or speak.

But there was only stillness from the truck, until finally the door on the driver's side opened and Michael stepped to the running board and then down to the shoreline.

"I hope you were wearing your seatbelt," Danielle called, breathlessly, not feeling any of the levity the statement implied, yet sensing an instinct to keep Michael calm.

The boy nodded.

Danielle writhed through the tributary in the direction of the truck, and within a minute or so, she was standing next to the boy who had saved her.

Again.

She would save the gratitude for later though, when they were clear of this section of the cordon that had so quickly turned from a promising escape route into disaster. All Danielle could think of now was the safety of the Flagon.

"Let's go, Michael. There could be more out here. They might be watching."

But Michael was staring blankly over Danielle's shoulder, entranced.

"What is it?" she asked.

Michael blinked once and then nodded his head over her shoulder.

Danielle turned slowly, expecting to see a dozen or more of the monsters rising from the water on the horizon. Instead, she saw the barrel of a rifle pointed directly at her, and the second she turned, it lowered.

The man holding the gun was a soldier, shades across his eyes, his hat low, but as he removed the sunglasses and brought them low to his hip, a smiled drifted across his face.

"I knew it," he said.

Danielle felt her legs wobble and her eyes flood, but she managed to utter the man's name. "Dominic?"

4.

"What are you doing here, Dominic? How..."

Danielle struggled to form the questions in her mind, and she wasn't even quite sure that it was, in fact, Dominic standing before her. Perhaps her eyes were tricking her,

projecting to her brain some kind of person-level mirage.

"Listen to me, Danielle, I've got another hour and thirty-four minutes until my shift is up. At that point, my replacement—"

"Wait a minute," Danielle shook her head, confused. "Are you telling me you've been up there this whole time?" She pointed to the North tower. "You could see me? See how close I came to being eaten?"

"I could barely see the tip of my nose in all that rain. But then when it subsided, I heard the scream for help and saw the crabs moving in. That's when I left my post and came inside—both of which are against protocol, by the way—but..." Dominic looked around the empty area of the cordon, bewildered. "...now they're gone. There were dozens of them."

"Dozens?"

Dominic nodded.

Danielle knew that couldn't have been right, but arguing about the crowd size was way down on the list of worries right now.

Dominic looked to Michael. "And who do we have here?"

Danielle studied Dominic, a suspicious glare now crinkling the lines of her face. She ignored his question about Michael and cocked her head. "Why are you here, Dominic? And I don't mean standing here right now. Why were you up in the tower? Are you working for them?" Her look of confusion suddenly turned to disgust. "You're working for the military?"

"Danielle, it's a long story and—"

"I don't care how much time you have."

"I promise I'll tell you everything, but n—"

"Just the bullet points then. I'm not taking a step until I know what the hell is happening right now. It is good to see you, Dominic, incredible really, but this doesn't make any sense. And I have a lot of reasons not to trust you right now."

Danielle thought of her list again, noting there was one more goal she could now scratch off: Find Dominic.

Dominic closed his eyes and nodded, acknowledging the fairness of Danielle's insistence, and then he began explaining, his eyes wide and scheming.

"They never saw me, Danielle. None of the people who wanted me dead—who still want me dead—ever saw what I looked like. Other than Stella and the colonel, nobody else in charge ever saw my face." He paused, seemingly for effect. "And Stella and the colonel are dead."

Danielle realized she hadn't asked McCormick specifically about the fate of the colonel, only Stella. "I heard about Stella."

Dominic cocked his head, confused. "Heard? From who?"

Danielle shuddered off the question. "No. Not right now." And then, "So you saw it, Dominic? You saw her die?"

He nodded slowly, frowning, his eyes thin and weary as he recalled the event. "I saw it. Why?"

"It doesn't matter."

Danielle made a mental note to put a line through that item on her list as well. She had believed McCormick when he told of Stella's demise, but not fully, and for that reason, she had left the item unchecked. But now she knew for sure. One more piece of closure.

"But what does matter is my as-yet-unanswered question about how it is that you're here right now. And also, just so you're aware, you're damn lucky that horde of crabs showed up. Otherwise, you'd be a lump of dead flesh in that tower right now."

"What do you—"

"How did you come to be in that tower, Dom?"

Dominic took a deep breath and lowered his voice. "You heard about Stella, which means you probably heard about the D&W building. And our escape."

Danielle nodded. "I did. I even witnessed a few seconds of the latter item. Watched the helicopter fly out that day. I figured you were inside. Hoped so, anyway."

Dominic looked to the ground in shame. "We knew you were alive, Danielle, but—"

"I know. It doesn't matter. What happened?"

"Stella and the colonel weren't the only ones inside the lab that day. There were others. Some of whom were civilians, just working the job, not really knowing all that was going on there. But there were soldiers there also, protecting the place."

"Okay, so what does that have to do with anything?"

"The soldiers didn't make it out of the lab either, met the same fate as Stella and the colonel."

"How did you manage to take out a whole lab of soldiers?"

"There were only a handful of them, and I didn't do it on my own. I made some soldier friends of my own along the way; I'd have never made it a day out there on my own without them."

Danielle wanted to interject about her own adventure alone, and how she had made it, but she checked herself.

"So, anyway, there were dead soldiers, with IDs, and before we made a run for the helicopter, I made a point to swipe one of the badges. Everything happening inside that place was illegal, and surely classified, so there wouldn't have been many on the outside who even knew the guy was there, let alone that he'd been killed."

"Someone probably missed him?"

Dominic shrugged. "Not if he didn't have family, or if he had told them he was on a classified mission. Someday yes, but not while all this is still going on." Dominic held his hand out to the prison that was the cordon. "Anyway, he didn't look exactly like me—a decade younger maybe—but it was a close enough match to allow me initial access. At that point, I just kept my head down and did what I was told. Plus, I had the help of actual soldiers—also unknown by the current brass—and they helped me navigate the red tape so I could get tower duty."

Danielle looked at Dominic, her eyes narrow, questioning. "So you just walked right back into the lion's den. With a fake ID?"

"I thought it would be harder than it was, honestly, and under normal circumstances, I imagine it would have been. But we're way past normal, Danielle. They're running out of bodies out there. The cordon is expanding, breaking down; they're on the edge of losing control. This thing isn't going to last for much longer." Dominic shrugged. "And for that reason, leadership isn't really asking too many questions of those who are able-bodied and enthusiastic. If you're a soldier and ready to serve, you're up."

Danielle just nodded, trying to find any gaps in Dominic's story.

"And I don't mean to rush you, Danielle, but we need to be hustling. I'm guessing your story is even better than mine—and maybe you can tell it to me over breakfast one day—but right now we should be going.

Danielle narrowed her eyes and frowned. "You wish."

"Fine, coffee then," Dominic corrected, keeping a straight face despite the obvious joke. "Let's go."

"Why did you *want* initial access?" Danielle prodded, not moving.

"What?"

"You said the dead soldier's ID allowed you initial access? Access for what? Why would you have wanted to come back here? Why would you have wanted tower duty?"

Dominic snickered and furrowed his brow, bemused. "Why do you think?"

Danielle shook her head, eyes wide, genuinely confused.

"I was looking for you, Danielle." Dominic's face wore the same look of puzzlement as Danielle's. "Why else?"

Danielle fought back a smile, but her mouth twitched just a fraction up the right side of her cheek.

"I would have gone on the cordon raids, but I haven't been here long enough to qualify, so tower duty was the next best thing."

Danielle smiled in full now, but she quickly blinked away the moment, not ready to soften in front of Dominic just yet. Instead, she turned to Michael and held out a hand. "This is Michael. He's been my hero over the last day or so and has suddenly become a big part of this very long story that I'll tell you over *coffee* some time."

Michael gave a wave and Dominic returned it in similar fashion.

"So, what do we do now? How do we get out of here?"

Dominic gave a somber nod but then answered quickly. "It's not going to be easy. Well, actually getting outside the cordon won't be too tough, but from that point it's going to be tricky. So, let's handle the first part and get the hell out of this place before your friends return. Once we're outside the gate," Dominic pointed to a spot shrouded in shrubbery, "we should be safe for the moment. But at that point, we'll have to move. We'll only have a little over an hour to get some distance; once they find out I've left my post, they're going to start ringing alarm bells." He frowned and looked at Michael. "I'm not going to lie to you though, Danielle, having a kid with us is going to make it tough."

"Well then it will be like every other day inside this place."

Dominic smiled and shook his head as if in awe. He wrinkled his forehead, squinting. "How are you still alive?"

Danielle shrugged. "I don't know, but you were still looking for me, so you must have had a little faith I would be."

Dominic nodded, his eyes now glistening with something between joy and love. "Damn right, I did." He held his stare for another moment, and then he swallowed and nodded toward the gate. "Listen, both of you, we're going to have to be quick and quiet and you're going to have to listen to me."

Danielle shrugged. "Okay."

Dominic suddenly looked around him, studying his surroundings as if seeing the cordon for the first time. "This is the first time I've stepped back inside since our escape."

"Feeling weepy about it?"

"Not quite."

As they walked toward the cordon entrance, Danielle thought of the others from the original group. "Tom and James," she said, suddenly embarrassed she'd yet to inquire about them. "Are they..." she trailed off, hesitant to know.

Dominic nodded. "They're fine. Safe and secure."

Danielle took a deep breath and nodded. "Where are they?"

"If we can make it out of the camp, we should see them tonight. They're still in hiding, but they're comfortable."

"It can spread, Dominic," Danielle uttered, almost irrelevantly. "Did you know that?"

Dominic nodded. "Yes, I know. *They* know. That's why their expanding the cordon." He paused. "But how do *you* know?"

"I saw it. I saw a man...turn into a crab right in front of my eyes. They just cut him and he..." she trailed off, still disturbed by the memory of Davies' transformation.

"They say it has to break the skin for the turn to happen. That it enters the bloodstream."

"What does?"

Dominic shrugged and shook his head. "Their sweat, maybe? Oils from their skin? Whatever it is that carries the virus or bacteria or fungus or whatever. I'm not sure they even know yet. The scientists, I mean. But they're in there around the clock; I know that much."

"The lab?"

Dominic scoffed as he nodded. "Yeah, the lab. You did learn a lot in here. But like I said, I don't really know. We only get what comes out of the rumor mill."

Dominic stopped walking, and Danielle and Michael followed in turn. Dominic stared into Danielle's eyes, a look of sadness there, despair.

"They've escaped. Did you know that? More than one."

Danielle nodded.

"They think it's been contained for now, but...but they can't know for sure. And now...now they've decided to just clear the cordon out for good. They're going to begin daily raids, to just try and capture anyone left inside."

Suddenly, Michael's pained voice rang from behind Danielle, startling her.

"Have you seen a black man that looks like me?"

Danielle turned and put her hand across Michael's shoulders, pulling him toward her.

Dominic shook his head. "I haven't. Is he your father?"

Michael nodded.

"But just because I haven't seen him doesn't mean he's not alive. Did they capture him?"

Michael nodded again. "They took him from our house. Soldiers. Like you."

Danielle could see Dominic's desire to plead his innocence, to explain more clearly that he was an imposter, there to help them. Instead, he just gave a solemn nod and said, "If he went with them quietly, calmly, without too much of a fight, they'll have kept him alive for a while. How long's it been?"

"A few days."

"He won't have much longer then." Dominic gave Michael a stern look, as if he were a man his own age, and said, "We'll do our best to find him, okay?"

Michael took a breath, at least partially reassured. "Okay."

Danielle lifted her shoulders and expanded her chest. "Okay then, soldier, lead us out of this fucking place. I've still got a few things left on my To Do list."

5.

The gate to the cordon was about fifty yards through the brush, on the North side of the tributary, directly below the guard tower which had been constructed just on the opposite side of the fence. Danielle, Michael, and Dominic waded through the shallow water and were now standing by the border of the enclosure, where a thick chain snaked through the gate and fence. A padlock hooked through the chain with the bolt swung to the unlocked position.

Danielle reached for the gate to open it wide and Dominic grabbed her hand suddenly. She snapped her look to him and prepared a rebuke, but she could immediately see the color had drained from his face. "What is it?"

"Look," he said in a whisper, pointing to the edge of the gate.

Danielle followed his finger but didn't immediately register the problem; the giant gate was open slightly, less than a foot wide, leaving just enough room for a man to squeeze through.

Or a crab, she thought, suddenly seeing the potential issue.

"It's open."

"You didn't leave it like this? Are you sure?"

Dominic nodded. "I'm sure. I closed it. I didn't lock it, but I definitely closed it.

"Maybe it just swung open on its own then."

Dominic shook off the possibility. "It didn't. Look at the size of it. And the bottom of it wedges into the ground. You see?" He pointed to the thick bottom post of the gate that was at least three inches into the dirt. "Plus, it latches. Here." He pointed to a lock set on the interior of the iron gate. There's no way."

"So then one of the guards opened it? Is that what you're saying?"

He shook his head. "No. Nobody comes down here. Nobody's ever been down here as far as I know. Not since the construction was completed. There's never been a breach on this side of the cordon, and, until today, the corrupted almost never venture this far toward the perimeter. It's the reason I wanted this post. I figured if you were still inside and looking to make an escape, you would have headed in this direction."

"Guess you were right there."

"Plus, since there is so little action down this way, they started using just the one tower. The south tower has been all but abandoned."

"Look!"

Michael pointed to the muddy ground that led from the base of the gate and away from the cordon, off toward the freedom of northern Maripo County.

There was no debating the soldier theory any longer.

Footprints, dozens, maybe sixty or more, enough that they blended into a jumble of heel and toe indentations so as to be almost invisible, littered the ground. And with daylight quickly fading, the evidence was almost impossible to see with the naked eye, but as Dominic shined his flashlight to the forest floor, the markings were unmistakable. There was no question about it now: the crabs were out. If there had been a minor breach in the cordon before, it was now a full-scale jailbreak.

"You're probably gonna lose your job over this," Danielle said flatly, instinctively trying to bring a bit of flippancy to the moment.

"Probably," Dominic replied, equally deadpan. And then he asked rhetorically, "Since when can they open doors?"

"I was about to ask you the same thing."

The three companions exited the cordon and walked until they were clear of the trees, and then continued to follow the footprints through the mud until they reached an open field of tall grass.

Danielle was officially out of the cordon now, finally, and though she was far from safe, she took a deep breath, feeling like a paroled prisoner who's just exited the last gated entrance of a penitentiary. As she exhaled, she stared out toward the horizon and the cluster of lights blazing from the spotlights and trucks and jeeps that signaled military occupation.

"That's where we gotta go?" Michael asked, following his new protector's stare.

"That's where we gotta go," Dominic replied. "And then over the bridge to the lab. If your dad is...well, that's where your dad would be."

The lights were perhaps a mile in the distance, and Michael continued to study them for a few beats more. Finally, he asked, "How we gonna do that?"

Dominic looked at Danielle now, tacitly passing the duty of explaining this quest to her.

"Let's start by turning off the flashlight," she said. "No point highlighting the fact that we're coming." Danielle scanned the landscape for a moment. "And then we'll just start walking. They're working with a skeleton crew, right, Dom? So we'll just see how far we can get before we have to take someone out."

"Take someone out?"

Danielle shrugged.

"You are right about the skeleton crew, though. I think we should be able to get pretty close. And since I'm *supposed* to be here, I'm not going to raise any eyebrows if I show up. We're going to have figure out you two though, especially Michael. If they see the two of you, they're going to detain you, no matter what I say."

"Then they won't see us. We'll stay low in the grass until you can clear out the area, and then—"

"Clear out the area? How do you suppose I should do that?"

"I don't know, but I trust you can think of something. It's just for a few minutes so we can clear the base and get to the bridge. How's the bridge for guards?"

"Anything outside the cordon is technically unguarded, but there are soldiers milling around all the time."

"Then we should be able to get to the lab."

"You don't even know where it is."

"How many buildings could there be past the bridge that could be a lab? Just give us a gap. We'll find it."

Danielle was far less confident than her words suggested, but she knew Michael needed the hope. The truth was, she figured their prospects of making it past the camp and over the bridge at about one in ten, and finding and rescuing Scott, one in a hundred. Still though, she wouldn't know for sure until they tried.

Dominic nodded. "Okay. But like I said, the bigger issue is how fast we can do this. The next watch will be at the tower in less than an hour, so we need to get past the base and to the lab in under that. And then we have to free Michael's father from wherever they're holding him. And then find some type of vehicle that can take the four of us out of there to somewhere safe."

"That doesn't sound too bad?"

"Not if you're John Wayne."

"At least it's getting dark," Michael said, finding the silver lining in the gargantuan task ahead of them. "That should help."

"I would have agreed with that three minutes ago," Dominic said, "but now that we've—that I've—unleashed a plague of demons upon the world, I'm seeing the darkness as less of an advantage. And, can I add, they're probably hearing us talk right now?"

"Not that helpful, Dom." Danielle sniped.

"Let's just walk," Michael offered. "What choice is there now?"

From the mouths of babes, Danielle thought, and then nodded in agreement. A moment later, the three companions took their first steps into the tall grass and toward the base.

"If we walk quickly, I'm thinking we can reach the base in fifteen minutes." Dominic's voice came out low and distracted as he gave his estimate from his crouched position in the chest-high grass, which, on Michael, was nearly to his chin. Danielle could see Dominic from the corner of her eye, swiveling his head slowly from left to right, trying to spot whatever enemy might be waiting, approaching, and she noted how much like a soldier he now appeared.

"I guess your days of blathering on about *King Lear* are over, huh?" she ribbed, her posture with the rifle a mirror image of Dominic's. Despite the coolness of her remark, however, her adrenaline was racing.

Danielle couldn't see the smile from Dominic, but she could hear it in the former English professor's voice. "That, they are," he answered. "And your nights of serving country-fried steak to mummies is a thing of the past too, I guess."

Danielle couldn't help but laugh aloud at the retort, and when the chuckle finally subsided, she replied, "Yes, soldier, those salad days are far behind me now."

The three continued to tread quickly through the stalk-like grass, with no one speaking a word for what was probably five minutes, and when Danielle finally looked back to the cordon barrier to judge how far they'd traveled, she saw a wispy sway in the grass, the tip of each blade glistening for a flash in the moonlight before passing the glimmer down the field.

The sway in the field continued for several yards, and Danielle followed it with her eyes as it rippled west and then ultimately disappeared into the darkness.

Just a breeze, she thought, *that's all*. But the plunge in her stomach suggested the movement was more than the wind could have caused.

And what breeze, exactly? The air was as tranquil as a prayer.

Danielle decided to speak up. "Did anyone see that?"

Michael stopped and turned, now facing in the same direction as Danielle. He moved in close to her, his right shoulder now pressing against her. "What? See what?"

"I don't know, I..." Danielle looked down at the frightened boy, his body now frozen in place, wedged to her sternum. "It's okay. I just...it's fine. It was just the wind."

"You *saw* the wind?"

Danielle looked forward to Dominic, who had continued walking and was now several paces ahead, his focus still on the space in front of him. She swallowed and nodded at Michael. "It's fine. Let's go."

Danielle released her right hand from the rifle and held the gun by her side in her left. She then took Michael by the hand and began to march, hurrying the pace by double.

They had taken a dozen steps, maybe fewer, when Danielle suddenly felt a surge of fear begin building in her groin, rising through her stomach like a storm on the sea, barrelling through her chest before finally settling as a burning blush on her face. She kept her eyes straight though, her mind focused on Dominic and the ground ahead, but her attention was quickly redirected to Michael as he summoned her name in a whimper.

"Danielle?"

She looked down at the boy, but her eyes were instantly drawn to the ripple of grass approaching in the distance. It was a different version of the swell Danielle had seen earlier, larger, now undulating like an ocean wave as it rippled directly toward them.

"Run!"

But it was too late. Within three paces of their escape, Michael's body disappeared into the night, the grip of his palm and fingers ripped away from Danielle's as if he'd been sucked into the mouth of a tornado.

Danielle was spun like a top by the wave, but she stayed on her feet. She looked down at her empty hand for an instant, disbelieving, and then she rotated her body methodically, making a full circle as she searched for Michael and the thing that had kidnapped him.

But she could see only the unmoving blades of dark grass before her now.

Michael was gone.

"Michael!"

She quickly put the rifle sight to her eye and flipped on the light, and then Danielle began walking frantically through the field, taking a few steps in one direction before turning and searching in another, trying to cover every inch of ground in front of her.

"Dominic!" she called over her shoulder. "It's Michael!"

But Dominic was already beside her, and within seconds, he pointed to a spot about fifty feet to the left. "Look."

Danielle followed Dominic's finger but could see nothing. "Where? Do you see him?" She was now on the verge of tears.

"No, not Michael, but the crabs are there. I can tell by the sway. There are at least a few of them."

"We have to find him Dominic!"

"How did he—"

"Danielle!"

It was Michael, and he sounded close, maybe fifteen yards in front of her now.

Danielle walked quickly but cautiously toward the sound of his voice. "Again, Michael! Call out again!"

"I'm here."

Michael's second call was calmer, and now came from a spot just to Danielle's left.

She turned slowly and shined the light into the grass, and there, sitting upright and slightly forward as if listening to a campfire story, was Michael. The arms of two ghosts were draped around his head and neck, and they were stroking his head and face slowly, as if trying to soothe a baby to sleep.

But their attention was on Danielle now, the beasts staring at her with eyes that were blank and expressionless, and yet somehow taunting.

A tear hung impossibly beneath both of Michael's eyes, which were now pleading orbs of desperation. "They're....they're touching me," he said. "Am I going to die now?"

Danielle's throat felt like she'd swallowed a golf ball, but she quickly released the lump to her chest and shook her head in a shiver. "No, Michael. It's okay. *You're* okay. You're...you're not cut, are you?"

Michael shook his head, the tears that were dangling from his cheeks now raining down to the ground below. "I don't think so."

Danielle nodded and smiled weakly and then raised the rifle, aiming between the eyes of the crab to her left. "Just don't move, Michael. Just stay as still as you are right now."

"Danielle!" It was Dominic, his voice a screaming whisper. He softened his speech. "You can't fire. Not like this."

"I don't give a damn if they hear!" she snapped. "We'll figure out another way."

Danielle wrapped the inside of her top knuckle around the trigger and crooked her neck as she stared through the sight."

"It's not that. You can't get them both with one shot. The second you hit one, the other one might rip him to shreds."

Danielle was on the verge of panic now, her voice shimmying. "Why aren't they doing it now?"

"I don't know. These new ones, the ones that survived the melting, they're more erratic than their ancestors. Sometimes violent, sometimes calculating. And it could be they're changing again. I mean, it looks like they're holding him...I don't know, hostage?"

"What?"

"Maybe that's not the right word, but something is happening. They figured out how to work the gate. They could never do that before. Maybe they're getting smarter. So maybe they figure you won't shoot if they have Michael in their clutches."

"Well, they're damn wrong about that."

Dominic lifted his rifle and took the same stance as Danielle, and being left-handed, he was facing her in a mirror image. "Let's make it one shot then. We'll take them both out at the same time. That way they won't have time to react.

And one shot will be easier to explain when I get to camp. Bonus."

"Okay," Danielle agreed. And then, "I guess they're not that smart, huh?"

"Not smarter than a junior college professor who blathers on about King Lear, that's for sure. Which one you got?"

With her eye still to the sight, Danielle replied, "The one on your side."

"Got it. So I've got the handsome devil to my left. And Danielle?"

"What?"

"Please don't hit my bullet."

The notion of the criss-crossing rounds colliding in midair was a funny one, but Danielle felt no desire to laugh. She had the craving of an executioner now, poised to take the shot of her life. "I won't," she said.

"On three?"

"Sure."

"Don't move, kid," Dominic said, but Michael was already immobilized with fear. Then, as if tallying ducks on a pond, Dominic counted, "One...two...three."

6.

Danielle heard only one report from the rifles—a thunderous, deafening noise—but the sight of both crabs careening backwards and causing an explosion of dirt around them meant she and Dominic had been perfectly synchronized with their shots.

She lowered the gun for a moment and stared like a mad woman at the scene, and then she lifted it again and pointed the light of her rifle at the crab in front of her. That one was Dominic's shot, and she could see the glistening of its eyes as the blood from the quarter-sized wound poured down the center of its face.

Her shot, which had struck the crab on her right, was still moving, struggling like a netted fish, and as she moved into the space to clear Michael away and check him for injuries (God help them he wasn't cut), she could see the extensive damage her bullet had done to the thing's chest.

Michael had yet to move since the blast, and he was now sitting with his eyes closed, holding his knees as he rocked slightly from front to back.

"Let's go, Michael," Danielle said calmly, moving her hand to give a stroke of comfort to his head. She paused, however, imagining the hands of the crabs upon his face, figuring a touch like that from her could trigger the boy to panic. Instead, she put her hand under his left armpit and lifted, encouraging him to his feet.

Dominic had also moved into the kill space, but he was now standing over the fallen crab, the one not yet dead, and without a word, he pulled a large blade from his bag and stooped down by the monster. Danielle turned away, but she could hear the grotesque slice of the knife as it glided through the white skin of the beast, and she quickly spun Michael and escorted him away, back to the spot where she had fired the rifle.

Dominic joined them seconds later and nodded to Danielle, his face as serious as she'd ever recalled seeing it. "Now we *really* have to go," he said. "That was loud, and there are going to be inquiries as to what that was."

"Yeah. And there were *way* more than two of those things that got out," Danielle reminded, "so probably another good reason not to hang around."

And with that realization, Dominic and Danielle switched off the lights, and all three began to run toward the camp, no longer considerate of any soldiers who may have been standing watch.

Within minutes, they were only steps from the edge of the tall grass where the grounds of the base camp began. Danielle could see the dramatic line where the three-foot reeds had been mowed away and a new grass, trimmed to the height of a golf course fairway, became the property of the soldiers.

And beyond the manicured lawn, no more than fifty yards from where they huddled now, a long row of large military shelters had been constructed, perhaps eight in all, spaced about twenty feet apart and rising from the ground like giant, sage caterpillars.

And it was quiet.

"This is strange," Dominic whispered.

"What is?"

"I don't see anyone here." He poked his head above the grass again, looking toward the base, verifying that what he'd seen was, in fact, true. "I don't get it. There should be headlights blazing right now. Jeep engines running and commands being barked out."

"Personnel is thinner than you thought, I guess," Danielle offered.

Dominic shrugged, not convinced of the theory. "Maybe. Still though, we're keeping to the plan. The two of you are going to stay here until either I return to get you, or I give you a signal."

"And what might that look like? The signal, I mean."

"I'll give a whistle. Catcall style."

"Classy."

"Don't come out until you hear it. Promise me that."

"No, sir. 'Fraid I can't promise that."

"Danielle—"

"We will stay here for what I believe to be a reasonable amount of time, but after that, we're on the move. And full disclosure, it might not be that long. Certainly not a second more than ten minutes."

"Danielle, you—"

"Listen, Dom, I have no intention of becoming one of those things, or of becoming a meal for one, and I'm definitely not going to let that happen in the middle of a field *outside the cordon*." Danielle looked down at Michael. "We've come way too far to let that happen."

Dominic sighed. "Fine. Just keep the rifle high and your eyes peeled. I'll be as fast as I can."

And with those words, Dominic was off, heading west, away from the camp.

Within a minute, Danielle could see him again, clear of the tall grass, approaching the camp from the direction he would have had he been arriving from his post for the day. He had the posture and demeanor of a man who was supposed to be there, and Danielle grinned, proud of him, suddenly flattered by his efforts to find her again, feeling something that resembled love, though not in any romantic sense of the word. Of course, that wasn't out of the question either, but that was for another life, a future life, one she may never get the chance to live.

With her eyes, Danielle followed Dominic as he approached the line of jeeps parked outside the building, and there she could see a uniformed man approach him. He was flanked by two soldiers. The man pointed to the area from which Dominic had just walked, and Dominic turned and pointed there as well, shaking his head. She couldn't hear them, but the hand movements and body language suggested these men needed an explanation as to why Dominic was there.

And then the man in the middle, no doubt the highest ranked of the three, turned his back to Dominic and walked toward the shelter while the two soldiers grabbed Dominic by his arms, restraining him.

"Get the hell off me!"

Danielle could hear Dominic only faintly as the men struggled with him, but it was only a matter of seconds until they had Dominic on the ground, face first, one of the soldiers placing a knee to Dominic's back, pinning him there.

The man in charge then opened the door to the shelter and turned back to Dominic and the men restraining him. He made a gentle lifting motion with his hand, at which point the soldiers gripped Dominic at each arm and brought him to his feet again. This time Dominic did not resist.

Almost the second Dominic was up, another figure emerged from the entrance of the military building. This man was dressed in civilians' clothes and he walked forward with his head down and shoulders slumped, his hands low in front of him, fingers interlocked.

Just above the door of the shelter was a large spotlight that shone to the spot on the ground just outside the building's entrance, and though it was still some distance from where Danielle and Michael were hiding, she was almost positive she recognized this new character on the stage. And when he finally looked up to face Dominic, there was no doubt at all.

It was James.

He stared at Dominic for a few beats before finally lowering his head again, and Danielle could see easily it was a move made from shame, one that said he had betrayed a friend.

Danielle figured the army had finally found James in hiding—and likely Tom, as well—and through what was certainly a short interrogation, James had given up Dominic and his infiltration efforts. Danielle wanted to believe that he had been tortured, that he had listened to the clicks of a revolver against his temple, understanding that the next cylinder could have contained the lone round in the gun.

But in the depths of her heart, she knew it had never gotten that far. James was a good kid, and he had shown enough endurance to survive the snows when the catastrophe first struck, alone, before her group had found him on the road and brought him to the diner. And that, she conceded, was not an accomplishment to be discounted.

But in many ways, James was weak. It would have taken merely the suggestion of being put in a cage with one of the mutated humans to have broken him like a brittle twig.

And where was Tom? Danielle thought. *If they had caught James, they had likely caught Tom too. But if that was true, why had he not been paraded out in front of Dominic? Had they threatened him as well, and, when he'd defied them, killed him for not cooperating? And how did they find them? If no one knew what they looked like, how were they able to catch them?*

Danielle's mind was racing with potential answers to these questions, while also trying to find the next step to take in the current mission. Dominic wasn't coming back for them, that was for sure, so it would be up to her to improvise.

"What's going on, Danielle?" Michael asked, his mocha cheek only inches from hers as he stared through the grass at the scene occurring outside the shelter. "Who are those people?"

Danielle tried to invent a lie, but it sounded puerile in her head, and she immediately decided there was no gain in being anything other than fiercely honest with Michael from this point forward. "They're bad men," she said. "Like the ones that took your father. They and others—who in a lot of ways are even worse—are the ones responsible for all this.

But Dominic isn't like that, okay. He was just pretending to be to save me. And now we're going to save him. You and me. Got it?"

Michael licked his lips and nodded, slowly now, his eyes narrow and focused. Danielle recognized the look of resolve in the boy's face and knew it well. It was the place one arrived when a fear has finally been conquered. She had arrived there months ago, and now she had a companion.

7.

Danielle and Michael stooped low behind a jeep that had been parked in the rear of the shelter where Dominic was currently detained. It took them five times as long to arrive there than it would have had they taken the direct route, but such an endeavor was far too risky, even if the grounds were as clear as they appeared to be.

Instead, Danielle led Michael in a wide loop around the end of the row of shelters and then north toward the river, before finally doubling back and arriving directly behind Dominic's building.

Along the way, Danielle had witnessed Dominic's replacement in the tower, marching toward her post, and Danielle wondered how long it would take for her to notice the breach in the cordon.

She may not notice at all, she thought, *not if she bypassed the gate check and went directly to the tower.*

Unless that sea of grass began to swell again.

But that concern was far from a priority, and Danielle turned her attention from the shelter now and looked across the river where the relative stillness of the camp was offset by what appeared to be an ensuing state of alarm, a melee. Dozens of soldiers were off-ramping from the bridge, their rifles raised, waving and barking commands as they fanned out in every direction.

Danielle couldn't see the source of their agitation, but she assumed it was to do with the ghosts that Dominic had inadvertently released a little more than an hour earlier. It was a fact now: the crabs—the corrupted—were not only free of the cordon, but they had now made it beyond the bridge and the natural barrier of the river. That was the reason that the forward base, the place where she and Michael were now, was virtually empty.

At the hub of the commotion across the river was a free-standing building that Danielle quickly determined was the aforementioned lab. It was a monstrous construction, especially considering it had been built in only a matter of months, and even in the relative darkness, Danielle could see the ivory whiteness of the thing, so unlike the khaki green of the shelters around her. She instantly thought of the D&W building that Davies had mentioned before his demise. It was the place where this nightmare had been hatched, a structure she had barely noticed in all her years of living in Warren County, despite its size and sprawling footprint.

But it rose in her mind now like the behemoth it had always been, and she could only imagine what had gone on in there, and what was going on now in its sister research lab, which was currently lit up like a Christmas tree.

Danielle turned to see that Michael was looking past the bridge as well, and she could see the concern and dread in his face.

"We're going to get him, okay?" she assured.

"How?"

"I don't know exactly, but Dominic and I will figure it out. I promise you. But the only way we can do that is with Dominic, so first things first, yeah?"

Michael nodded and turned back on his heels, his body tight against the front jeep's tire as he and Danielle studied the camp system.

Other than the guards and the officer who had ordered Dominic taken—and James, of course; she couldn't forget James—Danielle hadn't seen anyone else come or go from any of the shelters. And it wasn't for lack of visibility; from where they were situated currently, she could see the back ends of the shelters all the way down the row in each direction.

None of the other shelters mattered right now, however; Dominic was in the one that was less than fifty feet away, and she had to be swift with her efforts.

"I'm going in," she said solemnly, a phrase that sounded corny to her ears the moment she said it, something she would have uttered to Tom just before she went in to clean the diner's bathroom.

"I'll cover you," Michael answered.

Danielle smiled at Michael's follow-up cliché, and then considered for a moment that perhaps people really did talk like that in these types of situations.

"You do that."

Danielle stood quickly, looked left and then right, and then sprinted from the cover of the jeep. Within seconds, she was standing next to the shelter, the beam of light from the roof shining down on her as if she were doing stand-up in a comedy club.

But there was no one anywhere on the outside to spy her, so she held her spot and then turned and gave a thumbs up to Michael.

She moved a few steps toward the rear door of the shelter, making sure to keep on the hinged side of the portal, just in case someone opened it and stepped outside. She would have to make a move within a couple seconds, of course, were that to happen, but at least she would have the advantage of surprise. She placed her ear to the door.

And then she heard the screams.

It was Dominic, and his cries of distress were quickly followed by the voice of a man, surely the commanding officer who had ordered him arrested.

"Again, soldier, I only want to know two things: why you're here impersonating another soldier, and who else is with you."

"I'm...I'm not impersonating anybody, sir," Dominic replied. "I don't know what you're talking about."

Something banged against the shelter door and Danielle recoiled, and as she did, her mind flashed back to the roof of the Maripo Mazda and the crab that had pounded relentlessly against the steel door.

But no one exited the shelter, and Danielle slowly tipped her ear back against the door and listened. There was a scuffling sound inside now, the scramble of feet, like an anxious dog scurrying on linoleum. It was followed by the rattle of what sounded like chairs being knocked to the floor.

And then Dominic screamed again, and this time it was blood-curdling.

"Just a scratch and you'll be one of them, you know," the commander yelled, making sure Dominic could hear him over his own wailing. "We've done it before; rest assured that's true."

There was a pause, during which time Dominic's screams crescendoed for a beat and then subsided. Danielle closed her eyes in distress.

When Dominic was finally quiet, the CO continued. "But not to James here, because James was smart. You told us everything we wanted to know, isn't that right, son?

There was no reply, and Danielle could almost see the dishonor in James' eyes.

"Yessir, James here answered our questions right quick. Same as that helicopter pilot. Still can't believe y'all allowed that boy to live. Had to know he was gonna spill eventually, no matter what he told you. Especially when one of these freaks is standing in front of you. Look in the eyes of one of these things from a few feet away and just about anyone'd be persuaded, I figure."

The scuttling again from inside the shelter, and this time Danielle took the opportunity to slam a fresh magazine into the bottom of her rifle, the noise from inside drowning the sound of the gun action.

"So, once again, soldier, tell me why you've infiltrated my unit, and who else is with you. If you do that, I'll make sure Officer Stanwick tucks that thing back into its cage."

"I'm Richard Gerard."

Dominic's voice wavered with fear; even through the muffle of the door, Danielle could hear it.

"It's right there on my badge. I'm here because this is where I was told to be, sir."

"Look at this picture, son." The CO's instruction contained just a trace of irritation now, but he quickly regained his composure. "We already know that picture ain't you.

James already told us that. Have you been listening? That picture might have fooled us before because we wasn't paying attention, but James here already gave us your name. Your first name, anyway. Ain't that right, James? Dominique, ain't that it?"

"Dominic," a voice chirped. It was James.

"I don't know who this person is," Dominic replied, continuing to play what Danielle considered an impossible game of chicken.

The officer laughed. "I can see this ain't you, boy. Even if James hadn't told me as much. You really think you can pass for being born in 1992?" He laughed again, more heartily. "No offense."

Dominic's ruse was up, and Danielle couldn't help but picture the scene unfolding inside the shelter. The crab was chained or leashed and likely raging in its constraints, and no doubt it was standing in front of Dominic, being edged ever closer as the interrogation drew on. Whether Dominic was tied to a chair or to the ground, she couldn't know, but she could imagine his fear as he looked into the black eyes of the crab, which were likely locked on him like a circling shark.

"It's an old picture," Dominic continued, and Danielle couldn't help but roll her eyes and shake her head.

"That ain't you!" The irritation from the man in charge was now full-blown anger.

"Sir?" Another voice, one of the inferior officers.

"What is it?"

"Richard Gerard. Stationed at D&W. It's not known for sure what happened to him, but it's assumed he was there when...when it happened."

A pause, then the CO asked, "So, then, Dominic something-or-other, can we stop this now?"

There was a pause, Dominic considering the offer, perhaps, and Danielle held her breath, anticipating.

And then, through the door, she heard his voice again.

"Fuck you."

There was a pause and then, "That, Dominic, was the wrong goddamn answer."

As if triggered by the CO's words, Danielle took a deep breath and nodded her head in a quick, quivering burst, as if physically agreeing to the idea that had just swelled in her mind.

And then, without any more hesitation, she made the move, gripping the knob of the door and pulling it open.

In the second it took for Danielle to clear the door and enter the shelter, she formed a picture in her mind of what she expected to see inside. The location of the CO and the soldiers; the weaponized crab; Dominic.

But it was James who Danielle saw first, sitting near the front of the shelter, behind Dominic, leaning forward in his chair as if listening to a solemn newscast on the radio. He looked up at Danielle and met her eyes, and in a flash, his face transformed into a smile. It was as genuine a smile as Danielle had ever seen. The smile a toddler gives when he wakes from his nap to see his mother standing over his crib.

To her left, by the door, sitting at a computer with his back to Danielle, was one of the inferior soldiers, and as he moved his hand to pull his sidearm from his waist, she squeezed of a shot.

The bullet streamed past his face and tore through the canvas that formed the far wall of the shelter.

"That was on purpose!" she screamed. "The next one is in your fucking eye socket!"

The soldier nodded and put up his hands.

"Get up! Lay your weapon on the table and move there!" She flicked the barrel of the rifle toward the front of the shelter.

The second soldier had no play to make on Danielle, since in his hands he held a long metal pole with a ring that had been clasped around the neck of a crab. The beast had it eyes directed forward, toward Dominic, and it appeared at the moment to be relatively stable.

"You let go of that pole and I swear to god I'll make you watch that thing eat you from the inside out."

The soldier shook his head slowly. "I'm not moving, ma'am."

With the crab and soldiers under control, Danielle brought her attention to the commanding officer.

"Throw your weapon to me," she instructed. "And if I have to ask again, there will only be two people alive in this shelter to comply with my orders."

The CO threw his hands in the air, shoulder height, showing his immediate deference, though Danielle could see the mockery in his movements.

"Yes, ma'am," he said, composed, something close to a smile on his lips. "Never argue with a woman with a gun, that's my motto. Especially not if it's bigger than mine." He pulled his pistol from his holster and tossed it at Danielle's feet.

She looked at Dominic and saw that he had no restraints around his body or legs. "Dominic, let's go." She then looked at James. "You too, young man."

James stood first, and as he did, the CO moved like a panther and snatched the pole from his inferior officer, taking the reins of the enslaved crab and turning it toward Dominic, shoving it close, perhaps a foot or two away from his face.

The creature began twitching furiously now, snarling in its muted, grotesque way, the proximity of a human body appearing to have awakened its ferocity, as seemed so often to be the case with the beasts.

"You see my finger right here?" The CO nodded to his hand. "I've got it pressed down on this button that controls that collar around its neck. You know what that means? It means it's a grenade now. You shoot me, and this old boy gets loose on your friend's face. If that's alright with you, then have at it. Otherwise, drop that goddamn rifle. And I won't ask again either."

Dominic had begun to stand just before the CO had made his move, and Danielle could now see the zip ties around his wrists.

"Sit down, Dominic," the CO said, nothing but contempt and command in his voice now. He looked back to Danielle. "Here's what you're going to do, miss, you're going to lay that rifle on the—"

In an instant, before she could consider any of the unintended consequences of the action, Danielle aimed and fired a round, striking the yoked crab in the back of its head, just to the right of center.

The crab went limp in an instant, its dead weight pulling the restraint down to the floor, forcing the CO to release the yoke which fell impotently to the ground. The crab collapsed at Dominic's feet and lay there like a puddle of speckled milk, the blood from its wound seeping to the floor in a river of red.

"Guess you didn't think that out too well, huh?" Danielle asked.

The officer looked at Danielle with a mixture of rage and awe, and then he shook his head, his jaws clenched. "Stupid bitch. Stupid fucking bitch! You're the ones responsible for this. You're the reason those things are out of the cordon now. Escaping past the fucking lab for Christ's sake!"

Danielle raised the rifle again and took three steps forward until the point of the gun was pressed against the officer's head. The officer to her right, the one who'd given up the reins of the crab, made an instinctive move toward her, but he needed only a stern look and a smooth shake of Danielle's head to back off.

"This is your fault you piece of shit," she said. "And before you and I part ways, you're going to tell me the name at the top of the list."

The officer's eyes were closed now, and Danielle could smell the fear rising in him. He hesitated and then shook his head, his brow crinkled. "What the fuck does that mean?" he asked quietly.

"Just what I said. I already know about Stella Wyeth and the company she worked for. Well, I know the name anyway. D&W, right? But what I don't know is the person at the top. The person in charge of all of this."

The CO scoffed. "You think I know that guy? Why would I know him?"

"I'm not implying you go skeet shooting with him on the weekends, but my guess is you know a name."

"It's some jackoff in Belgium. Shit, I don't remember his name, but he's the head of the parent company that owns D&W. It's not a secret. You can get it off the fucking internet."

"Yeah, well my internet's been down for a while."

"You'll never get past the bridge. There's soldiers everywhere."

"Really? Because from what I can tell they seem a little preoccupied at the moment."

"They've got it under control."

Danielle ignored him. "Also, I'm going to need your clothes. All of yours. So let's get to stripping."

Without argument, the CO began to undress, and the two soldiers beside him followed his lead.

"Just a question for you though, sergeant. Something that's been bothering me every day that I've been inside."

Without looking at Danielle, the CO said, "It's major."

"Who gives a fuck?" Danielle asked rhetorically and then got to her actual question. "I want to know how this was possible. How this *is* possible. I want to understand how no one has stopped this. Where are the elected officials? Where are the whistleblowers? How could all of this corruption not be exposed by now?"

The CO stopped undressing and stared up at Danielle. He gave her a bemused smile, genuinely confused by the questions. "Whistleblowers? Stopped it? What in Satan's hell are you talking about? Stop what? *We're* the ones trying to stop it."

"But you were the ones who started it!"

The CO shrugged. "It's a lot more complicated than that, but even if that were true, which I'm not admitting it is, it doesn't matter at this point. Nobody on the outside cares now. A few conspiracy nuts on TV maybe, but not the masses. Maybe in a decade they will, but not today. People just want their world to be safe, to keep the evil contained, so when they see tanks and jeeps and men with guns surrounding a piece of land, they know that's what we're trying to do." He paused. "Y'all have made that a lot harder to do though—you and Mr. Dominic. But my men will clean up the mess you've made, because that's what they do. And if they can't clean it up, if one or two of them get past, we'll just move some folks out and extend the cordon further. We'll take over the state if we need to."

"How can you do this? Under whose authority?"

He shrugged again. "I just follow my orders, ma'am, and my CO just follows his. That's the way it's always been." He pursed his lips. "But if you're asking how the public can go along with what's happening here, it's like I said, they just want to be safe. You'd be surprised how effective a leaked snippet of drone video can be. Every few weeks or so just drop a few seconds of grainy footage of a couple of these mutants running around the streets of Maripo, it tends to get everybody back in line. Better in here than loose in their cul-de-sacs."

"You're the fucking monsters," Danielle quipped, seething now, almost wishing the man would lunge at her so she could shoot him between the eyes. But he was sitting on the floor now, stripped to his underwear with his arms draped over his knees, no longer a threat. Danielle turned to the soldier on her left. "Where are the zip ties?"

The soldier looked sheepishly to his CO for consent, but the unit leader had lost interest in his command, so the soldier moved quickly to a short foldout table containing a variety of loose items. He picked up a handful of ties and then returned to his spot.

"Tie up your boss and then move on to your brother there," Danielle ordered.

Danielle watched as the soldier pulled the nylon cords tight around the wrists of both men, and when he was done, she said, "It's your turn now. James, you got this?"

James nodded and tied the remaining man's hands quickly.

"Michael's waiting for me," Danielle said, "so let's do this and get out of here."

She cut the ties from Dominic's wrists and then picked up the shorter of the two inferior soldier's uniforms, and then Dominic and James each grabbed their bundle of clothes, silently figuring out which size was most appropriate. In a few minutes, the three companions were donned in their respective uniforms, indistinguishable from any other soldier in the camp.

"Let's go," Danielle said, and the three walked to the front of the shelter.

Danielle opened the door, but before she walked out, she looked back to the men on the ground behind her, their hands in front of their t-shirted bodies, bound at the wrists.

"If I see any of you outside of this shelter," she ran her eyes up and down the men, "—and you won't be hard to miss—I'll shoot you in the chest. And I won't hesitate."

She thought of her list again as she met the eyes of the CO. And then, somewhat irrelevantly, said, "Belgium, huh?"

Find Dominic

1.

~~Find Dominic~~.

Kill Stella

1.

Danielle studied her list for the first time in days, and she felt a surge of pleasure at the progress she had made, thankful that she had taken the time to put her goals down on paper. *That had made all the difference*, she thought, paraphrasing a line from her favorite poem.

This latest goal wasn't her accomplishment, of course, though she figured she had played at least some part in it. And besides, it was all about results, right? Hitting your numbers. And she was a company girl, so who cared who got the sale?

She moved the pen from Dominic's name to the one just below it and then drew a line through her goal, feeling the sting of a tear as she made the mark.

~~Kill Stella~~.

That was that.

"I'm ready."

Danielle was jolted back to the moment by the sound of Michael returning from a cluster of trashcans which he had used as cover while he relieved himself.

She spun around and looked at Dominic and James, sitting up stiffly in the back seat. "You guys good?" she asked.

Both men nodded, though it was obvious that Dominic was still shaken by his captivity, and Danielle now feared whether he would be ready for the next challenge, only minutes away.

Danielle nodded back and smiled weakly, and then stuffed her list into the breast pocket of her uniform.

Two more goals to go, she thought. And then she would be done.

The first goal was an original, but the second one was a recent addition, unwritten.

Danielle tucked her hair tightly into her cap and then turned the key to the jeep, and as the engine rumbled to life, she let loose a scream, a staccato burst of vocal energy for the battle ahead, and then sped toward the bridge and the lab on the other side.

*Rescue Scott

1.

Rescuing Scott Jenkins wasn't on Danielle's original list—obviously, since she'd only met the man within the last week—but the instant Michael Jenkins saved her life and became her charge, it quickly became an ad hoc mission to save the boy's father.

She'd also decided the new goal was even worthy of its own line on her list, and she made a mental note to add it later, an addendum below the last goal.

Danielle brought her attention back to the bridge and pulled the jeep to the edge. She shifted it to park and idled, still on the forward-base side of the river. The group had already made the decision to turn the headlights on as they drove across, figuring that keeping them off would only attract unnecessary attention on the lab side. But the commotion across the span—which had seemed to be spiraling into chaos less than twenty minutes ago—now looked to be placid by comparison, brought under control by the soldiers, just as their CO had declared.

But the sudden quiet was wrong, almost impossible based on what Danielle had witnessed earlier, and she sensed there was still confusion spinning around the lab. In any case, they would know soon enough.

Danielle shifted the jeep back into drive and began the trek, accelerating slowly, using this new window of disorganization to begin the crossing. She drove at a steady pace, and in less than a minute, they were across the bridge.

From there, she followed a dirt road toward a large gravel parking lot that had been built on the east side of the lab, in the opposite direction of a group of four soldiers who were standing nervously over two dead crabs.

That's only two, Danielle thought. *There were a whole lot more than that a few minutes ago.*

She anxiously began scanning the rest of the grounds for signs of other crabs, other groups of soldiers. But there were none.

The prints by the cordon gate had suggested ten times as many crabs had escaped, but she quickly realized why the area was so calm. The crabs had fled, and the rest of the soldiers had followed them. They could be a mile away by now, more, dispersed into a dozen different directions, wandering down suburban side streets like rogue bands of Guinea baboons.

Danielle shuddered at the thought but quickly forced her attention back to the mission. Crabs on the loose in society was a problem—for sure—but it wasn't hers to deal with at the moment.

She shut off the engine but left the keys in the ignition and then immediately looked to Michael, giving instruction that he was to stay quiet and low while the adults went inside. He was the only one not in disguise, she explained, and he was far too young to pull off the charade even if he was.

"We tried that before and look what happened," he complained, referencing the same instruction she had given him inside the cordon: to stay put in the pick-up truck while she ventured off to attack the barrier.

Danielle smiled. "What happened was you saved me. Remember?"

Michael frowned and dropped his head, knowing he'd unintentionally set Danielle up for that reply.

"What do you think would have happened if you were with me and not in the truck? Who would have come in at the last minute and mown those bastards down like crabgrass?"

Michael grinned and his eyes grew wide. "*Crab* grass?"

Danielle exploded in laughter, not intending the play on words. When she settled, she put a hand on Michael's face. "Just please stay here. Please?"

Michael sighed and nodded. "Fine."

She gave a loving pinch of his cheek. "Good."

"But Danielle..."

Danielle waited, searching the boy's eyes.

"Bring him back. If he is alive, if he isn't one of them, don't leave without him. Please."

Danielle felt a panging constriction in her chest, but she took a breath before it turned into physical emotion. "He *is* alive. I have a very good feeling about that. And if I didn't plan to bring him back, we wouldn't be here right now. Okay?"

Michael nodded.

Danielle looked to Dominic now; his eyes were distant as he stared out the side of the jeep.

"Dominic?"

Dominic met Danielle's eyes, but his stare was vacant.

"Hey!" she snapped, trying to bring him to life. "You know this place, right? You need to be the one leading this thing."

Dominic swallowed and nodded, but Danielle was unconvinced.

"Listen, I know that was terrifying, Dom, what just happened back in the shelter. Trust me, I do. But we need you to be good now. *I* need you to be good. I need you to be the Dominic that convinced a group of scared strangers to leave Tom's Diner all those months ago. The Dom that jumped into an icy river to save James, someone you barely knew, and then later infiltrated a military unit to save me."

Dominic nodded again. "I got it, Danielle. I'm fine."

Danielle could still see him wavering and she sighed. "Remember the day we left the diner in the box truck and drove you to your house? You found your wife that day, just as you had hoped, except it wasn't your wife. You remember?"

Dominic closed his eyes, fighting the memory. "Of course."

"Do you remember how close you came to it that day? And also how close you came to dying?"

He nodded. "I remember that too."

"But you didn't die. You left shaken that day, for sure, but that fear quickly turned into strength. And it was that strength that helped keep you and the rest of us alive. You led us to the bridge and found a boat to cross the river, and then you fought off those things with, may I say, stunning bravery when they attacked us from the water. It hadn't been a day since you saw your wife cruelly changed into something...less than human...and you were amazing. And then you found Tom and James again. And a way out of the cordon. *You* did all that, Dominic, and that's the guy we need now."

"I only made it out of my house that day because of you," Dominic reminded. "Don't forget that, Danielle. It was *you* that saved *me* that day, not the other way around. You're the strong one in this group, not me." He snickered and gave a bemused smile, not understanding how she couldn't see the obvious truth of his words.

"We're both strong, Dom. That's why we can do this. That's why we're going to do this."

Dominic shrugged, a show of conceding the point, and then said, "And there's something else you're forgetting."

"What's that?"

"That day, in my foyer, I didn't know about the whole contact thing. The way it can spread through cuts in the skin." He swallowed and inhaled, holding the breath in his lungs for several seconds before exhaling. "Not that it would have mattered, I guess. I was in a different state after I saw her." He frowned and flickered his brow. "I really just wanted to die."

Danielle sighed and nodded, giving his words a moment to settle. "I know you did, Dom. And yet here you are. You didn't die that day and you didn't die back at the shelter a few minutes ago. And that's all we can really hold onto right now. The fact that we're alive. What else is there?" She shrugged. "We just keep going. That's all we can do." She paused and then added "And since you're the one that led us out of the cordon, we'll call it even on who saved who."

"*Whom*," Dominic corrected.

Danielle frowned and raised an eyebrow. "Really?"

Dominic furrowed his brow and shook his head. "Besides, you just saved me again, Danielle. Like ten minutes ago. So now I owe you another one."

"Like I said, we'll call it even." Danielle looked over at James now. "You, on the other hand, you still owe me a couple."

James frowned and nodded earnestly. "I know."

Dominic laughed aloud, and with that sound, Danielle could see a spark return to his eyes. It was a flicker of the old Dominic that Danielle had just described, and she knew it was the flash they would need if they were going to bring Scott out of the lab alive.

"Hey!"

The shout sounded close, coming from the darkness to their left, in the direction where the soldiers had been congregated. Danielle squinted through the night, trying to find the source of the call, and soon a flashlight beamed to life. Seconds later, it was accompanied by the crunching of approaching footsteps.

"Where the hell have you guys been?" the voice asked. "And why are you just sitting there? We've got a fucking catastrophe over here." The man spoke with just the hint of an accent, his tone calm and low, a striking contrast to the foul language he was using.

"The major ordered us to check the lab," Dominic said. "We already know about the breach, but our orders are to lock down the lab first and then lend support."

"Who gives a shit about the lab?" the soldier asked as he stepped into view. He was probably thirty, Hispanic, shorter than average but well-built, and his eyes were dripping with suspicion. "Nothing you can do in there anymore."

Danielle wasn't quite sure what that meant.

"And the Lab's not gonna mean a fucking thing if we don't track down the ones that got past."

Danielle spoke up now, trying to sound authoritative, careful not to use any nomenclature that might give her away. "CO said you guys had it under control. Guessin' that isn't the case?"

The soldier tipped his chin up, looking even more skeptical than before. "Nah, it ain't the case," he said. He was staring past Danielle now to the seat beside her. "Who is that?"

Michael.

Danielle turned to see the boy hunched low in the seat, his face turned toward the door of the jeep, pretending to sleep.

"He's, uh, we—"

"We found him in the cordon," Dominic chimed in. "I saw him during my patrol, and we detained him. So now he's my problem, and it's the other reason we need to get inside the lab. He's just a kid so orders are to make sure he's taken care of. And, as you can see, he's not doing so well."

The soldier continued his study of Michael, the expression of doubt on his face unchanged. "Is he cut?"

"Says he's not. And I didn't see any blood when I caught him."

"I don't..." The soldier stopped mid-sentence, his attention caught by something in the direction of the bridge. "What the fuck is that?"

Danielle directed her gaze toward the bridge now and immediately saw the reason for the soldier's distraction. Not yet halfway across the short span of concrete, running toward them with a face of despair and horror, was the CO from the shelter.

The major was still in his underwear with his hands tied in front of him, and behind him, perhaps fewer than twenty yards away, was a crab—an escapee from the cordon, no doubt—propelling himself forward, slamming its hands to the ground as it erupted forward, tracking the major like a missile of animal flesh, gaining ground with every bounding step.

The sight was surreal, and Danielle felt almost paralyzed as she kept her eyes fixed to the chasing crab.

The corrupted.

Next, a flicker of movement came from the grounds on the opposite side of the river, from the shelter where Danielle and James had tied up the soldiers and ordered them—upon penalty of death—to remain.

Danielle redirected her focus there, and her eyes immediately landed on the vision of two more crabs, this time emerging from the door of the shelter like a pair of attacking, white bees. They were furious in their gestures, their arms and necks spinning and flailing wildly, and even from that distance, Danielle could see the thick, red streaks that extended from their mouths to their chests.

And when they turned and began running toward the major, she knew he was as good as dead, and that they were all in very serious trouble.

"Get to the lab!" Danielle screamed. "Michael, go!"

The soldier who had approached them ignored Danielle and continued gawking at the approaching monsters, finally lifting his rifle to get a better view through the sight.

"Major Branks?" he whispered, disbelieving.

Then, in an instant, he seemed to figure out what was happening, and that the 'soldiers' beside him were the enemy.

But by then, it was too late.

As he turned toward the quartet of impostors, he was instantly met by Michael's pistol, which Danielle held extended in her right hand, the end of the barrel meeting him just above the eye. "Hand it over," she commanded. "Right now!"

The soldier hesitated for a moment, during which time Danielle cocked the hammer and pressed the barrel deeper. He sighed and lowered the rifle and handed it to James, who had sidled up beside him.

Danielle stepped back from the soldier now, keeping the pistol on him, and she checked the bridge again, where the crabs were halfway across and only steps from the fleeing major.

"Michael, get inside. Now."

Michael hadn't listened to Danielle's original command, and his eyes now lingered on the bridge as well, captivated by the hunt.

"Michael! Now!"

Michael finally turned and looked at Danielle, and then he ran toward the front of the lab without looking back.

Seconds later, the screams of the major shattered the air like a rod of iron through stained glass.

Danielle wanted to turn away from the carnage as well, but she was compelled by the savagery, drawn to the finesse and speed of the monster as it leapt from the pavement of the bridge and enveloped its body around the torso of the officer, its thin, gangly arms wrapping around the large man's neck before bringing him to the ground with ease.

The major continued to scream, even as his face smashed into the unyielding ground; within seconds, the other crabs were upon him, tearing at his clothes and skin with unrelenting hands and teeth, ferocious, angry, remorseless.

It was all over in seconds, but it was a long enough spell that the images would live forever in Danielle's dreams.

Danielle turned her attention back to the soldier in front of her now, prepared to return the rifle since he was currently unarmed and thus defenseless from the attacking ghosts (though she suspected he had another weapon on him somewhere). It was a fool's decision, she knew, but she simply couldn't leave him stranded to die the way the major and his men had. She was already responsible for those three lives, and she couldn't bring herself to allow another to end so easily.

But before she could make the offer, the soldier, without concern for the gun that was still pointed at him from behind, began a full sprint in the direction of his commanding officer whose arms had already been torn from his trunk.

Danielle had no intention of shooting him, of course, and, in fact, she felt a sudden and deep sympathy for the man. She felt pity for all the soldiers, really, including Davies and McCormick. They had lost touch with the good in their hearts. At least that seemed true for most of them, excluding, perhaps, those in the highest of ranks, those pulling the levers that kept this secret machine of death up and running.

And yet, despite the misguidances of the rank and file, there still existed admirable qualities in these men and women, things like duty and valor and solidarity. They were simply missiles who had been programmed toward the wrong target but whose lives still had purpose, even though many would pay that price in the end.

She watched now as the other three soldiers ran toward the bridge, without hesitation, head-on in the direction of the oncoming crabs as if prepared to meet them like Saxon soldiers repelling a horde of Viking invaders. Two of them had high-powered rifles, so, unlike the major and his subordinates, Danielle had no reason to doubt that the crabs would be dead within seconds.

And once the rogue crabs were eliminated, the soldiers would be back for her and her friends, and they would have little concern for Danielle's current pangs of compassion. She and Dominic and James and Michael would be seen as traitors in their eyes, the reason for their current predicament, and potentially infected with the new strain of snow monster. Without question, they would be shot on sight.

A torrent of doubt flooded Danielle now, and she suddenly felt an urge to abandon the goal of rescuing Scott, to take the jeep and escape while they still had the window.

But even if she had wanted to follow her cowardice instinct, it was too late now. Michael was already inside.

Danielle steeled herself back to the present, ready to shift her focus from the bridge to the lab and Michael, who was already inside. For all she knew, he was already in the clutches of other crabs, perhaps even his newly converted father.

She turned to begin her run toward the building, but as she rotated her head, from the corner of her eye she saw a sea of white emerge from the tree line of the abutting forest, fifty feet or so from where the soldiers had just been gathered around the dead crab. To Danielle, it looked as if an avalanche had suddenly erupted from the border off trees, seeping out like melted marshmallow and now flowing directly toward the bridge.

Ghosts, an army of three or four dozen, who had likely been hiding in the gloom and watching the soldiers all along, waiting for the moment when their defenses became compromised or their attention re-directed—as it was now toward their major—launched their attack.

Danielle wanted to scream, to warn the men of the terror that was approaching behind them, to give them at least a chance of survival.

But she simply couldn't take the risk. Screaming was likely to draw the crabs' attention toward her and her friends, and even with the guns with which they were armed, it wasn't enough to hold off so many; they would all be dead within minutes.

So, instead, she watched silently, helplessly, as the group of forty or more crabs flowed as one toward the bridge, like a rapidly moving cloud, a swarm of dusty ghouls, gaining on the unaware warriors with every breath.

"Let's go," she said solemnly, encouraging Dominic and James to hurry toward the lab.

Halfway to the front door of the large white building, Danielle heard the first gun shots, followed by a single scream. Whether it was the scream of the soldier whose head she had put a gun to only minutes earlier, or one of the others, she couldn't know, but that first one was quickly followed by three additional cries, in rapid succession, each one more heartrending than the last.

2.

"Michael!"

Danielle's voice was barely a whisper, but it carried through the chamber like thunder, seeming to drift into every corner of the space.

The inside of the lab was a giant, un-partitioned room, cluttered and well-lit, with walls and floors as white as the exterior of the building. Occupying the center of the large space was row after row of tables that had been separated into three columns, with each of those extending all the way to a barrier wall at the back of the building. On and around the tables was evidence of work and invention; computers and monitors, microscopes and robotic arms, notebooks and pens lying next to half-filled beakers.

Giant aluminum ducts ran the length of the ceiling and connected into various metal chambers that had been hung near the building's support columns. Fluorescent lights lit up the room like a football stadium, and the glare from them sent a wave of pain through Danielle's head. It had been a long time since she'd seen fluorescent lighting, she realized, and it was having its way with her.

What was missing from the room, however, were people. There wasn't a soul; it was as if the place had been suddenly abandoned, mysteriously, a Lost Colony of scientists.

On each side of the lab, running the length of the room along each wall, were tall, clear chambers, about seven feet high and circular in design, like giant pneumatic tubes. Danielle hadn't noticed them at first, but now they struck her like a hammer, sending a shiver of sickness through her belly and torso.

She took a few steps to her left, toward the side wall that was closer to her, until she was standing in front of the tube that was nearest the entrance. It was empty, but as she studied the strange tube further, she got the general gist of its purpose.

They were built to hold people—or crabs, perhaps—though for what purpose exactly she couldn't decide.

Danielle moved down to the next tube, and then the third, examining them more closely. These next two chambers were of the same design, also empty, and each had a set of narrower tubes hanging from the tops and sides of the interior, devices used for breathing purposes, maybe, or possibly as a channel to fill the chamber with fluid.

She looked across the room now, over the busy tables and view-obstructing columns, and on the opposite wall, about four chambers from the back, she saw something move in one of the chambers.

"What *are* these things?" James asked, still studying the tubes nearer to them, not noticing Danielle's gaze. "Are these for people?"

Danielle didn't answer, her eyes still fixed on the movement in the far chamber. She took a few steady paces across the lab and then, steadily, she began to run.

Danielle maneuvered nimbly past the long tables, vaguely anticipating some mutant creature—the result of some black-ops research, maybe—to leap from behind one of the tables at any moment and begin to gnaw upon her neck.

But she reached the occupied tube unmolested, and as she viewed the contents, she felt a scream begin to burgeon in her throat. She threw a hand across her mouth and closed her eyes, shaking her head.

"No," she whispered. "Please God, no."

Seconds later, a voice from beside her asked, "Who is that?"

Danielle opened her eyes in horror and looked down at Michael, instinctively putting her arm around him as her eyes filled like a lake.

"Don't look," she said.

But Michael moved out of her arm and studied the tank further. "Do you know him? Dominic?"

Danielle was confused at first, and then she realized Michael was in denial, unwilling to accept that she hadn't saved his father after all, that he was instead floating like flotsam in a tube in front of them.

She looked back to the chamber, to take in the reality for herself, and instantly realized it was she who was wrong.

The man inside was black, like Scott Jenkins, but upon further inspection, she could see this person was older, sixties maybe, and quite a bit shorter than Scott, likely some other poor citizen of Warren County who'd had had the misfortune of surviving the snows and staying alive for months after.

About his condition, however, she was not wrong.

The man's eyes were wide, frozen in fear and confusion, and Danielle could only imagine the terror that had gone through his mind at the moment of his death.

The chamber itself was filled with a thick, yellowish liquid that was certainly some type of preservative, and the corpse floated in it as if drifting through space.

"I don't think so," Dominic answered. "He doesn't look familiar. But...look at his face. His features. They're..."

"Coming apart," James finished.

Danielle studied the corpse's face further and she could see what her friends were referencing. The man in the chamber was missing his right ear, most of his hair on both his head and face, and his right eye wasn't the dark brown color of his left, but rather the black onyx of the crabs'.

"It's like he was in the process." Dominic swallowed and took a deep breath. "I guess we know what this place is for then."

"They're trying to stop it?" Michael asked. "Trying to find a cure?"

Dominic frowned. "I wish I thought that, Mike. And I suppose it might be true in a way. But I'm guessing they're more concerned with controlling the change than curing it."

Michael nodded, though it was clear he didn't fully understand. "So, is this where all those ones that attacked the bridge came from?"

"What do you mean?"

"I don't know. I mean, all the soldiers that are supposed to be guarding this place are gone, right? Chasing the things that we let out of the cordon? So, if they're chasing the ones from the cordon, where did all the ones come from that came out of the trees? The ones that attacked the bridge?"

Danielle understood Michael's point, but she quickly realized he had his theory backwards. He was right in that the soldiers *had* been chasing crabs, but the ones they were chasing had escaped from the lab not the cordon. The ones from inside the cordon were the ones that had attacked the major and his men, the ones that had hidden in the forest, waiting to ambush.

Either way, though, it all ended in the same place, which would eventually be a catastrophe for the world.

"Where is everyone else though?" James asked. "If that's true, that the soldiers ran off to hunt the crabs, why aren't the...I don't know...scientists still here? Or whoever was running the show in this place? I doubt the same people who were conducting these experiments ran off to hunt those things down. Seems like a different skill set to me."

A dull thud came from somewhere deep in the building, beyond the back wall, and the group turned as one toward the sound.

No one said a word as they stared at the barrier, watching the wall as if expecting it to melt away, or perhaps lift off into space.

The thud boomed again and this time there was the faintest of noises accompanying it, a sound that was high-pitched and twangy, like the hidden harmony in a song.

"Did you hear that?" James asked.

"I heard it," Dominic answered. "It sounded like a voice to me. Coming from behind the wall."

"Look!" Danielle pointed to the corner where the far wall met the back partition, and there, as clear as a housefly on an ice cube, was a large metal door with the words KEEP OUT written on the front.

Dominic nodded. "Let's go."

They walked quickly to the door and stood beside it, with Dominic taking the lead and resting his hand atop the knob.

"What are we waiting for?" Michael asked anxiously.

Danielle had a bad feeling about what was on the other side, but there was no point making a case of caution at that point. They were going through no matter what.

"Be ready for anything," Dominic instructed. "All of you."

Dominic turned the knob and pushed the door in slowly, and Danielle knew instantly by the smell that they were in for a show of revulsion.

As Dominic pushed the door wide, a large room slowly came into view. It was the remaining section of the lab—which, Danielle guessed, was about a quarter of the building's entirety—and, in seconds, she could see where the breach had occurred and the crabs had escaped.

The back door—a thick, metal block that was at least twice the size of the one they'd just opened—was gaping wide, and a clear path to the world stretched out beyond it.

The cool night breeze reached the interior opening almost immediately, and the moving air helped to moderate the odor of death that hovered somewhere inside.

No one took a step toward the threshold, the instinct of restraint filling each member of the group like rainwater in a well, the atrocity beyond looming large in their imaginations.

"I guess we have the answer to the question about the soldiers," Dominic said, nodding toward the opening in the back of the room. "They're not off chasing the ones from the cordon; they're chasing the ones that were in here. I doubt they even know about the ones that escaped from inside."

That had been Danielle's speculation, of course, but as she thought about the theory further, she remembered the major's words and how he had blamed them for the breach. "What about the major?" she asked. "He said it was our fault that they were out. That we were responsible for everything."

Dominic shook his head. "I think he was speaking more...I don't know, cosmically. That because we didn't co-operate with the state or something, that's why their experiment turned into the clutter of shit it is today. I don't think he knew about the horde that escaped by the tower though." He paused and then flicked his eyebrows. "Well, not until it was too late anyway."

"So, what happened in here then?" James asked.

Danielle considered the question quietly, and then quickly surmised the lab workers had lost control somehow, had underestimated the intelligence of the crabs perhaps, and then the monsters had staged some kind of mutant mutiny, escaping from whatever restraints had held them shackled. And once they were out, the crabs had overpow-ered the staff in the room and escaped through the back.

It's just like at the gate, she thought. *They had figured out how to open the door.* Maybe it was as she'd expected: they were getting smarter.

There was no way to be a hundred percent sure about her intelligence hypothesis, of course—it was possible that one of the lab techs had opened the door in terror after the melt down and then fled like a rabbit from a wolf, allowing the beasts easy access to the world.

But she knew in her heart that wasn't right. The crabs had opened that door, and they were the rabbits now, luring the soldiers from the camp, leaving it vulnerable, decimated.

And what then? Did they just run to daylight, fleeing to the hills before wandering off to the next county, either west or north, bringing destruction to the unsuspecting civilians in their path? Or perhaps they had hidden and waited in the hills, preparing to double back to the river when the area was clear?

The possibilities were too big to consider, too cataclysmic, so, instead, Danielle took a brisk step forward, pushing past Dominic and through the threshold until she gained the full view of the room.

And the scene was as horrific as she had feared.

The first object her eyes met was a hand, so cleanly severed it looked like a prop from a bad horror movie, though with a bit more detail perhaps, hair around the knuckles, poorly manicured nails.

Within seconds, her sightline was filled with the entire massacre.

Blood and clothes and thick chunks of flesh littered the floor in front of her, covering the ground like a beach of gore that led gradually to a sea of carnage. A headless corpse sat slumped near the center of the room, the dead torso bent forward, balancing itself upright, while other bodies—their heads still fastened to their necks—splayed wildly throughout the room, eyes bulging, appearing as if to be drowning in the slaughter. Everywhere were sections of ears and bones and breasts and necks, each body part lining the floor like pieces in an abstract art gallery.

Danielle whipped her face around as if she'd been slapped and then hung her head, her eyes closed, trying to erase the images. She then turned and walked vigorously back to the interior door, exiting the room and gathering Michael along the way. Without a word, she led him to the front of the lab and the door through which they had originally entered.

She stopped at the entrance and attempted to slow her breathing, which was now teetering on panic.

"What did you see?" Michael asked

Danielle closed her eyes again and took several more slow breaths, trying to focus on nothing but the flow of air in and out of her lungs. In a few moments, she felt gathered and then looked at Michael, answering, "It's going to be okay. I promise. I just...I just ha—"

"What did you see?" Michael repeated, his voice more insistent this time.

"It was..." She took another gaping breath, exhaling slowly. "It was very bad, Michael." Her voice wavered now. "I don't really know how to—"

"Danielle!"

The voice came from the back room—the Murder Room, as Danielle would always remember it. It was Dominic.

Danielle let her eyes linger in the direction of the call for a moment, as if considering whether to answer. Finally, she said to Michael, "Stay here. I'm going to make sure everything is...okay."

"But it's not okay, is it?" Michael's voice was laced with despair. He moved to one of the lab stools beside him and sat. "Remember what you told me, Danielle. You were going to bring him out. You were going to bring him back to me."

"I know I said that, Michael, but—"

"Danielle, there's someone alive back here!"

Danielle couldn't help but let her lips drift into the tiniest of grins as a set of teardrops suddenly materialized, perching at the edge of both eyes. Before Michael could say another word, she turned and ran back to the door that led to the massacre.

As she approached the entrance, she saw James standing outside, his face as white as chalk, and she knew he'd made the mistake of entering and was now back outside again, recovering.

Danielle rushed past him and through the door for the second time, now hopeful as she lifted her eyes above the floor and to the right side of the room where Dominic was standing.

The walls.

She had been so hypnotized by the destruction on the floor below her that she hadn't noticed the walls of the room, which were queued with the same clear tubes that had lined the walls in the front of the building.

And inside one of them was a man.

A black man.

And he was alive.

There was no doubt about it this time. It was Scott Jenkins.

3.

"Scott?"

Danielle yelped the name, startled, not quite believing the man in front of her was actually the subject of their mission.

Scott Jenkins' nose was barely an inch above the fluid inside the tank, and hearing his name, he lifted his chin so that his face just cleared the liquid. His eyes were slits, exhausted, and he appeared to be naked, though the murky yellow solution was nearly opaque, clouding his lower body. To Danielle, it looked as if he were floating in a vat of rusty urine.

Scott's eyes met Danielle's for just a moment, but they shifted away quickly, as if he didn't recognize her. He then looked at Dominic but lost interest in him just as quickly. His eyes darted to the ceiling for a moment and then to each side of him, down the rows of tanks. Danielle thought he looked mad, and if he had witnessed the obliteration in front of him—which she couldn't imagine he hadn't—how could he not be?

Scott looked back to Danielle again, and then his eyes immediately drifted just over her shoulder, where they stopped and transformed into a gaze of longing and sadness. He coughed once and then started to cry.

Danielle turned to see Michael standing behind her, his cheeks flooded with tears.

"I'm guessing this is him?" Dominic said.

Dominic's words were a mood-breaker, but Danielle was grateful for them. They didn't have time for sentiment; they had to get moving.

"How do we do this?" Danielle asked. "How do we get him out of there?"

"I'll assume you're asking me because you think I know? And you would be wrong about that."

"What? Haven't you been in here before?"

Dominic shook his head. "Been on these grounds many times, but never actually stepped foot inside." He paused a moment. "I've been to a place very similar though, except that spot was a bit more airplane hangar than laboratory. I'll have to tell you that story some time. Over coffee, maybe?"

"Not breakfast?" Danielle bantered. And then, "So you've never seen these tubes before?"

He shook his head again. "Nope."

Danielle walked to the tube that held Scott and studied it in full, scanning it from top to bottom and then back to the top. "Look there." She pointed. "See it. It looks like it latches in the back."

In the back of the tube were three sets of thin hinges equally spaced from top to bottom. She let her eyes adjust through the liquid until she spotted the cut in the plastic that formed the huge rectangle of a door.

"Do you see it?"

Dominic nodded. "I guess we just open it then, right?"

"What if it hurts him somehow? To just take him out so abruptly?"

Dominic shrugged. "I don't know, Danielle. What choice is there?"

As Danielle considered the alternatives, a sound of pattering footsteps came from just outside the back of the lab.

Danielle instinctively grabbed Michael and pulled him down, kneeling with him next to the tube. She then motioned for Dominic to do the same. He followed.

From their angle in the room, Danielle could only see about half of the opening in the back door, but as she continued to stare toward it, she saw the first crab pass the opening, followed by three more. They seemed to be unaware of the open lab though, instead focused in the direction of the other monsters that had escaped from the area.

They're going to join them, Danielle thought. *They're going to ambush the soldiers from behind, trapping them.* And then an afterthought. *I hope they bought a ton of ammo.*

Two more crabs entered the frame of the door and disappeared, and this time Danielle counted a full minute. She then counted another, then one more, allowing time for any other straggling members of the cordon group to pass.

But no more came into view, and after another minute passed and she felt it was safe, Danielle finally stood from her crouch, never taking her eye off the door. Finally, she looked down to Michael and encouraged him to stand with her.

Danielle checked the door one last time, an afterthought before preparing to continue with the rescue of Scott. And just then, a moment before she shifted her eyes away from the rear entrance and back to the lab, the bony, white shoulder of a final, trailing crab appeared in the doorway.

The creature took a step as if to follow in the path of the others, but before it disappeared into the night, it stopped and lifted its head, searching for a smell, or a noise perhaps, some movement of molecules that had drifted in on the wind at just that moment.

The crab stood in place for several seconds, hunched and chasing the scent or sound, until finally it turned and faced the building. It lingered there for a few beats and then moved to the threshold of the door.

Danielle pushed Michael back to the floor, dipping down beside him a second later, but just before she dropped, she caught a passing glimpse of the crab's black eyes. Perhaps it was her mind's concoction, but they appeared searching, hungry.

"Shit!" Dominic whispered, now crouched next to them. "It's inside."

"It'll leave," Danielle answered; it was more prayer than belief.

From their position on the floor by the tube, they could no longer see the crab, but they could hear it as clearly as a gong as it moved through the doorway and forward into the wide space of the room. Danielle imagined its chimp-walk gait, its spastic head and neck and eyes, and she knew it wouldn't be long until the mutant made its way toward the slaughter its brothers and sisters had wrought.

"Where is your rifle?" Dominic asked.

Danielle looked to the floor, and when she didn't see it there, she immediately remembered that she'd left it back by the front door with Michael. In her haste to see Scott, or whoever it was that was still alive in the Murder Room, she had forgotten to grab it.

"Shit!"

Dominic nodded and held up his pistol. "All right, stay close then."

They continued listening to the erratic scurrying of the crab as it searched the lab, banging into stools and carts and white boards, and later sounding as if it were attacking various pieces of furniture, testing them to see if there was life somewhere inside.

Suddenly the lab went quiet, for just a moment, and then the slapping of bare feet on tile began to crescendo quickly. Danielle knew it was only a matter of seconds before the crab entered their corridor and they would meet it face to face. She didn't have a weapon, but Dominic was armed, and she knew he wouldn't hesitate to fire on sight. And if his aim was pure, that would be that.

Dominic held the pistol high in front of his face, like a cop entering a drug lord's nest, his hand steady, level. The footsteps of the crab sounded just around the corner now, and Danielle could almost see the white goblin before it entered her vision.

But then, for a reason Danielle couldn't have guessed, it stopped. Just when the showdown seemed destined to come to a head, the sound of the crab's feet ceased.

Seconds later, the slapping rhythm began again, this time fading with each moment that passed. It was backtracking in the direction of the door, and after another thirty seconds or so, they heard a stool move on the opposite end of the lab, near the door that led out of the lab and into the night.

Danielle held her breath and stood, just to about three-quarters height, tall enough to see over the worktables. She stared toward the door, and there she could see it, the crab, shuffling out the door, giving up the hunt.

She waited until it was fully outside, and then she gave it another few beats until the crab was completely out of sight. She nodded. "Okay, it's gone. But we got lucky. We need to make this happen now."

Dominic and Michael stood, and Danielle immediately rushed to the back of the tube, committed not to waste any more time.

She felt along the plastic outer shell and quickly found the lock. "Michael, stay in front where your father can see you. Talk to him. Tell him he's going to be okay."

Michael paused. "Is he?"

"Yes," she answered emphatically, and then, "I think so." She turned to Dominic. "You stand beside me. When I open the door, you need to be here in case he falls. I'm not sure how he's standing up right now, and I don't want him to collapse and crack his head open." She paused. "Do you think there's a blanket in here somewhere?"

Dominic looked around the room until his eyes fell on the back wall and a red package next to a fire extinguisher. He nodded in that direction. "Right there," he said. "Fire blanket."

"Perfect. Grab it."

Dominic sprinted to the wall and grabbed the blanket and was back in position next to Danielle within moments.

Michael was well into the story of how he and Danielle and Dominic had come to be there, and how he had used his dad's truck to kill some of the monsters by the cordon fence.

"Not gonna punish me for taking the car without asking, are you dad?" Michael asked. But Scott wasn't in on the joke, not there yet, and he only shook his head in response to the question.

"Ready?" Danielle asked, but before anyone could answer, she took a step to the side of the tube, lifted the pin on the latch, and opened the door.

The fluid gushed through the opening like a waterfall, flooding the surface by the tube in large splashes before flowing into the lab and shallowing out into the open space, finally becoming little more than a thin, wide puddle across the floor.

Danielle watched with anticipation as the water level in the tube decreased rapidly, and soon she could see that Scott was, in fact, being kept upright artificially, held in position by two restraints, one under each arm. The manacles were holding Scott prisoner, she knew, but they were also the reason he hadn't slipped beneath the yellow solution hours earlier and drowned.

Danielle averted her eyes as Scott's nude body became exposed, but the moment the water reached about shin level, she squeezed into the tube and unlatched the restraints on either side, freeing him.

His body collapsed straight down, but Dominic was there to catch him, as instructed, and he quickly wrapped Scott in the blanket and led him down gently to the floor. Dominic kept the man's head turned, keeping him from witnessing the slaughtered scientists that were only a few feet away.

"I got you, buddy," Dominic said. "Just hold on; we'll get you some clothes ASAP."

"Dad, do you think you can walk?" Michael was standing over his father now, his voice calm but stern.

Scott looked at his son, his eyes still wild and scared, but there was sanity in them now, recognition, and he nodded affirmatively to the question.

"Okay, then I need you to get on your feet and walk with us. Just a few steps until we're outside. We have a jeep and then we're gonna get out of here."

Scott swallowed and studied his son's face, seeming to take in each word with great concentration. Finally, he spoke. "I can do that."

Danielle could see the restraint in Michael, the lump in his throat, and she was impressed by his understanding that it was his poise alone keeping his father balanced, at least for the moment, and it would be his continued composure that would give them any chance of escaping the nightmare.

"Okay then," he said. "Let's get to it."

With Dominic and Michael flanking him, Scott got to his feet with surprising promptness, which Danielle took as a good indicator of his strength. Once upright, he looked over to the bodies surrounding him on the lab floor and then groaned and shuddered. He made a motion as if to vomit, but the wave passed.

"It's okay, dad. We're gonna be outta here in a minute. Just let the man lead you. His name is Dominic. Say hi to him, dad."

Scott looked to his left and nodded. "Hello, Dominic."

Dominic already had his shoulder propped under Scott's arm. "How you doing, Michael's dad? One hell of a boy you got there. One hell of a boy."

Scott gave a quick, bewildered nod, as if agreeing with the truth of the words, but needing to shake the notion into his brain. "Yes. Yes, he is."

"The jeep is in the front," Danielle said. "We should head that way."

With that, the three companions—now four with Scott Jenkins—exited the Murder Room and headed to the door at the front of the lab, with Dominic backtracking momentarily to secure a pair of pants for Scott from one of the mutilated corpses.

When he caught up with the others, no one asked questions, and he broke the uncomfortable silence by asking, "Where is James?"

"He was right here when I came in," Danielle answered, looking frantically about the lab as she strode toward the front. "Michael, did you see him leave."

Michael shook his head. "No. He was here when I came in too."

They reached the front door and stopped to deliberate. "What do we do about James?" Danielle asked the group at large.

Dominic shrugged. "He must have gone outside to wait. He wasn't looking too good coming out of that room."

"I guess we'll know soon enough."

Danielle opened the door and stepped out to the lab grounds, and her eyes shifted reflexively to the bridge and the remnants of the butchered soldiers. Only part of the bridge was illuminated by the shelter spotlights, but in that light, Danielle could see portions of their bodies hanging at gruesome, unnatural angles. They were all dead, that was obvious, and the crabs responsible were gone.

Danielle imagined the fear and pain they must have experienced as they were ripped apart, and a sudden pang of guilt returned, the guilt for not having warned them of the hunters approaching from the forest. Or maybe it was something else. Maybe, she considered, it was guilt for not feeling worse about their deaths. Or the deaths of McCormick and Davies and the scientists inside the lab.

Or death in general.

Danielle sighed and then blinked away the existential thoughts, and the guilt was soon replaced by a wave of gratitude for the distance between her and the corpses, a gap which spared her the details of the soldiers' ruin, if not the fact of it.

She brought her attention to the ground in front of her now and realized the crabs weren't the only things that were gone.

James was gone too. And so was the jeep.

4.

"What?"

Danielle felt the nervous rise of laughter in her belly as she viewed the empty lot, and then she walked until she reached the spot where the jeep had been parked earlier. There, she did a full turn in the open area, looking for evidence of the missing vehicle.

"He took it." Dominic seethed, gritting his teeth as he stood with Michael and Scott just outside the closed front door of the lab. "I can't believe he took it! Goddammit! I was this close to forgiving him for selling me out, and then this? How could he..? Goddammit!"

The conclusion didn't sound quite right to Danielle: James simply fleeing by himself into the night, leaving them stranded amid the peril they were currently facing. But she didn't argue; after all, James had looked sick outside the Murder Room, and scared, and since he had already treasoned himself once by giving up Dominic's espionage plan, it wasn't unreasonable to think he had abandoned them again.

"We should have left him in the shelter. I knew it. We should have let the crabs tear him apart like they did those bastards on the bridge. And when I see him, he's going to wish we had."

"We don't know that it was him." Danielle spoke the words as if they'd been programmed, without conviction. "Or if he did take it," she continued, turning back toward the lab to face Dominic and the Jenkins, "maybe he..."

The sentence seized in the back of her throat as her nervous system was suddenly activated, triggering her heart and breathing to race like a missile. Her face flushed for a moment and then ignited with a burning red fear as she stared toward the side of the laboratory. She felt the need to rub her eyes, to clear the vision in front of her, to be sure what she was seeing was real.

But she kept as still as possible, trying to slow her respiration, fearing that any motion would generate an attack from the twenty or so crabs that were standing in front of her.

"What's wrong?" Dominic called. "Danielle?"

Danielle gave a short quiver of her head, a signal that talking was a bad idea at the moment. She then tipped her head gently forward, and Dominic followed the direction of the nod, looking to his right.

The crabs that were clearly visible to Danielle were blocked by the wall of the lab from Dominic's vantage, and he couldn't see them from his position at the lab door.

But Dominic recognized there was trouble, Danielle could see it in his face, and as he took a step forward, he craned his head dramatically toward the side of the lab.

"Stop, Dominic," Danielle hissed.

"What is..?" Dominic was compelled to learn the mystery now and ignored the warning. He took several more paces until he could see the side of the building, at which point he stopped, frozen.

"Oh...no."

Seeing Dominic enter the scene, the crabs stirred in agitation, and then gradually they began moving forward, just a step and a half or so before stopping again, at which point they continued to sway and bounce vaguely on their haunches. They studied the two humans before them for a moment, and before Danielle and Dominic could devise a strategy for dealing with the danger, the group of crabs began to disband.

The most distant crab from Danielle, the one farthest to her left, loped off in the direction of the bridge, continuing until it reached the outer point of her peripheral vision before it disappeared in the night. The other crabs followed suit, fanning out until they created a wide semi-circle, creating an arch over the group of fugitives like an umbrella of ghouls.

But Dominic and Danielle weren't trapped, not quite; the barrier of crabs only prevented them from going forward in the direction of the lab and beyond. Behind them, if they chose to run, was open space, and if they were fast enough and could keep their footing, it wasn't unreasonable to believe they could make it to the river before the crabs were upon them.

But that option didn't really exist, at least not in Danielle's mind. Scott and Michael were her responsibility now, and they were still on the stoop of the lab entrance, just now becoming aware of the threat that was hovering less than fifty feet away.

The father and son could retreat, Danielle supposed, go back inside the lab and wait there until the beasts scattered from the lot in pursuit of her and Dominic. But there was no guarantee the crabs would come after them if they ran, and Danielle was reluctant to divide the group unless she was offered no other option.

Within moments, however, when a giant thump rattled the large metal door of the lab, the option of returning to the lab was obliterated as well.

At the crashing sound of the entrance, Scott and Michael cowered like dogs in a thunderstorm, the older Jenkins dropping to his knees and covering his head with his arms. Michael simply froze and stared back at the door.

"Michael!" Danielle shouted. "Get away from there!"

Another thump pounded the door, and this time Michael pulled his father's arm up, lifting him to his feet, and father and son dashed away from the lab, reaching Dominic and Danielle in seconds.

The four survivors stood huddled now, teetering on helplessness. Danielle was still unarmed, and she felt naked as she studied the crabs, which seemed to be encroaching, though their movement was nearly undetectable, like the hour hand of a clock.

Dominic pointed his pistol at the door now, his hands trembling in anticipation of the flood of white enemies that would be coming through it in a matter of seconds.

"We have to go," Dominic said. "We have to run."

"My dad can't run," Michael pled. "We have to stay. We have to...to fight them off." His voice was weak, unconvinced of his own words.

"No, Michael," Scott answered instantly. He coughed once and cleared his throat. "Dominic is right. They're coming. You can see 'em. They're gonna get to us eventually. These ones standing here and the ones coming through the door." He gave a disdainful look toward the crabs and shook his head. "All of us are going to die if we just stand here. Not enough rounds in that Glock to take them all out."

"If we run, you're running with us, Scott," Danielle explained. "Running without you was not part of Dominic's suggestion."

Dominic didn't confirm the truth of Danielle's declaration, but Danielle didn't care. She had no plans on leaving Scott to die alone.

"I appreciate you saving my boy, but you're gonna need your ammo for you. I'm only going to slow you down. Michael's right, my legs are weak. Not sure I can run."

Michael had begun to cry, and Scott smiled, trying to soften the situation. "Hey, Hey? You're gonna be alright, Mikey. You are. You're my boy. You're a survivor. And you're going to survive today. You're going to get out of this place and help Danielle and Dominic find the people who did all this. Find the people who killed your sisters and your mother."

Danielle spoke up, interjecting with pragmatism so as not to give the heartfelt moment a chance to breathe. "You know, I once read a story of a mother who fought off a seven-hundred-pound polar bear to save her children. Seven-hundred pounds. These kids were outside playing hockey, this bear attacks them, and she literally put herself in between the animal and the kids and fought the thing off with her bare hands."

Scott stared at Danielle, seemingly bewildered by the impromptu tale.

"So, the point is, if she could do that, I think you can manage to run a few hundred yards on tired legs."

Scott shook his head slowly, frustrated by Danielle's stubbornness. He then sighed and shrugged. "Guess I can try."

"Good."

"But you don't wait for me. If I go down, or fall behind, you keep going."

Danielle nodded absently. "Sure."

"Say it," Scott commanded.

Danielle rolled her eyes. "Fine. If you go down, we keep going."

"Or fall behind."

"*Or* fall behind."

The rattle of the lab's door handle brought everyone's attention back to the threat at hand, and they scrutinized the silver knob as it wiggled erratically back and forth.

"I think we should go," Dominic said.

Danielle looked at Scott. "Go," she said. "That's how we'll do this. You go first to get a head start."

"Don't cheat on our deal, Danielle. If I can't keep up, then—"

"I want to see how they react when you run. If they start chasing you as soon as you start running, then we'll know that's their strategy." She paused and looked at Michael. "Would you rather we experiment on Michael instead?"

Scott gave a suspicious look. "Fine. But don't waste your ammo on—"

"Go!"

Scott hesitated a beat before finally turning and facing the river, and then he looked back at Michael one last time. "I love you boy." Then back to Danielle. "Where do we meet?"

Danielle grinned. "That's my dude," she said and then gave a stern nod. "There's a place about a mile up the river. They used to rent kayaks and rafts and things like that. Can't remember the name, but you can't miss it. It's in an—"

"Maripo Adventure Company. I know the place." He paused and raised an eyebrow. "What? You think black folks don't kayak?"

Danielle snorted a laugh, and before she could banter back, Scott was off, slowly and limping, but at a pace that wasn't beyond hope. It was his stamina that Danielle worried about, however. He was malnourished, dehydrated, and without water and calories to burn, he wouldn't make it far if the ghosts suddenly gave chase.

As if triggered by Danielle's concern, the crab to her left twitched its head up, then forward, like a dinosaur trying to catch the scent of its scurrying prey.

"You see that one?" Danielle asked.

"I see it," Dominic answered, hovering the Glock .9mm somewhere between the fan of ghosts on the lot outside and the ever-bulging door leading to the lab. "But I can't cover everything. And it's too far anyway. I can't hit it from here. Not with a pistol."

The nervous ghost clicked its head up again and then looked over to the monster beside it, and, if Danielle hadn't known better, she would have sworn it signaled to it with a nod.

The second ghost snapped its head forward now, and then opened its mouth wide in what appeared to be a massive yawn. There was a moment of stillness between them, and then, in unison, both crabs took three quick steps forward, appearing ready to explode into a gallop before stopping suddenly, reminding Danielle of a sprinter false starting at a track meet.

"Dominic!"

"I see them!"

The same crabs began moving forward again, now at a walking pace, but this time they kept going, slowly accelerating as they progressed, clearly testing what the reaction of Danielle—and more importantly Dominic—would be.

Within seconds, the two crabs were off, quickly reaching the slope that led to the river, steadily closing in on Scott.

The rest of the horde held their place in the fan, but Danielle knew it wouldn't be long before their strike would be unleashed as well, and at that point, Scott would be right, there wouldn't be enough rounds to stop them.

Danielle took a breath and thought of the crab on the roof of the Mazda dealership. This was the moment she had trained for—not for the soldier in the tower (which had turned out to be Dominic)—and not to save herself. It was to save her fellow human, and at this moment, it didn't matter if the gun was a rifle or a .9mm pistol.

"Give me the gun, Dom."

Dominic examined Danielle, confusion wrinkled into his forehead. But he could see the tenacity on Danielle's face, hear the resolve in her voice, and he handed her the pistol without a word.

Danielle gripped the weapon and then stretched her arm behind her in a wide sweeping motion before bringing the pistol in front of her, holding her arms extended now, the gun at eye level. She studied the gangling target in front of her, galloping like a three-legged horse, the white sheen of its body making the mark relatively clear, considering the night sky. In a moment, she knew Dominic was right about the more distant crab; its yardage and wide route made that shot impossible. The nearer crab had also started at a distance too far to hit, but during its pursuit of Scott, it had adjusted its route, taking a more direct path across the hill toward the exhausted man. It was probably forty yards away now, a difficult pistol shot for anyone, especially in the dark, and particularly for Danielle, who had had little practice with this type of weapon in her lifetime.

But she cleared her mind and let out a breath, and when her body achieved a stillness she'd never felt before, she squeezed the trigger.

Danielle's body remained motionless, as if it were encased in concrete, and she watched in silence as the crab fell, first to its knees and then forward onto its face, its body dropping as if a switch had suddenly been toggled off inside its brain.

Danielle knew it wasn't a head strike though—it had likely struck its ribcage—but it was a direct hit, perhaps even piercing the beast's heart.

Danielle then moved the pistol to her left, trying to find the crab that was previously out of range, praying it, too, had move closer to her. She located the white blur quickly, but it had kept on its original route, and was now bounding at full speed and over a hundred yards away.

She took her eye from the gun and looked across the hill at Scott, helplessly. She put her hands on her knees and bent at the waist, doubled over, feeling sick to her stomach.

She looked to the ground now, and then to Michael, who had also looked away, not wanting to witness the violent death of his father.

No! she thought. *I need to give him a chance.*

She stood tall and turned again toward Scott and then cupped her hands around her mouth. "Scott!" she called. "Turn around!"

Scott wasn't quite halfway to the water, and upon hearing his name, he stopped and turned toward Danielle, and then immediately rotated a half turn to the pursuing crab, which was now fewer than thirty feet away.

Danielle could see the defeated slump of his torso, and then the instinctive recoil of his neck and shoulders. But the retreat was only momentary. His body quickly became a pillar, the posture of resignation, with no intention of running.

"No!" Danielle screamed. "Keep going!"

But the crab was only steps away now; running wouldn't make a difference.

"No!"

Danielle said the word in a moaning plea, and then tears began falling in large, silent drops onto her cheeks.

The despair lasted only a moment, however, as it was quickly replaced by a surge of anger that entered her chest like the burn of turpentine. She stiffened her torso now, preparing to turn back to the pack behind her and start emptying the Glock's magazine into as many crabs as she could.

But before she could make the pivot, she heard three loud pops explode above her head, and in the distance, within an arm's reach of Scott Jenkins, the pursuing ghost dropped from the landscape and into the darkness of the field.

Danielle blinked several times and then wiped frantically at her eyes to clear the blur of tears that had accumulated, and when she removed her hands, the vision of Scott standing alone, unscathed, remained. He was in the exact same place on the hill, and the chasing crab was now a dead lump at his feet.

Danielle had no idea what had just occurred, and certainly Scott didn't either, but both seemed to understand the danger of examining the mouth of a gift horse.

"Go!" Danielle called instinctively, and with the command, Scott turned and continued running down the hill toward the river.

Danielle turned back to the lab now for answers, figuring it was Dominic who had somehow secured a rifle and taken out the crab on the hill. But Dominic stood empty-handed and continued facing the surrounding group of crabs, which seemed to have retreated slightly but otherwise stood their ground. The rattling door had also become suddenly still.

Danielle continued scanning the grounds for an explanation, still confused by what had just occurred, and then finally Dominic pressed an elbow into her side and nodded upward.

Danielle followed the motion with her eyes, and there, on the roof, with a rifle slung across his shoulder, was James.

5.

James turned the rifle on the horde now and popped off another round. Then another. And within seconds, before the monsters could process that there was danger in their environs, four or five crabs were lying dead on the ground.

But they sensed the threat quickly, and the moment they did, they scattered like moths, with most of the monsters heading the way of the bridge, the direction in which they were currently facing, while others (the smarter ones, perhaps) hesitated for a beat and then turned and retreated, following the same path of the lab escapees, abandoning the footprint of the military complex and escaping themselves into the world of the living.

A third group, however, consisting of a half dozen or so of the corrupted, took neither course of escape, and instead headed directly toward Dominic, Michael and Danielle.

Danielle fired her weapon and hit one of the middle crabs in the shoulder, stopping it cold in its path, and then finished it off with a second shot, striking it in the face this time, exploding its nose and cheeks like a tomato.

"Dominic!" It was James, calling from the roof.

Dominic looked up to see the young sniper pull a handgun from his waistband. James held the weapon high, displaying it for verification, and then he threw it down like he was tossing a beanbag. It wasn't a lesson in gun safety, Danielle thought, that was for sure, but Dominic caught the pistol softly, cradling it into his palms before engaging his fingers and snapping off several rounds in the direction of the zombie assailants.

Three more of the attacking group fell to the ground like fleshy bowling pins, leaving only two of the crabs on their feet now, both of which had slowed their pace to a lingering gait, seeming to re-consider their aggression.

But it was too late for them also. In seconds, James squeezed off several more shots from the rifle, maximizing his perched position atop the roof, and the final pair of freaks fell dead in the dirt.

The lot in front of the lab was clear now—of both crabs and soldiers—but Danielle knew her group's work was far from done. There was an assembly of crabs heading toward the river, and though they had started in the direction of the bridge, Danielle could see that they had now changed course and were headed in the direction of Scott. He would never outrun them; she and Dominic and Michael—and now James—were his only hope.

As if reading Danielle's mind, Dominic was already staring down the hill to the dark water, his face sullen. "They're too far ahead. We'll never catch up to them in time."

"Well, we're going to try," Danielle replied. "He's a smart guy, and he seems to know the area. He'll be able to...hide. He'll hide until we find him."

"Hide where? There are no buildings out here. And there certainly aren't any between here and that kayak place."

"We're going to try, Dominic!" Danielle snapped, and then she immediately glanced to Michael who wore a look of resolve on his face, supporting her notion. He nodded at Danielle.

"Wait a minute," Dominic said.

Danielle shook her head, frustrated. "What? We have to go."

Dominic smiled. "James!"

Danielle turned to the roof and looked up to the spot where James had been standing only a minute ago. He was gone.

But in what was no more than ten seconds, a blaze of yellow light lit up the trees to the left of the lab and then turned and shone on the group of three standing in the middle of the lot, exposing them like escaped convicts. All around them was a sea of dead monsters.

A few seconds later, the jeep pulled up beside the huddle of three and stopped, James in the driver's seat, hands gripped around the wheel as if he were trying to crush it.

"Put it in park," Dominic ordered. "I'm driving. You're riding shotgun."

James shifted the jeep to park as instructed and moved right, seemingly relieved by the command.

"Really, Dominic?" Danielle asked, guiding Michael into the back and hopping in after him. "After what he just did, you still don't trust him? I think he's earned your forgiveness."

Dominic shot Danielle a brief look of puzzlement before shifting the jeep to drive and pulling off toward the river. "I trust him fine, my dear, more than ever. It's just he looked a little nervous there in the cockpit." He looked at James. "Is that right, Annie Oakley?"

James nodded.

"And besides, he can't shoot and drive at the same time, and we need someone who can take these fuckers out on the move."

6.

Dominic drove the jeep toward the river with abandon, bounding and bouncing down the hillside like a rally car racer, nearly flipping the vehicle on one occasion, which finally prompted an admonishment from Danielle.

"Killing us before we find him isn't going to help anybody."

But Dominic's recklessness settled immediately when he reached the bottom of the hill, at which point he downshifted the vehicle to a crawl and began cruising slowly along the shore of the river, keeping as close to the water as possible without risking getting stuck somewhere along the muddy bank.

James unbuckled his seatbelt and pushed himself up to the back of the seat so that he was nearly standing. He held the rifle to his eye as he swiveled his head slowly, searching.

They continued deliberately along the firm ground of the bank, barely moving at ten miles an hour, and though Danielle wanted to encourage a bit more urgency to the drive, she knew if they went too fast they stood the risk of missing Scott cowering somewhere in the dark.

When several minutes passed, however, with still no sign of the man Danielle had vowed to rescue, the seeds of panic began to grow inside her belly.

"Where is he?" Michael asked rhetorically, as if verbalizing Danielle's unease.

Danielle felt the instinct to answer, to re-assure the boy that his father was safe, but she stayed quiet, knowing that only finding Scott Jenkins would satisfy as an answer.

"Anything?" Dominic asked, glancing at James.

James shook his head, keeping the gun poised.

The empty fields and foliage displayed by the jeep's headlights were the only thing visible now; otherwise, the landscape surrounding them was a blanket of black ink, and a palpable hopelessness began to grow inside the vehicle.

But within a half mile, the thick grass and foliage turned to a wide path of short weeds, and then a gravel lot, not unlike the one in front of the lab.

Dominic slowed the jeep even further, and soon the headlights lit upon the beginning of a dark wooden walkway lined with low railings on either side.

"Stop here," Danielle barked. "This is the place. It's not as far as I thought."

"This is what place?" James asked.

"Pull up a little more."

Dominic inched the jeep along a few more feet until the beams of the jeep illuminated the door of a small wooden structure which extended out onto stilts over the river. Above the door was a sign that read The Maripo Adventure Company.

"He's here," Danielle announced. "He's gotta be."

"I sure hope that's not true."

It was James again, and before Danielle could question his meaning, a spark of terror flushed her as she spotted a bobbing of white in both windows that fronted the store, entering and receding from the panes like tiny moons quickly fading in and out of the night sky.

They were crabs, of course, there was no question on that, and they were already inside the shop where Danielle had told Scott to meet them.

"Shit!" Dominic grumbled.

"We have to go find him!" Danielle cried. "I told him to—"

"Wait!" James ordered. "Listen."

Danielle began to protest, and then to ignore, but as she began to exit the jeep and head toward the kayak shop, she heard the noise James had just referenced.

It was the familiar sound of ghosts moving in the night, crowding and hording like raccoons scuffling in a dumpster. It was a sound Danielle knew well by now, though on this occasion the noise seemed magnified somehow, as if the absolute darkness was acting as an amplifier.

The ghosts were still several yards away, not visible in the range of the headlights, but they were certainly close enough to be upon the jeep in a matter of seconds if they chose to attack.

Danielle pictured the monsters grouped together in their tight huddle of re-animated corpses, looking up at them from just outside the perimeter of light as they tore apart some unfortunate deer or dog or disoriented drifter.

Or Scott Jenkins.

It was the most likely answer, of course, and the image of his slaughter brought a wave of sickness over Danielle.

But Danielle was quickly snapped back to the moment when Dominic turned off the headlights.

"Why did you do that? They already know we're here. The only difference now is that *we* can't see."

"I can see," James said, his eye still pressed tightly to the rifle sight. He was using the night vision of the scope to view what Danielle and the others could not. "There's a group just to our left. They look like they're...feeding."

Danielle felt the prickle of tears again and quickly wiped them away.

"There are probably four of them there. And maybe another three by the shop. They're going in and out of the kayak place. It's like they're looking for something?"

"No," Michael whimpered.

Danielle took a breath, buoyed with hope. If they were looking for something, there was a chance it was for Scott, which meant he might still be alive. "What else? Do you see any sign of Scott?"

James shook his head. "No, but I obviously can't see inside the place." He paused, and then, "Oh, shit. Shit! They're coming, Dominic! They're coming!"

Dominic flicked the headlights on again, and for an instant, only the empty storefront occupied their line of sight.

But that quickly changed. From the left corner of the jeep's headlight range, the first of the crabs from the feeding group entered the view, its face almost a complete mask of red. A second later, the remaining feeders became visible, sprinting, and they were soon joined by the three searchers from the boating store.

And they were coming fast. Before Danielle could blink, the closest crab was less ten yards away.

James fired the first round, immediately killing the lead one on the left. But the crabs were coming from all directions now, with some of them weaving erratically, serpentine and staggered, while others took a more direct route to the jeep, seeming to sacrifice themselves like ants in a colony.

"Drive, Dominic!" Danielle yelled, and without hesitation, Dominic shifted the car into gear and sped forward, slamming into the two crabs that had come at the jeep from point blank range. The impact was severe, damaging the crabs badly and possibly killing them; but the force also catapulted James over the windshield frame of the jeep and into the grass, the rifle sailing somewhere into the darkness.

"I meant in reverse! Jesus!" And then, "James! James, are you okay?"

James stood slowly, seemingly uninjured, but then he immediately turned and began to run as three of the attacking ghosts closed in on him, their red mouths wide and gnashing.

Within seconds, James and the crabs were all outside the glow of the headlights, and Danielle could now hear only the sound of running footsteps.

"Look out!" Dominic called.

Danielle turned to see two crabs directly beside her, their hands groping forward like crazed prisoners begging for help through iron bars. Instinctively, she recoiled into Michael who was sitting on the other side of the jeep, and then she steadied the pistol on her attackers. She fired off the remaining four rounds in the gun, making direct hits with the first two shots, and quickly lamenting the waste of the two superfluous bullets.

Danielle's eyes were wide, but her vision was blurry from shuddering, and she took several hyper breaths as she stared at the now open space in front of her, expecting more of the monsters to appear at any moment.

Trembling, she asked, "Are there any others?"

"Besides the ones after James, I don't think so, but I lost count."

Danielle looked at Michael for a more definitive answer, but he only shrugged and shook his head, his face sheened with horror.

"Okay, assume there are then. I'll go for James."

"I'll go," Dominic said. "I'm the one—"

"Go find Scott. Take the jeep right up to the building. But be careful. There could be more inside. I saw..." Danielle broke off her instruction and stood in the back of the jeep, squinting as she leaned forward and stared down to the river. The dark water now had a soft patina of moonlight across it, giving it just a glint of visibility. "Look!"

Dominic and Michael followed Danielle's finger as a dark shadow moved slowly across the water. It was black and formless, moving with insouciance, like a boat on the River Styx.

The three watched the movement in silence, in horror, and when it began to turn inward and approach the shore, Danielle expected it to suddenly transform, to grow and rise from the water like some mythical beast from a Norwegian folk tale.

"Hey!"

The call came from the water, impotent and desperate.

"I'm down here!"

The figure on the water was still just a vague silhouette, but Danielle now knew it was a boat. A kayak. And that Scott Jenkins was inside.

"Dad!" Michael called.

"Go, Dominic. Go get him. I'll meet you upriver. James couldn't have gotten too far, so don't leave me here."

"I'll never leave you again, Danielle, so if you don't show, I guess we'll meet again somewhere in Paradise."

Danielle felt a grin begin to form, but her face wouldn't allow it. Instead, she simply replied, "I'll show."

Dominic nodded, and with that, Danielle hopped from the jeep and quickly located James' rifle. She picked it up in stride and then turned to begin the chase.

7.

Danielle was behind the two crabs in seconds, and the moment she saw them, she unleashed a shout that was some mixture of duck call and Apache war cry, an attempt to turn their attention from James to her.

She hadn't seen James yet, and she took that as a good sign. If these crabs were the two that had given chase after the crash, which she assumed they were, it meant James had managed to evade them thus far.

Hearing the cry, the crabs turned like cobras, as if their necks had been spring-loaded, and they were now facing Danielle. Then, with perhaps a single beat of hesitation, they attacked, rushing her like rottweilers in a dog pit.

Danielle positioned the rifle on her shoulder and fired off two rounds—*pop! pop!*—quickly, methodically, sending the two crabs to the dark grass below. She checked her breathing, her heart rate, noting the steadiness of both, and, in that moment, she realized how much easier the chore of killing became each time she did it.

She stood in place and scanned the area now, searching for James. But, despite the emergence of the moon, the landscape in front of her was still a charcoal blanket, so Danielle continued forward, her head on a swivel as she searched for her companion.

As she strode, a new energy began to well inside her, fueling her lungs and powering her legs forward. And though she and her group were far from out of the woods, she had a sudden sense of accomplishment and triumph. Her mind was clear now, and the air suddenly smelled differently. Perhaps it was her proximity to the river, she considered, but on a deeper level, Danielle knew it was the smell of something else: Freedom.

Danielle felt the suppressed grin from earlier begin to form again, and this time she allowed it to materialize, spreading in a thin line just above her chin. It wasn't humor or cheer that she felt—not exactly—but it was something, something real, the manifestation of the new vitality inside her perhaps.

Danielle broke into a light jog now, the rifle flat across her chest, her index finger resting lightly on the trigger, ready to finish the mission.

But she barely made it twenty yards when a dull groaning sound came from somewhere in the dark, stopping Danielle cold. She held her breath and lifted her chin, listening. She presumed the noise had come from James, but the modulation of the sound brought with it the aura of dread.

James' name was on the edge of Danielle's tongue, but as she prepared to call it out, the groan from in front of her rang again, and this time it was accompanied by another noise. It was the familiar sound of scuttling again, the lifting and shuffling of feet, the huddling of bodies.

Danielle's mind spooled back to the forest inside the cordon, beside the tributary, when she stood in the pouring rain and watched the crabs feed like hyenas on the mutilated buck.

But the sound she was hearing now was louder, wider, and Danielle knew instantly there were far more crabs standing in front of her now than there had been earlier in the forest. And it wasn't just their movement she heard; although the crabs were essentially mute, they clicked and snorted and cleared their throats like every animal, and the noises from the group ahead suggested a throng of ghosts—double the bodies, perhaps—were just a few yards beyond.

Where the hell did this group come from? Danielle thought. *There had only been a dozen or so outside the lab.*

"Danielle?" The voice was a whimper; James.

Danielle couldn't see him, but she knew by the intonation of his voice that his situation was dire, and she imagined the poor man surrounded by the chalky horde, their smooth, bony hands already upon him, perhaps.

"There are so many," he cried. "Oh, god."

Danielle felt her heart sink now, James' desperation sapping the new energy from her entirely. He had acted so bravely on the roof of the lab, a true hero, but this was the James she had known since the diner, a scared boy who wanted nothing more than to survive.

"Where...where did they come from?" Danielle asked.

"I...I think they're the ones from the lab."

"No. What? The lab? But...*we* were inside the lab. Only one came inside, and that one left without noticing us."

Several seconds passed with only the sound of heavy breathing until finally James spoke again, his voice weary now, defeated. "No. You got lucky."

"What?"

"I...I went outside, after I saw the massacre of the doctors in the back room, I walked back outside, and just as I was leaving, I could see this horde, dozens of them—the ones around me right now, I guess—passing by the lab. They were heading away from the camp. They were leaving the base for the outside world."

These were the ones Danielle and Dominic had released from the cordon. Danielle knew it to her core. They had shown them the way to freedom. They had released them upon James. Upon the world.

"So, I waited. I waited until they were gone. I waited as long as I thought it would take for them to pass by the lab. And then I drove the jeep around to the back to pick you up. But...I don't know, I guess I left too early. I guess maybe they heard the sound of the engine or the tires on the gravel. But they heard it. As soon as I was around back, I could see them turn. First it was just one, turning and sprinting, and then they all started racing back to the building. One entered, and then they all followed like lemmings. I called to you, to warn you, but you were already gone."

"We went out the front. We must have just missed them."

"It was a miracle. Right when you were leaving, they were coming in." James paused and took several heavy breaths, trying to stay composed as the white killers circled around him. "Anyway, I hid from them and then shut the door behind them, and then as long as you shut the front door—which you did—we had them trapped inside. I...I didn't think they would be able to get out."

Danielle had forgotten about the bulging door in the front of the lab, and she hadn't really thought about where that inside group had come from in the first place.

And then another thought emerged: *they've learned to open doors.*

Or maybe they had just broken through, she reconsidered, the sheer weight of the bodies having been too much for the door to hold.

It didn't matter now, of course; they were out, and Danielle took three more steps in the direction of James' voice, and then three more, until finally she could see the dull outline of James and the mass of bodies around him.

They were circling him like hyenas, swaying and bobbing in their usual way.

"Danielle, go."

Danielle ignored him. "I'm not going. I'll shoot as many as I can, and while I'm firing—"

"No!" James interrupted, and then he instantly settled his voice. "No, Danielle. And you have to stop talking. They're focused on me now but that won't last if you come closer. There's nothing you can do for me now. You know I'm right. If you can see them right now, if you can see how many there are, you know. Please go."

"I can—"

"No. It's okay. I never planned to leave this place alive anyway. It wasn't meant to be. I gave up Dominic. I betrayed him. And Tom. And you."

"You didn't betray me."

James ignored Danielle's correction. "This was always going to be the way it ended for me. But not for you. Your fate is to escape. To survive. The fact that you're still alive after all this time is proof of that. You have to feel that deep down, right?"

The circle began closing and Danielle raised the rifle, clicking the round into place as she aimed.

"If you do that, you'll end up dead too." James paused. "They'll be on me before you get two shots off, and then they'll come for you."

"James—"
"Did you find him? Did you find Scott?"

Danielle hesitated, reluctant to concede to the change of subject. "Yes," she answered, and with that she saw James' figure stand tall and proud. She could almost see the smile form on his face.

"Thank god."
"I'm so sorry, James. I thought—"
"I know. Just find Tom now. Dominic knows where he is. And then get away from here. As far away as you can."

Danielle sighed. "Okay," she said, fighting the crackle in her voice.

"And one other thing, Danielle."
"What is it?"
"Find the people who did this? The ones at the top. The ones Stella talked about." He paused for a beat, and then the stern advice melted into a whimper. "Oh, god."

The crabs' arms began extending now, their fingers fondling James's chest and neck, his thighs and hair and face, and then the first one stepped forward in a wild lunge, its teeth latching onto James' right shoulder.

James screamed in pain and terror, and with that, the rest of the crabs swarmed on him like piranha.

Danielle closed her eyes for a moment and then looked to the ground, avoiding the gruesome finality to James' life, praying the screams from her companion would end.

She waited until they did and then turned and ran toward the river where the boat with Dominic and Scott and Michael was approaching the coastline.

She stood on the bank of the river and thought of James' request for revenge, and then, to no one, she said aloud, "It's already on my list."

Epilogue: Kill the Bastard

The Bastard could very well have been a woman, of course, but Danielle had liked the term when she'd added it to her list months ago; the stinging sound of the word de-personalized the goal somehow, reducing the villain she sought from person to monster.

But the person's gender was beside the point; all Danielle had cared about was finding and killing the mastermind behind the destruction of her home, her community, her life.

And now, quite possibly, as the news was beginning to break everywhere, the world itself.

And, it turned out, the person with whom they had made an emergency appointment and were only minutes from seeing was, in fact, a man, Lucas Maes, CEO of the Bern Group, the innocuously sounding name of the parent company that owned D&W.

Dominic and Danielle were early for their appointment and both sat casually outside of the CEO's office, Dominic reading a newspaper, Danielle reading over her list one more time.

Goal 1. ~~Map the Cordon~~
Goal 2. ~~Find a Rifle~~
Goal 3. ~~Kill a Crab~~
Goal 4. ~~Kill a Soldier~~
Goal 5. ~~Escape the Cordon~~
Goal 6. ~~Find Dominic~~
Goal 7. ~~Kill Stella~~
Goal 8. Kill the Bastard

Goal 9. ~~Rescue Scott~~

She folded the paper again and tucked it into her purse, a thin clutch of a bag that Danielle had bought at the airport not more than an hour before their flight to Europe.

Tom was safe, and he and Scott and Michael had remained at the hotel while she and Dominic headed into the city for their meeting. During the four or five hours they were estimated to be gone, Tom's job was to find a house to rent in the country, available immediately, somewhere the five fugitives could stay for a while without too many questions being raised.

But those arrangements would last a week or two at most, functioning only as a place of brief respite while America exploded into chaos. After that, they would have to move underground, and then across the border to The Netherlands or Germany, or perhaps south to Luxembourg.

They were lucky to have made it out of the United States, of course, which they had done by way of a six-thirty flight on the morning following their escape from the military siege of Maripo County.

Tom and Dominic had quietly renewed their passports during their time underground (Dominic under his military pseudonym), as if always knowing this day would come. As for her and the Jenkins, it was lucky for them Michael had insisted Danielle grab the emergency bag from the safe room. Just as he'd mentioned, it was supplied with passports—his and his father's—as well as over forty thousand dollars in cash. And, it turned out, Scott Jenkins had been married to a white woman, one who looked enough like Danielle that she could pass for Donna Jenkins in a pinch. So, using her passport, Danielle, too, had a way out of the country.

At the airport, they had purchased five tickets to Brussels (roundtrip, so as not to raise eyebrows), and were completing the sale at the very moment news of violent murders just outside the now famous cordon began to break. By the time they landed in Belgium, the news was everywhere, and the full effort of the American military was engaged.

Danielle doubted even a full-scale war would be enough in the end, though. The army hadn't been able to control the ghosts inside the cordon, and now that the monsters were scattered over dozens and possibly hundreds of miles, their capture and killing seemed nearly impossible.

Danielle had made a call to her parents in the cab on the way to the Bern Group headquarters—it was the only phone number she'd remembered by heart—and had told them without cushion that the country and continent were no longer safe. If they had the means, which she prayed they still did, they needed to leave immediately.

But truth told, she doubted they were still alive, and as she uttered her warnings into the phone, the words sounded brittle to her ears, benign, as if they were landing in a void, prepared to be extinguished forever somewhere in the infinite space of digital oblivion.

And then another thought arose, one even more existential than that of her parents' demise, and an itch of guilt began to percolate in her mind.

Had she abandoned her country? Her fellow citizens? Knowing the danger that was now flooding toward schools and

synagogues and stadiums and shopping malls, had she done
enough to inform the people that were in its path?

She'd done nothing, of course, so the answer was 'No,'
but whatever feelings of responsibility she had assumed released their grip on her conscience almost immediately. It
was an impossible task; she had no means by which to com-
municate such peril to a mass audience, and now that she was
a cordon fugitive—and future illegal immigrant to Belgium
and beyond—she was destined for a life of silence.

All she could do now was the next best thing.

"Mr. Gerard?" The secretary behind the desk stood and
removed the headset from her ear.

Dominic dipped the paper and glanced up nonchalantly,
legs crossed, ankle resting on his opposite knee.

The secretary smiled. "Mr. Maes will see you both now."

The smile was a nervous one, Danielle noted, and it was
obvious that concern was now simmering in the office like
soup on a stovetop. That was fine, though; it had to be that
way. A man like Lucas Maes would have never seen her and
Dominic on such short notice. Not unless the end of the
world was the topic and he was the one who stood to answer
for it.

"It's actually just my partner who will be meeting with
him," Dominic replied, walking toward the reception
counter as he spoke. When he reached the high lip of the
desk, he gave a wide smile. "I'm just here as a consultant."

The secretary tilted her head, her face wrinkling into
folds of confusion. "Oh, I see. Very well."

She smiled again and nodded, resetting her demeanor, and then pressed a button below her desk, unlocking Mr. Maes' door with a concise buzz.

Danielle was already waiting at the door, and at the rumbling sound of the lock unbolting, she gripped the office handle and turned it, keeping the door closed but disengaged. With her access to the office now secured, she nodded to Dominic, who quickly walked behind the reception desk. From there, he reached across the secretary's shoulder and ripped the phone cord from the wall.

"What are you..?"

"Your choices are as follows," he said, his voice stiff, low. "You can sit in that chair and keep as still as a desert mountain, or you can speak again, at which point I cut you with one of those letter openers there and pour this into the wound."

Dominic held up a small vial that could have been anything, but was, in fact, apple juice, heavily diluted.

"And then you'll know what it feels like. You'll know what all those people had to feel when they became the monsters that you and your company created. Then...then you'll understand why we're really here."

The secretary's face curdled slowly as Dominic spoke, finally ashing over to a color as white as the crabs themselves. Any doubt that had lingered in Danielle's mind about The Bern Group and their role in the felonies unleashed on her home was all but smothered now.

"And for good measure..." A phone suddenly appeared in Dominic's hand, and he presented it to the secretary like a magician, holding it out in front of his face. "Smile."

He snapped off several pictures and then immediately began bouncing his thumbs onto the screen, typing. "And now my associates know your face. Your name. Which means we know everything about you and your family. So, an hour or so from now, when people begin to ask, I'd be very careful about how much you remember from this incident."

The woman couldn't speak, couldn't move, and she simply nodded.

"Is my appointment here or not?" the muffled voice from beyond the door shouted. "Lina! There's something wrong with the phones!"

"May I borrow one of those letter openers?" Danielle asked, staring harshly at the secretary, her voice low and calm.

The woman quivered her head a few times and stared with terror at the two letter openers that lay in perfect order beside a metal file organizer. Dominic grabbed one and tossed it to Danielle who stuffed it into the small of her back.

"We'll have to be quick," she said to Dominic. "And they'll have our pictures on camera. We might not get out of here at all."

Dominic nodded, his face alert, anxious. He then said, "You don't have to do this. You know that, right?"

Danielle frowned. "I do."

She turned toward the office now and opened the door, glowering as she took in the face of Lucas Maes, who sat like a king at a large, oak desk that sat at least ten yards from the entrance. His was the face of malevolence, she thought, though she couldn't have identified what characteristics, exactly, displayed the quality.

She would ask a few questions first, of course, just to be sure, and if by some twist of the story it turned out he wasn't The Bastard on Danielle's list, she had no doubt he would know the name of the man or woman to whom the moniker applied.

But to her core, Danielle knew he was the one. There was something in the dip of his head as he stared up at her, the glare he shot her for just an instant before dropping his gaze and smiling as he looked down at the coffee on his desk. It was a look that was both eager and condescending, dismissive and disgusted.

Danielle focused again on the thin metal blade pressing against her skin, and she played out in her mind the sling she would make on it with her right hand as she reached across the desk and pulled Lucas Maes' head forward with her left. That would be the moment of truth, she knew, the last move before she jammed the steel fin into the back of his neck. Perhaps she would picture Stella's face as she twisted the blade inside his skull, seeing as she'd been robbed the pleasure of accomplishing that goal personally.

Danielle suddenly felt the urge to pull the list from her handbag, to feel the crinkle of the paper in her fingers, to read the words one last time before she completed the final task.

But she resisted, and instead walked confidently into the expansive office that overlooked downtown Brussels.

She closed the door behind her.

"Mr. Maes?" she said smiling, her eyes stinging with the burn of revulsion. "I'm Danielle. It's so very nice to meet you."

Dear Reader,

Thank you for reading! I hope you enjoyed The List as much as I enjoyed writing it. Please consider leaving a review on Amazon. Your review doesn't have to be long.

To stay in touch with me and learn about my other books, giveaways and special sneak peeks, visit my website: www.christophercolemanauthor.com

Made in the USA
Las Vegas, NV
24 November 2024